CW00551276

1

Santiago Tales

Joan Fallon was born in Scotland, but spent most of her formative life in the south of England. After a brief spell working in industry, she became a teacher and later a management consultant specialising in Behavioural Studies.

She now lives in the south of Spain, where she has become passionate about both the language and history of her adopted home.

She is the author of:

Daughters of Spain
Between the Sierra and the Sea
The House on the Beach
Loving Harry

(all are available in paperback and as ebooks)

JOAN FALLON

Santiago Tales

Scott Publishing

ISBN 978 0 9570696 6 4
First published in 2013
Scott Publishing
Windsor, England

ACKNOWLEDGMENTS

Although 'Santiago Tales' is a work of fiction, I would like to acknowledge the help I received from the following sources:

In September 2011, June Holland walked the *Camino de Santiago* from Roncevalles to Santiago de Compostela. It took her five weeks. My sincere thanks to June for the time she spent talking and sharing her experiences with me.

An invaluable book for pilgrims and writers about the *Camino* is 'Camino de Santiago' by John Brierley, first published in 2003.

I am indebted also to the various postings on the internet by pilgrims who wanted to record their experiences, in particular 'Camino de Santiago in 20 Days' by Randall St Germain. My thanks and admiration to them all.

WEEK ONE
DAY 1

CHAPTER 1
BETH

For a moment Beth thinks she is back in the hospital, the bed is hard and there is that constant undercurrent of people murmuring and the noise of doors opening and slamming shut. She opens her eyes, and blinks, trying to take in the surroundings. No, not the hospital, now it comes back to her. She is in Spain and she is on her own; for the first time in her life she is travelling alone. There is no Joe to accompany her, to laugh and joke and make the journey easier. Where is he today, she wonders. What is he doing? A wave of bitterness hits her and she can feel the bile churn in her stomach. He is probably busy with the bloody Test Match, as usual.

She sits up and looks around her. The room is spartan, clean and freshly painted; the floor is tiled in black and white squares. She is on the bottom bunk of one of two sets of bunk-beds that are cordoned off from the rest of the accommodation by a couple of partitions, one on each side. The man in the bed next to her is already up and dressed; he is lacing his boots, carefully winding the cord around his ankle and tying it in a double knot.

'Hi, hope I didn't disturb you,' he says with a lazy smile. 'I want to get off early, before the hordes.'

He has an American drawl.

She realises it is barely dawn, yet, just out of sight, people are already moving, stretching, coughing and making those early morning sounds that are so universal.

'Not really. It sounds as though everyone is already awake so I might as well get up as well,' she replies.

'You'll see, it's better to get on the road at first light; it's cooler for a start.'

'I'm not tempted to lie in, anyway,' she tells him. 'This bed is as hard as a board.'

'Not exactly the Ritz, is it,' he says.

She watches him stuff his sheet and pillowcase into his rucksack, roll up his sleeping bag and strap it on top, then hitch the whole pack onto his back.

'*Buen camino*,' he says and is gone.

'*Buen camino*, have a good walk,' she hopes that will be true. Right now she has doubts about the wisdom of her actions. It had all seemed so straightforward when she was planning it at home. She and Joe were experienced walkers; besides walking the length and breadth of England over the years, they had spent hiking holidays in the Pyrenees, gone hill climbing in Wales and, before she became sick, had been considering walking in Nepal. So the *Camino de Santiago* had seemed just another trip, no more difficult than any other. The only difference is that now she is doing it on her own.

She has been meticulous in her preparation, building up the strength in her legs by walking ten kilometres a day and occasionally fitting in a longer walk of thirty kilometres. Sometimes she drove over to Exmoor and walked across the moor; on other days she walked along the coastal path or took the country lanes into Barnstaple. She feels ready for whatever this trip could throw at her. But there was one aspect to which she has not given much consideration: the fact that she might wake up in a room full of complete strangers.

It was not until she was on the bus, reading through the guide book about the pilgrims' *albergue* where she was planning to spend her first night, that she realised that this converted medieval hospital offered travellers one hundred and twenty beds to choose from, all of them in a single, enormous dormitory. The thought of sleeping alongside more than a hundred other pilgrims filled her with an irrational anxiety. She is a light sleeper and so fastidious at times that Joe called her 'the princess' and not always in an affectionate way, either. She knows she often irritated him with her pernickety ways, like insisting that he and Luke drank their beer from glasses rather than cans and that he set the table with matching cutlery and not whatever came to hand. How on earth was she going to manage with the nightly grunts and snores of so many people around her, not to mention the smell of all those bodies in such close proximity? She had felt nauseous thinking about it and, if it had been possible, would have turned back then and there. But the bus to Pamplona only ran once a day so she had no choice but to check in along with all the other pilgrims.

They were all so young and enthusiastic; it had exhausted her just to look at them, with their gaudy, new rucksacks and clean hiking boots. As they strode along, their bright, eager chatter interspersed with the clicking of their poles on the asphalt road. There seemed to be so many of them, coming from all directions, as though all the youth in Europe were converging on the *Camino de Santiago* that autumn evening. No wonder the young man in the next bed wants to get off early, she thinks.

In fact, as she now realises, her fears about the hostel, or *albergue* as it is universally known on the *Camino*, were unfounded. She had barely noticed the young man last night, nor the occupants of the other two beds and, although it was not a perfect night, it certainly had not been bad enough to deter her from making the journey she has planned.

She pulls on her shorts, finds some clean socks in her bag and then puts on the traveller's most important item, the boots. The boots are old and scuffed, but they are comfortable. She is a seasoned walker she tells herself; she has walked many miles in these boots, not hard walks, but she has put in the distance. Walking helps her to relax; it has a way of stopping her thoughts racing and her imagination tormenting her with bleak images of the future.

She steps out into the pale morning light; there is a slight mist that hangs damply in the air, causing her to shiver. She slips the waterproof poncho over her head and sets off, following the arrows that guide her on her way. They are numerous but seem almost superfluous, what with so many pilgrims all moving in the same direction. She joins the straggly procession of bright clothes, fluorescent jackets and shiny poles that, if seen from above, must create the impression of a long, multi-coloured snake, winding its way down the hillside. The pilgrims' boots make a muted rumble along the cobbled streets like the growl of some mystical animal. Is this what she wants, she asks herself, to be just one more pilgrim in an anonymous crowd? Maybe it is. Maybe she can lose herself here amongst all these strangers.

She follows them to the edge of the town where some of the pilgrims have stopped to have their photos taken by a road sign that proclaims, almost with an inanimate glee, '*Santiago de Compostela 790 km*'.

'*Look how far it is, almost eight hundred kilometres. Will you make it?*' the sign challenges her. '*Are you up to this challenge?*'

She feels defeated before she starts and once again considers the possibility of aborting the walk.

'Want me to take your photo?' a young girl asks.

'No thanks, I don't have a camera,' she tells her.

'Well on your mobile phone then.'

'No mobile either, sorry.'

'No mobile.'

The girl could not be more astonished.

'But what if something happens? What if someone wants to get in touch with you?'

She shrugs. She had heard the same argument from Joe.

The pilgrims are spacing themselves out now; the snake is breaking up into segments. Some walk in small groups, chatting, others in pairs and some, like herself, walk alone. All the advice she has read tells her how important it is to walk at her own speed; she knows if she tries to keep up with some of these youngsters she will soon be exhausted. She wants to pace herself; there is a long way to go: seven hundred and ninety kilometres, she reminds herself.

Soon she finds herself walking on a dirt road through damp woodlands where dark ferns cover the ground and squirrels dart from tree to tree and there, in the middle of the path, shaded by oak and elm trees, is an ancient stone cross, covered in lichen. This is the Pilgrims' Cross, built to guide and protect the pilgrims and to purify the forest from evil. She is in the Sorginaritzaga Forest, the Oak Grove of Witches. Ahead of her, deeper in the forest, is the site of a witches' coven. This is where, in the sixteenth century, the Catholic church ordered nine people to be burnt at the stake for witchcraft. She shivers at the thought and walks a little faster.

This is the Atlantic Pyrenees, a softer, rolling landscape than its eastern counterparts. At first the walk is not hard, the path slopes downhill but according to her guide book, now that she has left Roncevalles the path will start its steady climb uphill until it reaches Alto de Mezquiriz, the highest point on this stage of the *Camino*. From there on, it will be downhill again, all the way to Larrasoaña.

Today is her birthday. She has not told anybody. There is nobody here to tell. She is fifty. Fifty years and what has she done with her life? My God, what has happened to all those youthful plans and ideas that she had? She had trained as a journalist and planned to be a foreign correspondent; that was her aim. That was what they talked about when she was at university. That was all she ever wanted to be. Most of her friends were in the English faculty but only a handful of them wanted to be journalists; the rest used their English degrees as passports to jobs in teaching, at the BBC or, in one guy's case, with the Royal Shakespeare Company. She wonders what has become of them now? Have they made a success of their lives or are they, like her, bemoaning the fact they have reached their half-century without really achieving anything? And what of her? Instead of becoming the anchor-woman on Channel 4 News, she became pregnant and married Joe.

She is tired already and decides to rest. Thinking about her birthday has made her feel sorry for herself, something she tries to avoid. She knows there is no point in dragging over the past but it is hard not to.

She sits on a boulder by the side of the path and looks about her. Ahead she can see the gleam of the river Erro, as it snakes its way through the valley towards the sea. The path twists and turns down the mountainside but, apart from a splash of red in the distance, probably the last of the pilgrims disappearing from sight, there is no-one about. Despite the sun, which by now is climbing steadily higher, she feels herself shiver. Even on the moors she has never felt as isolated as this.

She gets up. If she follows the path, it will take her to the river's edge where she can fill her water bottle. Gingerly she makes her way down the scree-covered slopes until she reaches the bank. The river is fast-flowing and the water tumbles over the rocks, creating mini-waterfalls that sparkle in the sunshine; she crosses it carefully, hopping from one stepping-stone to another until she reaches the far side. The grassy river bank is dry and spotted with wild flowers. She sits down again, letting her rucksack slip from her shoulders onto the ground beside her. There is no-one about. A silence hangs in the air like a spell waiting to be broken. Without moving, she watches the fish, swimming back and forth among the shallows. A flash of iridescent blue catches her eye, telling her that her presence has disturbed a kingfisher. She waits and sure enough he returns; the prospect of a meal is too tempting for him and, almost before she is aware, he has caught himself a fish and flown away. The sight of this lovely bird cheers her and for no reason she finds herself smiling. It would be nice to stay a while longer and watch the sun continue its climb across the sky, pushing the early mist out before it, but she needs to get on. And besides which she is hungry. She has not eaten since the cheese roll she had on the bus, the previous night. She leans forward, dipping her hand in the river. The water is crystal clear and as cold as ice; it has come straight down from the mountains. Beth unscrews her water bottle and fills it. Then she splashes a little on her face and gets up.

The path carries on through leafy woodlands until it crosses a main road. Ahead of her she sees a church spire; she has arrived at the tiny hamlet of Gerendiain. Time to stop and have breakfast.

There are some pilgrims ahead of her; possibly they have already made a stop and are now on their way again because they do not hesitate but stride purposefully through the cluster of houses. She wanders into what she assumes is the main square, a tiny area bordered by stone houses and finds a café. An elderly couple are sitting at one of the tables, their rucksacks and pilgrim staves at their feet.

'Hello there,' the man says.

He looks like a retired schoolteacher, with his carefully combed white hair and round spectacles.

'Hi.'

The woman looks at her and smiles.

'You looked whacked,' she says.

She is eating a large toasted sandwich. The smell of the cheese is mouth-watering.

'I suppose I am,' Beth replies.

She sits at the table next to them.

'My name's Jill,' the woman tells her. 'And this is my husband, Dennis.'

'Hi, I'm Beth.'

'Your first time on the *Camino*?' Dennis asks.

She nods. She wants to attract the attention of the waiter, who is chatting to a group of pilgrims on the far table. At last she succeeds in catching his eye and he comes across.

'One of those,' she says, pointing to the woman's half-eaten sandwich. 'And a large black coffee.'

The waiter says something in Spanish, or it may be Basque, whatever it is, she does not understand. It does not seem to matter because he goes away and soon returns bringing her the sandwich and coffee.

'This is our third time,' Dennis tells her, proudly. 'The first time we only did the last hundred kilometres but it was enough to get our certificates.'

'We were still working, then,' Jill adds. 'We could only get a couple of weeks off.'

'Now we're retired we're doing the whole thing.'

They are a pleasant couple but Beth does not really want to chat. She is hungry and tired. It is surprising how much the walk has taken out of her. She takes out her tablets and pops one in her mouth. Jill is watching her but does not comment.

'The second time we did the *Camino del Norte*,' Dennis continues. 'We got the boat to Santander and walked down from there.'

'Yes, but this time we wanted to do it properly,' Jill goes on. 'We've allowed ourselves two months, so we can do all the detours and everything.'

'Going to go on to Finisterre afterwards too.'

'Sounds good,' Beth says.

She is enjoying the sandwich and the coffee is hot and strong, just as she likes it. She feels her energy returning.

'You feeling better now, dear?' Jill asks.

'Yes, I'm fine. I probably let my sugar level get too low. Maybe I should have had breakfast before I set off this morning.'

'We always do. Good breakfast at six and then on our way,' Dennis tells her. 'Then a stop for coffee when we feel like a break.'

'We like to take our time,' Jill confesses. 'After all, now we're retired we've got time to stop and smell the flowers.'

She giggles.

She must have been quite a pretty woman when she was younger, Beth thinks, looking at her upturned nose and almond eyes; now her skin falls in soft folds and fine lines criss-cross her neck. She is wearing a wide hat made from a bright yellow cotton; it casts a golden glow on her face.

'Where are you heading for?' Dennis asks.

'Larrasoaña.'

'That's about another fifteen kilometres,' he tells her. 'You should get there in time for lunch.'

The waiter comes over and gives him the bill.

'Well we're off. See you in Larrasoaña, maybe.'

'Yes.'

'*Buen camino*,' Jill says, tugging her hat securely onto her head. 'I'm sure we'll bump into you again. You'd be surprised how often you meet up with the same people.'

'*Buen camino*,' she replies.

She finishes her breakfast and pays the waiter.

'You are *inglesa*?' he asks her as he counts out her change.

'Yes.'

'Lots of *inglesas* walk the *Camino*,' he says. 'Now the weather is good. No rain.'

'And not too hot,' she adds, picking up her rucksack.

'Good luck. *Buen camino*,' he says.

'Thank you.'

She sets off down the path after Jill and Dennis, but there is no sign of them now.

She walks steadily for the next two hours, stopping only occasionally to refill her water bottle from one of the many fountains on the way or just to sit and listen to the skylarks for a moment or two. She thinks of what Jill said about having time to stop and smell the flowers; if this trip is to make any difference to her life she has to learn to do just that.

As she approaches Larrasoaña the countryside becomes more cultivated and she is walking through pastureland, dotted with herds of grazing beef cattle. A pair of buzzards circle high above her, disappearing and reappearing as they fly up above the clouds. They remind her of home. For a second or two her eyes fill with tears as she thinks back to the days when she and Joe would walk on the moors, listening to the mewing call of the buzzards circling above them. How she had loved him then.

*

She and Joe had met when she was working for the Bideford Gazette, her first job, straight out of university and starry-eyed. Joe, older than her and incredibly handsome, was already an established journalist, writing the sports column for the Gazette and freelancing for a range of other papers. She fell for him straight away. It was hard not to. He was tall and broad-shouldered, a very macho man with a natural designer stubble, no matter how often he shaved. It was not only George Michael that could make her heart flip in those days, Joe had sex appeal and more. But it wasn't just that she loved him, she admired him too; he had it all: if not fame, then respect and recognition from his peers. He had what she wanted, a successful career in journalism.

They lived together for a while, in a tiny fisherman's cottage by the harbour. She remembers that cottage with affection because, despite the damp walls, the draughty windows and general lack of space, they were very happy there. She continued to write her column on local events. Every summer she attended garden fetes, writing up the winners of the lightest sponge cake, the best plum jam, the biggest marrow, the ripest tomatoes. Beth, together with the pimply youth the Gazette employed as a photographer, attended the local schools' sports' days, recording the winners of the egg-and-spoon race, the high jump, the long jump, and whatever other jumping competitions they did, went to gymkhanas, swimming galas and, in the winter, Christmas concerts. It was not what she had set her sights on but she had Joe and that was what mattered; she was happy.

She wipes her eyes with the end of the scarf that she has twisted around her neck and tries to smile. At least she doesn't have to attend any more of those awful carol concerts. She gave up her job at the Bideford Gazette five years ago, when she first became ill and has not written a single word since then.

She checks the guide book. Ahead of her is the river Arga; so she is just over three kilometres from her destination. Unlike the previous river, the Arga is too wide and too deep to cross on foot but there is a narrow bridge spanning it, which according to a painted sign on the bank, has been the crossing point for pilgrims since the fourteenth century. As she steps onto the bridge, she cannot escape the sensation that she is following in the steps of a long line of pilgrims, stretching back for centuries. All who crossed here would have had their problems, their hopes and dreams; many would have been hoping for a miracle; some would have been seeking forgiveness. For an instant she sees herself not as a lonely individual but as part of a long tradition of pilgrims who have passed here before her.

She stops and looks up at the sun. She knows it must be almost midday but having no watch and no mobile she has to rely on the movement of the sun to give her some idea of the time. This is a new concept for her; she has always worn a watch and been tied to some timetable or other. Working with the newspaper there were deadlines to be met, appointments to be kept; everything, whether work or leisure, was noted in her diary and adhered to. The alarm clock woke her every morning and the clock in the lounge advised her when to go to bed. If the batteries ran down they were immediately replaced; she was never without some means of telling the time. Now all she has is the sun. She would never have believed how liberating it could feel to be free of time. It is as if, by leaving her watch behind, she has also left her troubles behind her too. Logic tells her that this is not the case, they are not gone, just suspended for the moment but that is enough to make her feel different. Already she can sense her cares slipping away; one by one she sheds them, like the skins of an onion.

It is well after noon by the time she arrives in Larrasoaña. The first *albergue* she stops at is full but the owner directs her to another at the far end of the town.

'We're always the first to get full,' he tells her. 'That's why we put some extra mattresses in the barn. You're welcome to one of them if you want.'

'No, I think I'll try the next place. *La Posada* you said?'

'Yes, that's right. You can't miss it; it's just past the main square.'

The walk through the town is pleasant: everything is clean and sparkling in the afternoon sun. The smell of baking bread floats out from a baker's shop, reminding her that it will soon be lunchtime. From one of the numerous small cafés and bars there is the smell of something tasty cooking in garlic and herbs; Beth feels her stomach rumble at the thought of food. As soon as she has checked into the *albergue* she will come back here and eat.

It seems that Larrasoaña, although small, has always been an important stopping place on the *Camino*; there are shops selling all the provisions that a hungry and footsore pilgrim might need and souvenirs for tourists who have wandered into its path. Beth notices the shape of a scallop shell carved on a pillar and stops to touch it. As she traces the grooves of the shell with her finger she understands why it has been adopted as the symbol of the *Camino*. The grooves, converging in a single point, are a clear metaphor for the many routes that lead to Santiago de Compostela and also, for that matter, to God. That is what they say. That is what the pilgrims believe. So they wear it as a badge. The Spanish even use the same word for pilgrim and scallop: *peregrino*.

As she walks on, looking for *La Posada*, she sees that the symbol is everywhere in this small town. The ubiquitous scallop shell is carved into the walls of buildings, alongside the armorial shields of long forgotten families; it is displayed in windows and painted on signs; it is carved on plaques that decorate the walls. She stops to look in a shop window; here there are posters of it and racks of postcards depicting the pilgrim's staff and the scallop shell to send home to family and friends; there are facsimile scallop shells to tie onto your staff, stickers to attach to your rucksack and even tee-shirts emblazoned with the emblem. It does not seem to matter that the pilgrims are easily identifiable by their clothing, their wide hats and walking poles, they are expected to wear the badge of the *Camino* as well. Oh well, people have to make a living, she tells herself.

It is not far to walk but by the time she arrives at *La Posada*, her back is aching from the weight of her rucksack and her calves hurt. It is time to rest; she has been walking since early morning.

'*Buenos días*,' she says to the concierge.

She pulls out her phrase book and reads:

'*Me gustaría un habitación. Soy peregrino.*'

She shows the woman the pilgrim's passport that she got in Roncesvalles; without it she would not be allowed to stay in the hostels.

'*Muy bien*,' the woman replies, taking the small booklet and stamping it with a rubber stamp. 'Follow me.'

The *albergue* is clean but the rooms are small and crowded; there are three sets of bunk beds in the room she is allocated. All the beds have been taken except one, the one by the door. She claims it for herself and sits down on it. All of a sudden she feels exhausted; she cannot face going out again into the town to eat. She has some bread that she bought in a previous village and two slices of cured ham; this will do her for lunch. She eats a little of the ham and then puts it away; she is too tired to eat any more. She unpacks her bedding and makes up her bed then she stretches out.

Well, here she is, miles from home. The first stage of her journey has begun. Despite her exhaustion, she feels a sense of achievement at what she has accomplished today. And tomorrow? What will tomorrow bring? Before she knows it, she is asleep.

CHAPTER 2

Beth is woken by the sound of someone climbing into the bed above her. Whoever he is, he smells of garlic and fried food. The mattress above her sags with his weight and a faint cloud of dust floats down and settles on her sleeping bag.

She rolls onto her side and sits up just as the door opens and a woman, wrapped in a skimpy towel, enters. Her long, dark hair is plastered against her head and drips water onto her skinny bare shoulders. Large grey eyes regard her curiously.

'You're awake,' the woman says. 'Hi, I'm Fran, Fran Rutherford.'

'Beth.'

'The showers are free now, if you want to slip in before anyone else.'

'Is the water hot?'

Fran wrinkles her nose and says:

'So so. Best to go now before it's all used up.'

'Thanks, I will.'

She pulls her wash bag out of the rucksack and, grabbing her towel, sets off for the bathroom.

'It's at the end, on the right,' Fran shouts after her.

'Hey, keep it down, will you. I'm trying to get a siesta,' a voice from the top bunk says.

'Siesta time's over. Sorry-o,' the woman tells him with a laugh. 'You shouldn't have spent so much time in the bar.'

Beth cannot make out his reply but it sounds rude.

The showers are communal but there is one set for men and another for women. She pushes open the door to the women's shower room and goes in. There is a stale smell coming from the drains and although it looks reasonably clean, the tiles are old and cracked and there are traces of mould on the wall. She is not keen to go in but she has to freshen up somehow. There is someone there ahead of her, using the end shower-head.

'You'd better hurry; the hot water's almost all gone,' the woman tells her as she rubs soap on her legs.

Beth hesitates. If she waits until the woman goes there may be no hot water but she is reluctant to strip in front of a stranger. The woman has her back to her so Beth takes the opportunity to undress and steps under the shower-head furthest away from her. She is right; the water is barely tepid. She soaps herself quickly and then waits until the woman finishes and leaves before she gets out.

By the time Beth returns to her room, Fran has gone and the man in the top bunk is lacing up his boots.

'Hello,' she says.

'Hi,' he grunts, without looking up.

'Given up on the siesta then?'

'Fat chance of getting any peace here; I thought I'd go and get some air instead.'

She dresses hurriedly, sitting on her bunk, so that she is out of his range of sight. It is awkward, dressing sitting down but she thinks she is going to have to get used to it. One thing is becoming very clear about this pilgrimage: she is not going to have much privacy. She slips on some sandals that she has brought to wear in the evenings and to give her feet a rest from the hiking boots then roots about in her bag to find a hairbrush. It is extra weight but she could not leave it at home; there is no way she can control her thick unruly hair with a comb. She peers at herself in the tiny compact mirror that she carries; a pale, thin face with wide-set green eyes stares back at her.

'Bye,' she says to the man but he does not reply; he is still sitting on his bunk.

Once outside she makes her way back to the main square. She has slept soundly and feels much refreshed but she is starving; now she needs to find a bar or a restaurant where she can eat. Most of them are already packed with hungry pilgrims; some of whom are sitting at the tables, others on the pavement outside, their rucksacks by their sides.

'Hi, over here. Beth.'

She looks round. There is the girl from the *albergue*, waving at her; she is sitting at a table with half a dozen others. Her long hair is loosely pulled back into a pony-tail and she is wearing a red tee-shirt with a black and white panda and the initials WWF blazoned across the front.

'Come and join us, Beth,' she calls. 'There's bags of room.'

They all move up to make a space for Beth to sit down.

'Hi,' she says, feeling a little shy in front of so many strange faces.

'We're in the same room.' Fran tells the others. 'In *La Posada.*'

They take it in turn to introduce themselves and shake Beth's hand. All, except one, a man with a strong Texas accent, seem to be English. Once the introductions are over, the American turns to her and says:

'So, Beth what brings you to the *Camino*?'

He is very direct. She is not sure she is ready to talk to strangers about her reasons for being here; she is not even sure she understands them herself.

'Oh, I've always liked walking,' she tells him, a little brusquely.

'So you're a walker then, not a religious nut.'

'Sorry?'

'I have this theory that there are two kinds of people that walk the *Camino*, those that are hoping for a religious experience and those that just enjoy a good walk. You sound like the latter.'

'So which are you?'

'I'm like you, I'm a walker. I don't believe in all that guff about miracles. Do you know ...'

'Don't take any notice of him. He's all hot air,' Fran interrupts. 'More importantly would you like some wine, Beth?'

'Red please.'

She smiles apologetically at the Texan as an older man, sitting next to Fran, pours out a glass of wine for her.

'We were just about to order some food. What about you?'

'Yes, I'm starving.'

'And you?' Fran asks, looking at the Texan.

'No, not for me. I ate far too much at lunchtime.'

He finishes his drink and puts the glass on the table.

'I'm off anyway. I want to catch up with some friends. They said they'd be in '*El Gato Blanco*' tonight. See you guys later, maybe.'

There is a chorus of goodbyes and then the chatter dies down while they discuss the menu, one recommending one thing and someone else another. In the end, the older man, whose name is Walter, takes charge and orders a selection of dishes for them to share and three more bottles of Rioja.

'That's it, sorted. I do like a decisive man,' Fran adds, with a wink at Walter.

Beth helps herself to an olive, then sipping her wine she looks around at the group. Now that the American has left there remain Fran, Walter, a middle-aged woman called Helen and a couple of twenty-somethings called Darren and Sheri, from Birmingham. Beth is wondering whether they all already know each other, when Walter turns to Helen and introduces himself.

'Been on the *Camino* before, Helen?' he asks.

'No, this is my first time, but I think I might do it again.'

'Enjoying it, then?'

'I'm not sure enjoyment is what it's about,' she replies, rather seriously. 'But I am finding it rather fulfilling.'

Beth wonders if she is a nun in mufti; she has a very serious look about her. Her greying hair is scraped back from her face and twisted into a knot on the back of her head and she has a rather severe pair of glasses balancing on the end of her nose.

'My wife and I used to go hiking,' Walter tells her. 'She would have enjoyed this. She died, you know, five years ago.'

'I'm sorry to hear that,' Helen replies.

'Heart attack.'

He pours some wine into his glass and starts to top up Helen's.

'No, no more for me,' she says.

'You're not driving are you?' he asks with a chuckle.

'I've had one glass, thank you. That's about my limit, I'm afraid.'

'I saw you in Roncevalles, I'm sure,' he says, 'in the church.'

'Probably. I spent quite a while in there. I like churches. In fact I plan to visit as many as I can on this pilgrimage. I shall take an extra day in León to visit the cathedral and possibly in Burgos too. I want to see as much as I can.'

'Why not. Best to make the most of it.'

'So Walter,' Fran says. 'You're a widower? You must miss your wife.'

'I do; we'd been married for forty years. You get so used to having someone around that your life is pretty empty when they've gone. I never realised, until it was too late, how much I relied on her; it was Nora who kept the home together.'

Beth thinks he looks sorry for himself and why not. His wife was the constant in his life that he never expected to disappear. Without her, life wasn't the same. She could relate to that.

'Is that why you've come on the *Camino*?' Fran asks.

'In a way. It would have been nice to have done it together, but that's not going to happen.'

'So you decided to come anyway?'

'Yes. I've got nothing else to do these days, so here I am.'

'Do you have any children?' Beth asks.

She can imagine him as a grandfather; he is a big, burly man and has a jolly look about him, although that may be due, in part, to the Rioja, for which he seems to have acquired quite a liking.

'Three. Two girls and a boy. Of course they're all married now. I've even got grandchildren: six, three of each.'

'That's nice for you.'

He smiles, ruefully.

'Yes, I suppose so, when I get to see them. They're all so far away. Life's different for young people these days. They want it all, marriage and a career.'

'Why not?' Fran asks, slightly defensively, Beth thinks.

Walter does not reply to this, instead he says:

'Anwyn, my eldest daughter, lives in China, so I hardly see her at all; she's at the pinnacle of her profession and has no plans to become a mother. My son got a job with Canadian television and lives in Toronto, with his wife and family and even Megan, my youngest girl is in Australia. She had a successful business as a beauty therapist in Cardiff but then she met this Australian, married him and moved to Sydney. Now they have a couple of kids of their own but we've never seen them. Only photos.'

'Trying to get away from you, were they?' Fran asks with a laugh.

Walter does not look very amused at this.

'It's a good job I've got Skype or I'd see nothing of my grandkids growing up,' he tells her.

'Ah, the wonders of modern technology.'

Beth thinks Fran is poking fun at him.

What about you?' he asks Beth.

'No grandchildren, thank God. Just one son; he's twenty-four,' she tells him.

'So plenty of time yet.'

He turns to Helen, who is studiously reading a thick guide book.

'And you Helen?'

She looks up and squints at him over her glasses.

'Me?'

'Any kids?'

'No, no,' she says, shaking her head.

She looks embarrassed at the suggestion. Beth notices that she does not wear a ring.

'That guide book looks a bit heavy to carry all this way,' she remarks, hoping to change the subject.

'It is, but I couldn't leave it behind. It's fascinating.'

'Helen's a teacher,' Fran says.

'Yes, I'm chronicling the stories and legends that are linked to the *Camino*. I intend to use them in my classes.'

'What do you teach?' Beth asks, although she feels she can guess at the answer.

'History and religious studies. My specialism is comparative religion, that sort of thing.'

'Does that cover myths and legends then?' Sheri asks. 'I love legends.'

'It depends. Comparative religion is about different people's beliefs after all. Centuries ago people believed in all sorts of things: witchcraft and dragons for example. In many cultures the myths and legends have become bound up with religion and it's not always easy to distinguish one from the other. Often the Church encouraged the integration of these beliefs rather than forbidding them. For example, they used to build their churches on old pagan sites and replaced many of the pagan festivals with religious ones.'

'Yes, do you know that they say Christ wasn't born on 25th December at all,' Sheri tells them. 'He was born in the summer. They just used that date because it coincided with the winter solstice.'

'Nobody is really sure of when Jesus was born, but you're right about the Winter Solstice,' Helen says. 'It celebrates the birth of the new solar year and was celebrated long before the birth of Christ.'

'So what about all this business with holy relics? You know, the finger of some saint or other having special powers?' Fran asks.

'Well there again, it depends on the religion. The possession of relics is important in some religions, the Catholic Church for instance, and not others. The presence of a holy relic in a church gave that church a special status; it was said that miracles could happen. And of course it boosted their congregations; people would come from all over to see the relics.'

'What exactly is a relic?' asked Walter.

Beth notices that he hasn't taken his eyes off Helen since the conversation began.

'In Catholicism it's something that has belonged to, or been touched by Jesus or a saint. It could be a piece of cloth, a small bone, a piece of the cross, anything that was in their possession.'

'So having the entire skeleton of St James makes the cathedral in Santiago very powerful?' he asks.

'Yes. That's why people have been making this pilgrimage for centuries.'

'Hoping for miracles,' adds Beth.

'Exactly, hoping for miracles.'

'But are they genuine?' Fran asks. 'How do they know if they're genuine?'

'Some probably aren't, but all of them have a story behind them. Some stories are true and some are legends, handed down by word of mouth for centuries.'

'So how did they get the bones of St James?' Sheri asks.

Helen smiles. Suddenly she doesn't look so plain and dowdy; the smile lights up her face. Beth thinks she would be so much prettier if she changed her glasses for contact lenses and put on a bit of make-up.

'Well, therein hangs a tale.'

At this moment the waiter returns with two plates of *jamon*, a large *tortilla* stuffed with the local asparagus and a plate of lamb stew with red peppers.

'Great, ham and eggs,' Darren says.

'And *'chilidrones'* adds Fran, 'the local speciality.'

As they eat Helen tells them that she has always wanted to do the pilgrimage to Santiago de Compostela but that she could never get away.

'I lived with my mother,' she says. 'She was bed-ridden for the last ten years but then she died last Christmas. Once I'd sorted out all her affairs I decided it was time to do something I wanted. So I started training and reading up about it and here I am. I have six weeks holiday and I'm spending it all here on the *Camino*.'

'Good for you,' Darren says, topping up his glass with more wine. 'So come on then, let's hear about St James and his bones.'

Helen clears her throat and casts a shy glance in Walter's direction. Beth sees him smile at her encouragingly.

'Well, as with all legends there is usually more than one version. In this one, James, who was one of the Twelve Apostles, sailed to Galicia and set up a ministry in the area near Padrón and Finisterre. They say that was how Christianity was first introduced to the Iberian peninsula, through James. Some people question why he chose to go to such a remote place to set up a ministry, but what you have to realise is that there was an important Druid settlement there long before Christianity.

However, as the story goes, James's mission was not very successful. There were few converts to Christianity; in fact only nine conversions are recorded. So, in the year 40 AD, James decided to return to Judea. When he arrived in his native land, he was immediately arrested and, this much we know for certain because it is recorded in the Bible, in Acts

12 verse 2, he was beheaded by King Herod Agrippa I in the year 44 AD. He is believed to be the first of the Apostles martyred for his faith.

Anyway, after his death, two of his disciples, Atanasio and Teodoro, took his body and sailed to Spain with it. They landed on the west coast of Galicia at the Roman outpost of Iria Flavia, close to Padrón, intending to take his body to Finisterre - the place that everyone believed was the end of the earth and, according to legend, the symbolic transition point between life and death. They asked the pagan Queen Lupa for permission to bury his body on her land but she sent them to the Roman legate at Dugium instead. The Romans threw the disciples into prison and took James's body. It seemed that the disciples' mission had failed. But that night an angel appeared and set them free. The disciples collected the body and made their escape, heading east, with the Romans in close pursuit. It looks as though God was on their side that day because, they say, as they crossed the river Tambre, the bridge collapsed behind them, making it impossible for their pursuers to catch them. The disciples carried James's body to a place called Libredon and buried it there.'

'So how did it end up in the cathedral in Santiago?' Darren asks.

'Well, no more was heard of St James until the year 813 when, one night, a shepherd called Pelayo saw a bright star that led him to a field in Libredon. There he found a burial site. He reported what he had discovered to the Bishop of Iria, Bishop Teodomiro, who immediately identified the site as being the burial place of the apostle James.'

'Very convenient,' Darren says. 'Now how would he know that?'

'Shsh, it's a legend,' Sheri whispers.

'Anyway, the bishop ordered a cathedral to be built over the remains. Then, when the king, Alfonso II heard the news he declared Saint James to be the patron saint of Spain,' Helen continues.

'So Libredon is the old name for Santiago de Compostela?'

'Yes exactly. In Spanish, Santiago de Compostela means Saint James (*San Iago*) of the field of stars (*campo de estrellas*) because of the star that led the shepherd to his remains.'

'And people make the pilgrimage to St James, hoping for a miracle?' Fran asks.

'Some do. Others think it's nonsense.'

'I think, despite what your Texan friend said, that most people have that hope at the back of their minds,' Beth says.

She is surprised at her own words. Until this moment she has never thought about miracles and certainly not in connection with herself. Is this what she is looking for? A miracle?

DAY 2

CHAPTER 3
HELEN

Instead of following her usual pattern of rising early, making herself a frugal breakfast in the *albergue's* kitchen and then going to the seven o'clock Mass, Helen decides that today she will go straight to the church. She snuggles down into her sleeping bag for a few extra minutes, thinking about last night. When they left the bar Walter suggested he walk back with her to the *albergue*; he had even carried her bag for her. She smiles to herself; she had felt like a school girl. How many times she had witnessed the young lads at her school walking beside their sweethearts and always carrying something for them, some token to show they cared, a tennis racquet, a laptop, a rucksack of books. It was a display of intent; they were laying claim to the girl of their choice and even she knew what they had in mind.

Walter is a nice man, a bit old maybe, but nice. She can tell he is lonely and, sadly, a little bitter. He had talked a lot about his children last night and how much he missed them but she knows it is really his wife that he misses.

She wriggles out of her sleeping bag and heads for the communal bathroom. It is a big *albergue* and, in her room alone, there are twenty bunk beds. One or two people are already up and about, but most are still lying in bed and, if the level of snoring is anything to go by, still fast asleep. Her leg itches where she was bitten some days ago and she scratches it gently. It was lucky that the bite was hidden under her trousers or they might not have let her in. When she arrived the previous afternoon she witnessed an angry scene between one of the pilgrims and the owner of the *albergue*; the pilgrim had some nasty bites on his neck and the landlord would not admit him. Bed bugs are the bane of the pilgrim's life; they cause nasty, painful bites which itch so much that it is impossible to sleep and the bugs, once ensconced in the folds of their clothes, are very difficult to shift. All the proprietors of the *albergues* are on the look-out for signs of the infestation. If a pilgrim brings bed bugs into a dormitory they multiply rapidly and are virtually impossible to eradicate, hence the harsh attitude towards anyone wearing the scars of a nightly fight with the vermin. She feels a bit guilty about her own bites, but consoles herself with the certainty that she has not brought any of the little beasts with her.

It does not take her long to get ready and she packs up her belongings and heads for the church. She is early and sits at the back to wait for the other celebrants to arrive. She has tried to attend Mass every morning since she started the walk. There was only one day that she missed, when she woke up with a raging headache and could hardly move. By the time the concierge had managed to hurry her out, it was too late to go to church. She had waited for the chemist to open, bought herself a couple of packets of painkillers and moved on.

She kneels on the wooden prayer blocks and goes through the usual routine: first she prays for her sisters and her brother; she prays for God's help on her journey then she prays for all the unfortunate people in the world: the sick, the disabled, the homeless and the poor. She prays for Walter too, that he will find peace and happiness and, finally, she prays for the souls of her mother and father.

Her mother was a strict woman. As she sits in this peaceful Romanesque church she can hear her harsh voice still, berating her for doing so little with her life. Nine months have passed since she passed away and, with her death, has come a peace that Helen had forgotten existed. She knows it is wrong to think ill of her own mother but she cannot help it. Her mother stole so many years of her life.

There are only a handful of people attending Mass today, mostly women and mostly old. Despite being the wrong side of fifty Helen feels young beside them. She follows those who are taking communion, to the altar. The priest is a young man; he smiles at her kindly as he raises his hand in blessing. Helen accepts the host and turns to leave. As she makes her way back to her pew she notices Beth standing at the back of the church, watching.

She is there again when Helen steps out into the early morning sunshine, sitting outside the café opposite.

'Hello there. I haven't seen you at Mass before,' she says, sitting down next to Beth.

'No, I don't attend Mass. I was just curious to see inside the church. It's very quaint.'

'Yes, I suppose it is; the whole town is rather nice, isn't it. Did you notice how it's centred on the *Camino* rather than around the church, like most other medieval towns?'

'Well now that you mention it, I suppose it is.'

The waiter comes over and hands Beth a large cup of coffee.

'Have you had breakfast?' she asks Helen.

'Not yet. I think I'll have some toast.'

She waves across at the waiter to come back and take her order.

'Did you sleep well?' Helen asks.

'As well as you can with everyone around you snoring their heads off.'

'Where's Fran?'

'Oh, I expect she's on her way. She had already left by the time I woke up.'

'Well I slept like a log. There's something about being here that makes me feel so relaxed; I can't explain it. I never slept like this at home.'

'You looked after your mother, didn't you say?'

'That's right. She died last year.'

'I'm sorry. Do you have any other family?'

'Yes. We're a big family; my mother had eight children in all, six of whom survived infancy. They're all girls except for one, Patrick, called after the saint, of course. Mammy was very religious.'

'So there were plenty of you to share the responsibility for your mother.'

Helen laughs bitterly.

'No, of course not. It fell to me, the middle one. There was no real reason why the responsibility of caring for Mammy should have fallen to me. It could have been Mary; she was the eldest, but she got pregnant and had to marry in a hurry. It could have been Rachel, but she was a wonderful musician and had no time to spend at home looking after Mammy. Then Ruth, who was two years younger than me, was called by God and joined a convent. That only left Martha, but when Mammy fell sick the first time, Martha was still at school, so I ended up looking after them all.'

'What about your father? Where was he?'

'Down the pub with his cronies.'

'Oh, I'm sorry.'

'Don't be. That's just how it was. She was my mother and I was happy to do my duty. After all who else was going to do it?'

41

She pulls out her guide book.

'The next stage is nearly twenty-one kilometres,' she informs her.

'Yes, I saw. We have to get through Pamplona too. I'm not so keen on that. I hate the idea of walking through busy towns.'

'It's said to be a beautiful city. I may stop and have a look at the cathedral while I'm there,' Helen says.

She has promised herself that she is not going to hurry this journey. This is her first time abroad and she wants to see everything. Talking about her mother has reminded her just how much she has missed of life.

'Shall we get going?' Beth asks.

'Yes, we can walk together until Pamplona, if you like.

Helen is pleased to have some company, at least for part of the way.

The first stage of the journey is a gentle stroll through the valley of the Arga river, along its tree-lined river bank. The path leads them downhill until they reach the village of Zuriáin, where they cross the river and begin a steady climb up towards Alto Cantera.

'Hang on a minute. I need to fill my water bottle,' Beth says.

She looks tired.

'Are you OK?' Helen asks.

Beth has that grey look under her eyes that Helen's mother had when she was ill. She wonders if something is wrong with Beth.

'I'm fine. Just need to stop for a minute or two and have a drink.'

There has been no shortage of drinking fountains along the route. This one is a simple tap coming out of a stone trough. Beth unscrews her bottle and fills it with the clear, cold water. Then she scoops some up in her hands and drinks greedily.

'That's wonderful,' she says. 'God, I was thirsty.'

Helen's water bottle is half-full so she tops it up and puts it back in her rucksack. She sits down next to Beth, who has stretched out on the grassy verge in the shade of an enormous willow tree.

'What about you Beth, do you have a big family?'

She has noticed that Beth is not wearing a wedding ring, although that is not as significant these days as it used to be, she tells herself.

'No, just my son, Luke. I've got no brothers or sisters and my parents are dead. They divorced when I was only twenty.'

'I can't imagine what it must be like to be an only child,' Helen says.

She remembers with sad affection the noisy, disorganised household she grew up in, a time when her mother was fit and strong and the hub of the home. There always seemed to be wet nappies hanging by the kitchen range and toys and books littering the floor. She can see her mother now, a baby on one arm, stirring the mixture for the scones that she baked for their tea. It had been a happy home despite the fact that there was little money and her parents bickered constantly about it. It was not until Mammy grew ill that everything began to fall apart. Helen had tried to hold it all together but she had not succeeded.

'You don't know any different. I left home at eighteen to go to university and I never returned,' Beth says.

'But weren't you lonely?'

'Not really, I made up for my lack of family by having a wide circle of friends. Then I became pregnant, so I got married.'

'Oh.'

'It wasn't like that. Not a shot-gun marriage. We were happy as we were, but Joe's mother wanted it. She's Catholic and didn't really approve of us living together.

She wanted her only son to be married in church and her only grandchild to be baptised a Catholic. So we went along with it. Joe loved his mother and to him it didn't matter one way or the other. I loved Joe and wanted to make him happy. It couldn't have been simpler.'

'So where is your husband now?' Helen asks.

She is curious. This is the first time that Beth has mentioned her husband. She wonders if they are divorced.

Beth does not answer. Instead she gets up, swings her rucksack on her back and says:

'I think we should be making a move, especially if you're planning to visit the cathedral. We've still got a long way to go.'

WEEK 2
DAY 12

CHAPTER 4
BETH

Beth has been walking for two weeks now and is still not half-way there. Her feet are beginning to give her trouble and yesterday was particularly hard on them. She is in Castilla y Leon now, the hot, dry centre of Spain. Today she leaves San Juan de Ortega, early, just after six and begins her walk along a path lined with oak and pine trees. Unfortunately the dappled shade of the woodland soon comes to an end and she is once more walking through open countryside. Ahead of her is the climb up towards the vast plain that is named the Meseta, but before she gets there she wants to make a slight detour to visit the village of Atapuerca. It was recommended to her by a man she met in the bar the previous night.

'They found fossils and tools in the caves that date back over a million years,' he told her. 'It's the earliest human site in Europe. You have to stop there. You can't be so close and not visit it.'

She has always been interested in archaeology. When Luke was at primary school she accompanied his class on a trip to Lyme Regis. They trekked along the shore picking up ammonites and the fossils of what the children were convinced were dinosaur footprints. They chipped and scraped and filled their little buckets with chunks of wet shale, shells and anything that could be carted back to school and identified. Then they picnicked on the beach and the children, all thoughts of prehistory banished from their heads, played cricket on the sand and splashed about in the rock pools. Luke still has the fossils he collected that day; they lie in the bottom drawer of his bedroom cupboard, alongside the drawings and notes that he made when the class got back to school: two ammonites, a fish skeleton and a piece of fossilised wood. She had tried to throw them out once but he would not hear of it.

It is after seven by the time she reaches Atapuerca; it is a small village, with stone built houses and red painted drainpipes. Flowerpots line the quiet main street, which is just beginning to show signs of life. Two alley cats jump out of a dustbin and hiss at her as they dash across the road and disappear. She walks on; she can smell coffee and follows her nose until, round the next corner, she sees a small bar with a couple of tables outside.

She sits down and orders some breakfast; there is a limited choice: bread, oil and goats' cheese. Despite the heat, which has been building up rapidly since she started out this morning, she is very hungry. While she is eating, her eyes rest on some information leaflets in a rack by the door; she picks one up and reads:

'The Atapuerca Mountains contain a number of caves, where the bones and stone tools of the earliest men in Europe have been found. In the year 2000 the area was declared an UNESCO World Heritage Site.'

There are photographs of their finds: jaw bones, skulls, teeth, leg bones, stone tools, even some fossils of dead flies and cave paintings. Luke would love this.

'Are you going to visit the caves?' the waiter asks.

He speaks excellent English but with a heavy Spanish accent.

'I'd planned to, but it looks as though I'm too early,' she replies, referring to the leaflet in her hand.

'Yes, they don't open until ten o'clock.'

'That's a shame. I can't possibly wait over two hours.'

'You're a pilgrim then?'

'Yes, my next stop is Burgos.'

'Ah, beautiful city.'

He takes away her empty plate.

'Anything else? More coffee?'

'No, that's fine, thanks. It's a shame but I really can't stay. Maybe another time, when I can spend the whole day here.'

'Yes, come back again, when the call of the *Camino* is not so strong.'

She looks at him. Is that what it is? The *Camino* is calling her, urging her along? Whatever it is, she feels she needs all her energy to get herself to Burgos. She places some money on the table and wishes him goodbye.

The soil is red-grey and baked hard by the sun; its corrugated furrows stretch to the horizon and beyond. Not even a solitary tree breaks the evenness of the landscape, flat, dry and un-ending. Above her is the sky, a blue that could have come directly from a painter's palette, unblemished by a single cloud. The path stretches ahead, a dry and stony track leading her on across this wasteland and, as she walks, a covering of fine dust soon begins to cover her boots and work its way down inside her socks, irritating her already, sore feet. She feels she could walk for ever and never arrive at her destination; there is nothing before her and nothing behind. Occasionally, she hears small rustling sounds or a scuffling in the scrubby hedgerow and catches glimpses of green lizards, striped in gold, scuttling out of sight.

She stops, frightened to move. Right in front of her, a snake is coiled up on the path, sunbathing. She does not know what to do? Is it poisonous? She tries to remember if there are any venomous snakes in Spain, but her mind has gone blank. She and the snake regard each other; she is sure there is malevolence in his glittering eyes. The snake seems disinclined to move from its sunny spot. But there is no way that Beth can make herself walk past it. She is terrified of snakes. At last she edges back a bit until she feels she is out of striking distance then bends down and picks up a small rock, which she tosses halfheartedly at the snake. The reptile is startled but not hurt and slithers away, disappearing under the nearest rock.

Well at least something is alive in this bleak and isolated place, even if it is only a snake or an occasional lizard. The solitude is no longer comforting; it is beginning to become oppressive and the track ahead offers up no sign of ever coming to an end. She would like to stop and rest but there is nowhere to do so. The bread she ate at breakfast, lies in her stomach like a stone and she can still taste the slightly rancid flavour of the cheese.

Her thoughts keep returning to Joe. From the time they were married it was his career that mattered; no more mention was made of hers. The plans she had had, but never done anything about, were put on the back burner and eventually forgotten. Joe had loved her then, she knew, but he loved her as his wife, not as a person in her own right. She had always known that but it had not seemed to matter at the time; she had a nice home, a wonderful son and a loving husband, or so she thought. It would have been churlish to complain.

Joe, on the other hand, began to cast his net more widely. He was a passable sportsman and his passion was cricket, playing it, writing about it, reading about it and watching it.   Within a few years of their marriage, he had established himself as an expert on the subject and was being sent to cover England's cricket side wherever they went. His career had flourished.   Nowadays his name was known not just amongst the cricketing fraternity but in the sporting world as a whole.   Joe had made it.   Joe Stuart was a name recognised by everyone.

She, instead, watched the television news and saw her contemporaries make names for themselves: reporting the Truth and Reconciliation Commission in South Africa, the first Gulf War, the second Gulf War, continuing unrest in Palestine, the Iraq War and now Syria.   She picked up the Independent and read the by-lines of   names she vaguely recognised from her days at university. There was no shortage of news to cover and no shortage of able reporters to do it. She admired their courage and tenacity and wondered, if things had been different, if she could have been one of them.

She tosses her head angrily, as if to banish these memories.   It does not help to dwell on the past she tells herself, but cannot stop the bitterness from returning and eating at her soul.

It is not easy walking in these temperatures; by the time she arrives at the peak, Alto Cruciero, over a kilometre above sea level, she can hardly breathe because of the heat and the exertion of her climb.   She is pleased to have somewhere to stop at last and look around her; to her right she has her first view of the city of Burgos. Despite what the waiter told her, it is uninspiring. All she can make out is a conglomeration of squarish buildings and busy roads.   She fills her water bottle at a fountain then sticks her head under the running water, splashing it over her face and hair, enjoying the sensation of it trickling down her neck and wetting her shirt.

Feeling more refreshed, she begins her descent and very soon enters the outskirts of the city. The stony path now becomes a dual-carriageway, which for the next ten kilometres leads her first past the airport, with its shiny new terminal and fleet of commercial aeroplanes, then alongside a railway line, through industrial estates and commercial shopping zones. She walks along the pavement, her head down, willing herself forward. The heat is overpowering; it reflects up at her from the tarmac like the heat from an oven and there is no shade to offer any respite. She walks slowly, her hat pulled down low over her eyes. Occasionally another pilgrim will pass her and make a comment in greeting; usually it is something along the lines of: 'What a bloody awful place this is.' Or, if they are English: 'Hot enough for you?' All she can do is smile and carry on. She does not have the energy to talk and anyway, the noise of the traffic is deafening. A high-speed train screams past her and she feels the vibrations ripple through her body.

She was only forty-three when they found the cancer. Too young for the routine mammograms the over-fifties are entitled to every three years, she eventually mentioned her concerns to a young woman who was standing in as a locum for her own doctor, a curmudgeonly man, whom she has known since she was first married. Dr. Michael, as everyone calls him to distinguish him from his father, the older Dr. Dewer, has worked in the tiny practice just outside Bideford, for thirty years. A practical man, he administers palliatives and common sense in equal measures. He has no time for 'women's ailments' as he disparagingly refers to them. So when Beth thought she had found a lump in her right breast she did not know what to do. There was no way she could envisage discussing it with Dr Michael. Verrucas, colic, bronchitis, broken limbs yes, she could happily talk to him about them, but her breasts, no. She had gone to the surgery that morning to book an appointment for Joe, who needed some vaccinations before setting off to India for the second series of the Test Match.

'Dr Michael is away,' the receptionist told her. 'He's having a few days holiday. You can see Dr. Binns if it's urgent.'

Beth hesitated.

'She's a lady doctor,' the receptionist told her, confidentially.

'OK. That'll be fine.'

'There's only one other person before you, so she shouldn't be long.'

Dr Binns was young and serious. When Beth told her she had felt a small lump in her breast she examined her and immediately arranged for her to have a mammogram.

'It's probably nothing,' she told her. 'But it's best to be sure. These things are best dealt with early.'

These things. She had meant cancer. Beth did not know how to respond. She was frightened, it was true, but she was also stunned. How could this be happening to her?

The next week she went to the hospital in Barnstaple and had the tests. Dr. Binns had already told her that the surgery would call her as soon as they had the results and so there was nothing she could do except wait. The next few days were agony; every time the telephone rang she jumped, expecting it to be the doctor. She had not told anyone about her fears. Joe was still in India and Luke was doing his A-levels; she did not want to worry either of them and she definitely did not want to discuss it over the telephone with Joe. As it was, she could not always be sure what Joe was saying when she rang him, the line was always so distorted. She would tell them afterwards, when the tests had come back negative and they could all laugh about it. But, when the results arrived, they were positive. She had cancer. The big C. Something that happened to other people, not to her.

At last she arrives in the city and, stopping at a small green, sits down and leans her back against the foot of an old stone cross. She needs to rest. By now, her water bottle is almost empty. She knows that some of her companions from the night before, are planning to keep going; they don't want to spend time in the city. They want to get through it and out once more into the peace of the *Camino*, but she is too tired to go any further. Besides, now she is here, she feels she must at least pay a visit to Burgos's famous cathedral. She pulls out her guidebook and locates an *albergue* that is in the centre; it sounds easy to find and is cheap.

      The *albergue* is modern and has a dozen rooms; the concierge takes her up two flights of wooden stairs to the top floor and shows her which bed is free. Beth showers, washes her tee-shirt and underwear in the sink, hangs them by the open window and lies down for a siesta. She hopes to get at least half an hour's sleep before anyone else arrives to disturb her then she will go and visit the cathedral. Burgos is known for many things, but probably the most important of them is the fact that it is the birthplace of the 11th century knight, Rodrigo Diáz de Vivar, or El Cid, as he is more commonly known.

It is after six when she wakes; she has slept all afternoon. Feeling refreshed she sets off to explore the city. Beth does not expect to run into Fran or any of her other usual companions. They have discussed the possibility of meeting in Burgos, but she thinks it is unlikely to happen. They have their mobile phones with them, so can keep in touch with each other; she, on the other hand, through her own choice, is incommunicado.

Her first port of call is the cathedral but she soon tires of wandering around it; El Cid's tomb is interesting but uninspiring and, besides which, she is by now very hungry. She steps out into the fading sunlight. A young girl sits, huddled on the steps of the cathedral, a begging bowl at her feet. Beth takes a coin from her pocket and drops it in her bowl.

'*Que Dios te bendiga*,' the girl says and gives her a brilliant smile.

There is a small restaurant quite close, tucked in the corner of the square; it looks clean and not too expensive, so she goes inside to ask for a table. It is deliciously cool in there; the air conditioner is humming contentedly and a current of cold air greets her as she opens the door. There are no other customers; it is still early by Spanish eating standards, barely eight o'clock. She orders a glass of wine and a lamb dish that is billed as 'Dish of the Day'.

As she sips the wine she begins to relax and finds that even her feet have stopped throbbing. She leans back and looks around her. The restaurant is typical of the area, with dark wooden chairs and tables and the walls are plastered with pictures of either bullfighters or saints. The door to the restaurant opens and a man and a small boy come in; they look Spanish but are obviously not locals. The man has a large rucksack on his back, which he places under the table. The boy sits opposite him. He seems a lively child. She guesses that they are pilgrims, like her.

'*Hola*,' the boy says to her. 'Are you going to Santiago?'

'Yes, I am. Are you?'

'We're going on a pilgrimage,' he tells her. 'We're going to pray for the soul of my Mama.'

'Oh,' she says.

'Jaime, don't pester the lady,' his father tells him.

'No, it's fine,' she says with a smile.

She looks at the father, waiting for some explanation.

'My wife, his mother, died this year. She drowned. It's as the boy says, we are going to Santiago to pray for her. She was born in Galicia and ever since we moved to Madrid to live she talked about one day going back to Santiago de Compostela. It was Jaime's idea; he said we should go there and pray for her. So we decided to do the pilgrimage.'

'Isn't it a long way for a child to walk?' she asks.

'We aren't going to walk the whole way. We took the train from Madrid to Burgos and we're picking up the *Camino* here.'

'Papa, I'm hungry.'

'OK, let's see what they have to offer. What do you fancy, chicken?'

'Hamburgers.'

'I'm not sure if they have hamburgers.'

He looks across at the waiter, who smiles and nods.

'OK, hamburgers it is.'

The door opens again and two couples come in. These are obviously locals because the waiter greets them with smiles and hugs. They sit at the table by the bar and begin to chat in loud, excited Spanish. Beth drinks some more of the wine and finishes her plate of lamb; the wine has made her sleepy and she decides to pay the bill and go back to the hostel.

She heads back towards the cathedral; the *albergue* is not far from there, if she remembers correctly. The air is fresher now and the scent of jasmine floats across from a nearby balcony. She can hear crickets chirping and the chatter of happy voices; someone, somewhere is playing a guitar. The town has come alive at last.

As she turns the corner she sees a dog, tied to a lamppost; it looks like Lucky. Well, if Lucky is here then so is Fran. Lucky is a Podenco bitch that attached herself to Fran, just outside Logrono, in the La Rioja region and they have been together ever since. An obvious stray, Lucky has now given her devotion entirely to her new mistress and follows her wherever she goes. She waits patiently outside bars and taverns until Fran comes out then attaches herself to her side and off they go again. At night Fran tries to choose an *albergue* that has some sort of outhouse or porch where Lucky can sleep and each morning when she goes to leave, Lucky is waiting at the door for her. She is an old dog; her tan and white coat is marred by a grey muzzle and she walks with an arthritic sashay.

Beth bends down and gives the dog a pat.

'Hi there, Lucky. Waiting for your mistress are you? I bet she's on the Rioja again,' she says.

'Actually it's not Rioja tonight. I thought I'd have a change.'

Fran stands in the doorway, a chunk of bread and a piece of chorizo in her hand. She bends down and gives the food to the dog.

'No don't gulp it all down in one go,' she tells her, but she is too late, the food vanishes in a flash.

'This is amazing,' Beth says. 'I never thought I'd run into you tonight. Not here.'

'It's a pilgrimage, isn't it? Miracles can happen. Anyway are you coming in or shall I bring my drink out here?'

'No, I'll come in,' Beth says with a laugh. 'But just for a quick drink; I want to be up early tomorrow.'

'It wouldn't hurt me to have an early night, either,' Fran says. 'This heat is killing me.'

Beth looks on Fran as a close friend now; they have seen each other almost every day since she started the *Camino*. They rarely walk together because Fran likes to go at a faster pace but they try to meet up each evening and talk about their experiences.

'So are you on your own?' Beth asks.

'As if. No, the usual crowd are here.'

Beth follows her into the bar; it is crowded and noisy, as always. She sees a few familiar faces and then picks out Walter's thick mop of white hair. He is beaming across at her.

'Well Beth, you managed to find us then.'

'Quite by accident, I have to admit,' she says, sitting down at the end of the table.

There is something rather nice about meeting up with these people every evening; she feels that they are old friends now, even though she has only known them a couple of weeks.

'So, what sort of a day have you had then?' Walter asks her.

'Hot.'

They laugh.

'Tell me about it,' says Fran.

'What will you have to drink? The usual?' Walter asks.

'Yes please, red wine.'

'You've missed tonight's story,' Darren tells her. 'All about El Cid.'

'El Cid. I remember seeing the film, donkeys' years ago. I was only a kid. It was Charlton Heston in the lead, wasn't it?'

'Yes, and he's been dead for years,' says Fran. 'My mum liked him.'

'I went to see his tomb,'Beth tells her. 'In the cathedral.'

'It's wonderful, isn't it,' Helen says. 'I could spend days there.'

'Well we're moving on tomorrow,' Walter replies, anxiously.

For a moment Beth thinks there might be something going on between them.

'I'm tempted to spend an extra day here, but then I'd never catch up with you again,' Helen goes on.

'So, you'll continue?'

'Yes, of course I will. But I might come back to Burgos one day. There's a lot I haven't seen.'

Beth thinks Walter looks relieved at this.

'So what have you been up to?' Walter turns to Beth and asks.

She tells them about her disappointing detour to Atapuerca and how she arrived too early.

'There you are. If you had a mobile phone you could have rung ahead and found out if they were open,' Fran says.

'Even a watch would have helped to remind me that it was so early. I had no idea of the time when I got there,' Beth confesses.

'Talking of which, it's time I turned in,' says Walter. 'I want to be up early tomorrow before it gets too hot. I'm too old to be walking in this heat.'

'Yes, we're off too,' says Darren. 'The old dear at our hostel made a point of telling us that she'd lock the doors at ten sharp.'

Just like at a dinner party, Beth thinks, when one says they're leaving, everyone leaves. She sips the rest of her wine and waits until they have gone. Only Fran remains.

'You're very quiet tonight,' she says.

'A bit tired, I suppose.'

'And you didn't have any wine either. Don't tell me you've been drinking water all night?' Beth asks with a laugh.

'I have actually.'

'Why is that? Did you have too much last night?'

'No. Well yes, actually, but that's not the reason. I'm pregnant.'

'What?'

Beth is astounded. She looks carefully at Fran; there is no sign at all. She is as slim as ever, skinny even with all the walking she's been doing.

'Well it doesn't show.'

'I'm only three months.'

'When did you find out?'

'Just before I left home.'

'Well, congratulations. That's wonderful.'

Instead of looking pleased she thinks that Fran is going to cry. That would be an even bigger surprise; Fran does not seem to be the sort to cry easily.

'Was it unexpected?' she asks her.

'It was really. In fact it was a bit of a shock for both of us. The last thing on our minds, right now, is having a baby.'

'But it's a good thing? Right?' Beth asks.

She is beginning to sense that this baby is not that welcome. She knows that Fran's boyfriend, Tim, is a highly paid management consultant, who works for McGrinleys and that Fran too has a high-powered job. So it can't be anything to do with money. Perhaps they just don't want children.

'So that's why you're not drinking?' she asks.

'It makes me feel a bit sick, so I thought I'd lay off it for a bit. Or at least not drink quite so much.'

'Well it can't hurt.'

She finishes her wine; it is time they were going.

'Do you know what it is?' she asks.

'No.'

'What do you want, a boy or a girl?' Beth asks.

'I'm not sure that I want it at all. I think I'm going to have an abortion,' Fran says.

Beth does not know what to say to this.

CHAPTER 5
FRAN

The rucksacks lay side by side on the bed. Now that she had started to pack hers it looked ridiculously small. How on earth would she get everything in? She removed a pair of trousers and hung them back in the wardrobe. That still left a pair of jeans, some shorts, two skirts, an assortment of tee-shirts and her underwear, not to mention six pairs of socks and some spare shoes.

'It's impossible,' she called through to Tim. 'I'll never pack everything in it. And it weighs a ton.'

The thought of lugging all that luggage on her back was demoralising. She would never do it.

He was in the bathroom cleaning his teeth. It was Tim's idea to do the *Camino*, the Way of St James. Some friends of his had done it the year before.

'You've got to try it Tim; it's great fun. We met these fabulous Scandinavian girls, legs up to their armpits and they could drink us under the table,' his friends said, smirking at each other.

Then they saw Fran looking at them.

'But really nice women. One of them was doing the walk for her grandmother, who has Alzheimers.'

'Seriously though, you should do it,' said another of his cronies. 'Brilliant exercise.'

'And the wine's good,' said another.

Tim and Fran were just going for two weeks; a month would have been better but Tim's boss wouldn't hear of it. He was not even happy about two weeks.

Tim's friends all worked at McGrinleys and thought they were a cut above the rest of Fran's friends, most of whom were in marketing, like herself. They drove flash cars, spoke in loud voices and expected everyone to stand in awe whenever they said anything. She couldn't understand what Tim saw in them. To her they were just callow young men with poor complexions and enormous salaries. They called themselves management consultants, when in fact they were the dogsbodies for the real consultant, who had a team of these assistants at his beck and call. She listened to their boasting and knew it for what it was because Tim would usually tell her about his own day in great detail. He loved his job and put everything into it, too much, she sometimes thought. She knew the long hours he spent trawling through accounts looking for ways to improve a company's rising costs, how someone else in the team would scour reams of paperwork looking for opportunities to improve efficiency, how they interviewed the workers and documented their jobs, writing and rewriting job descriptions that would increase productivity. Sometimes he would tell her about the redundancies they had recommended the company to make and they would argue back and forth about the morality of it all.

'Don't pack mine,' Tim said, coming out of the bathroom, water dripping down his legs and onto the carpet. 'I'll do it later.'

He put his hands on her shoulders and began nibbling the back of her neck. She turned round and kissed him, her desire flooding through her like wine. The rucksacks were pushed aside, their neatly packed contents spilling on the floor as he pulled her down onto the bed.

Later, lying side by side, damp from their exertions, she had told him.

'Tim,' she said. 'I have some news.'

He looked at her.

'About your job?'

She had applied for a promotion but so far her boss was dragging his heels on giving her a definite answer. She knew he was considering giving it to Kevin but as yet hadn't come up with a convincing argument for doing so. She was better qualified than Kevin, had worked there longer and was assumed by everyone else to be next in line for a manager's job. But she was not a member of the squash club and Kevin was not only a member, he had won the league for the second year running.

'No, it's not about work. It's about us.'

'Us?'

He lifted himself up on one elbow so that he could see her face. She swallowed and said, with a smile that stretched from ear to ear:

'I'm pregnant.'

He let his head drop back onto the pillow and for a moment just lay there. She leaned across and kissed him.

'Didn't you hear me? I'm pregnant. We're going to have a baby.'

At last he spoke.

'Are you sure? Have you been to the doctor?'

'Not yet, I've done one of those pregnancy test things. It was positive.'

She bounced up and straddled him, leaning forward so that her breasts hung down, almost touching his chest.

'Well say something. It's great news, isn't it? We always said we'd have kids, one day, didn't we?'

Her voice wavered; she was no longer feeling so confident. Tim pulled himself out from under her and started to put on his clothes.

'It might be a mistake. You can't rely on those pregnancy tests,' he said, buttoning up his shirt.

'What's wrong? Aren't you pleased that we're going to have a baby?'

'We're not going to have a baby. It's too soon.'

She felt something harden inside her and said:

'OK, if that's how you feel. *We're* not going to have a baby, *I'm* going to have a baby. But, just for the record, you are the father.'

She pushed past him and went into the bathroom and locked the door.

'Look Fran, don't take on so,' he said, trying the handle. 'Let's talk about this. Even if you are pregnant, it's not as though you have to go through with it. It's an easy procedure these days. The doctor will sort it all out for you. Look I'll go with you. We'll go tomorrow; I'll get the day off work.'

She sat on the toilet seat and began to shake. This was not what she expected. This was not fair. It was supposed to be the best possible news, a moment to be remembered all their lives. Well she would always remember it, that was true, but not in a good way.

'Fran, come out so we can talk.'

He rattled the door handle again.

'Don't be stupid now. Come out and we can discuss this like adults.'

She unlocked the door and yanked it open.

'Like adults? OK, so what do you want to discuss? That I murder our unborn child?'

'Don't be so ridiculous. This is just like you, to get so dramatic about things. Look all I'm saying is that I'm, we're, too young to start a family right now. We're not even married. Maybe in a couple of years, when I have a better job, when we've paid off the mortgage, then we can think about it. Get married, have kids, the lot.'

'All very well thought out, but you're forgetting one thing, it's already done. We are expecting a baby. Not sometime in the future when you have your career sorted to your liking, but NOW,' she was screaming at him by now.

'Look Fran, you're over excited, why don't you sit down and we can talk about this rationally.'

She ignored him and began to get dressed.

'Fran, you know I love you. But I just can't see myself as a father, not yet. I'm too young.'

He was pleading with her now but it made no impression.

'You're thirty-five. That's hardly too young. You talk as though you were a teenager,' she replied, pulling a teeshirt over her head and stuffing the rest of her clothes into the rucksack.

She took her passport and her wallet from the drawer and put them in the pocket of her shorts then she hitched the rucksack onto her back and walked out.

'Fran, wait. Where are you going? We have to talk about this.'

'There's nothing to talk about.'

'Where are you going?' he repeated.

'Santiago de Compostela. On my own.'

And here she is, miles from London and miles from Tim. But it is not any easier to make a decision about the baby here than it would have been if she had stayed at home. She has arranged to meet Beth today and walk with her for a bit. She was surprised when Beth suggested it; Beth normally likes to walk alone. She's a nice woman, although a bit reserved;

Fran has grown fond of her over the weeks. Beth has suggested they meet by the cathedral steps, so that is where she is heading. The streets are deserted; only the road sweepers and a few pilgrims, like herself, are about. As she approaches the cathedral, she sees it as hundreds of pilgrims before her must have seen it, bathed in the golden glow of the early morning sun.

'Over here,' Beth calls.

She is perched on a bench in the square.

'Have you eaten?' Fran asks.

'All that I want. Shall we get straight off?'

'Yes, OK. It's going to be another hot one today.'

Today's stage of the journey takes then further into the Meseta and up to Hornillos del Camino. What a name. It tells you everything about what they can expect. In Spanish, *hornillos* means gas-burner or hotplate. Nevertheless it is nice to leave the busy city streets behind them and get back once more to the open countryside. They walk in silence for a bit then Beth asks:

'How are you feeling today?'

'OK.'

'No morning sickness yet?'

'A bit.'

'Don't worry, it only lasts a few weeks.'

'Thanks, that's a great comfort.'

'So what does your boyfriend think about the baby?'

'He says he's too young to settle down and be a dad.'

'Oh, that's a shame.'

'I don't know, maybe he's right. We're both still young. There's plenty of time to have a family later on. He thinks it'll hold him back.'

'Have you been together long?'

'Two years. I thought it was going well. I suppose it was until I dropped the baby bombshell. I should have known how he'd react. He's very ambitious, you see. He has a good degree in Business Management, loads of diplomas and an MBA from the London Business School. He's worked hard to get where he is and his next plan is to widen his experience. He has already started looking for other jobs. What he'd really like to do, although he's reluctant to admit it to anyone but me, is to be head-hunted by some big American company.'

'So marriage and fatherhood don't fit in with his plans?'

Fran shakes her head.

'No way.'

'What about you?'

'To be honest, Beth, I have no idea what I want, right now. Normally I don't have any problems making decisions but this is beyond me. I just don't know.'

The path ahead leads them relentlessly through the burnt countryside; there is no sign of anything, not a house, not a living creature.

'This is a bloody desolate place,' Fran says, wiping her neck with her bandana.

'Well at least it's pretty flat here. I'm not look forward to climbing up there,' Beth says, pointing to a high, table-top ridge in the distance.

'Are those buzzards?' Fran asks, squinting up at the bright sky.

'Vultures, probably.'

'Great, waiting for us to drop dead, I suppose.'

'Not yet I hope.

Beth manages to laugh, although Fran can see she is already exhausted. Maybe the *Camino* is too much for her. It certainly is as tough as anything Fran has done before. Even Lucky is dragging behind. If only there was some shade.

'So why did you decide to walk the *Camino*?' Beth asks. 'Especially if you knew that you were pregnant.'

'I'd been training for it anyway; we were going to do it together. So I thought, why not; I needed to clear my head and have time to think about what's most important in my life: my career, Tim or having a baby. I'm beginning to realise I can't have them all.'

'Well it often comes down to choices. It would be lovely if we could have everything in this life, but it doesn't work out like that. Well at least for me it hasn't.'

'So anyway, I packed my things and set off for France the same day. I haven't spoken to him since. I thought about ringing him when I was in the hotel at the airport, to try to talk some sense into him, but then I thought, why should I. He doesn't want our baby; he wants me to have an abortion. I don't think he understands what he is asking me to do.'

'I'm sure he doesn't,' Beth murmurs. 'He probably just needs time to get used to the idea.'

'Get used to the idea? I don't think he realises that this is a child growing inside me. To him it's just an unwelcome condition that can be removed with pills or something worse.'

'Is he really so unfeeling?' Beth asks.

Fran does not know how to answer this. The truth is that this is not like Tim at all. She had been so shocked at his reaction that she hadn't stopped to think about what it meant to him. Maybe she should have waited and talked to him instead of storming out as she did.

'Who's that?' Beth asks.

There is a woman, dressed in black, sitting by the roadside. She is talking quietly to herself.

'Hi there,' Fran says. 'Are you OK?'

'*Si, si.* I'm fine. I was just resting. The heat is too much for me today.'

'Are you a pilgrim?' Beth asks.

'Yes. I'm on my way to Hornillos.'

While they talk to her, Fran takes advantage of the stop to pour some water into Lucky's bowl and watches as the dog drinks it down eagerly. There is a little left in the bowl so she tips it over the dog's head to cool her down then has a drink herself, from the bottle.

'Why don't you walk with us for a bit?' she suggests to the woman.

'Gracias.'

The woman picks up her rucksack and walks beside them. She is small and dark skinned, with large black eyes and even blacker hair that is pulled back into a pony-tail. A typical Spanish face, Fran thinks.

'Are you on your own?' she asks.

'Si.'

'I'm Beth and this is Fran.'

'Encantada. My name is María.'

'And this is Lucky,' Fran adds.

'So, María, where are you from?' Beth asks.

María smiles at them shyly.

'I'm from Las Palmas, in Gran Canaria,' she tells them.

'And have you walked the *Camino* before?' Beth asks.

Everyone asks this question; everyone wants to know who has done it before.

'No, this is my first time. My husband didn't think I could do it but I told him God would help me.'

She fingers the gold crucifix around her neck as she says it. She does not look a very sporty woman; she looks more like someone's mum, someone who would be a lot happier at home, cooking for her family than walking across Spain on her own. Fran wonders what brings her to the *Camino* and what her story is.

'I've been to the Canaries,' Fran tells her. 'A couple of years ago. My boyfriend and I went there to celebrate my thirtieth birthday. It was great, sun, sand and sex.'

She notices María look away at this.

'They are beautiful islands,' she tells them.

'So why are you walking the *Camino*?' Fran asks. She is impatient to know what María's story is.

'Four years ago my son disappeared,' María tells them. 'He was six-years-old. It was during the summer holidays; the children had only broken-up from school the week before. I was in the garden, hanging out some washing and Manuel was playing on his bicycle. He asked me if he could go outside and cycle down the lane. I said of course he could; we lived on the outskirts of Las Palmas, in a very quiet area. There was never any trouble there, hardly any traffic. He had played in the lane many times.'

She looks at them, her eyes pleading that they understand. Fran finds herself nodding in sympathy.

'I thought there was no harm in it. I told him not to go too far and I unlocked the gate for him.'

She pulls out a tissue and wipes her eyes.

'I stood at the gate for a few minutes, watching him cycle down the path. He was wobbling a bit and I was more worried about him falling off than anything else. But he wasn't frightened; he lifted his hand and waved to me. I thought he might fall off then because the bike swerved a bit, but he righted it and carried on. 'Look at me, Mama,' he called. I remember I laughed and said: 'Be careful now, *cariño*.' and I went back to hanging out the washing. When I finished I went out to look for him, but he was gone.'

She cannot continue. She is not crying but her voice is cracking and she can hardly speak.

Fran looks at Beth. They do not know what to say. How do you comfort a woman whose child is missing?

'And there has been no sign of him since?' Beth asks.

María shakes her head.

'Nothing. That's why I have come to ask God to grant me a miracle.'

Fran feels tears in her eyes. Is it possible? Do people really come on the *Camino* looking for miracles?

By the time they reach Hornillos they are all exhausted. Fran thinks she will drop if she doesn't stop soon. For the last couple of miles they have walked in a silence only broken by the quiet murmurings of María. Fran thinks she must be praying but it is hard to make anything out and anyway Fran's command of the Spanish language is very limited.

The first *albergue* that they come across has only one bed available so they say good bye to María and continue to the next one. This one is very smart, with newly painted shutters and bright green sunshades outside.

'Yes, we have some rooms,' the concierge tells them. 'Do you have your *credenciales*?'

They hand over their passports to be stamped.

'Is that your dog?' she asks.

'Well, sort of. I found ...' Fran begins but the woman interrupts her.

'Sorry, no dogs.'

She hands back Fran's passport.

'Dogs forbidden.'

'Don't you have somewhere outside she could sleep? A barn or a shed?'

'No dogs.'

'Oh well. Look you stay here, Beth. I'll try the next place. I'll see you this evening.'

'I could come with you.'

'No, stay here. You look as though you're about to drop. We'll meet up in the pub about eight, OK?'

'Fine. I'll see you then.'

DAY 14

CHAPTER 6
BETH

When she wakes this morning Beth feels refreshed but hungry and her leg is itching terribly. She pulls off her sheet and examines it. Bed bugs. Her leg is covered in their bites. She cannot hold back a scream and jumps out of the bed.

'You too?' the woman in the bed above her asks. 'I think we've all been bitten. I thought you were the only one who'd escaped, seeing as you never got up once in the night.'

'I was tired,' she says.

She shows the woman her leg.

'Wow, someone was feasting on you alright. Got anything to put on them?'

She shakes her head.

'Here, give them a spray with this. It's pretty good stuff.'

She takes the aerosol from her and sprays her legs.

'Make sure you check your bedding before you go to bed tonight,' the woman advises her.

'I certainly will. This is awful.'

She cannot put into words how she feels at the thought of these horrid little creatures feasting on her blood like that. It makes her skin crawl to think of it.

'Thanks,' she says, returning the aerosol. 'I think I'll be on my way.'

She cannot wait to get out of this *albergue*. She is not going to bother showering. She dresses, rolls her bedding together and leaves. This is not going as she planned.

Today she has twenty kilometres to walk, not far if she were walking the coastal path in Devon but here, in this furnace, it will take her most of the day. She is glad to be up early, hoping to avoid her fellow travellers, but everyone has the same idea, start early and walk while it is cool. Except it is never cool. She cannot believe it is September. Already the sun is trailing its fiery tail across the morning sky, stirring the birds to song. She fills her water bottle at a fountain before she leaves the town and sets off, the rising sun at her back. Before her lies a wide, flat expanse of dry, open land where the stubby remnants of harvested corn spread like a golden carpet at her feet. She can see a group of pilgrims ahead of her and the sound of their chatter floats back across the still air. A pair of skylarks, startled by her presence, fly up from the stubble, trilling their way into the cloudless sky. Within seconds they are nothing more than tiny dots above her.

Dr. Michael was back from his holidays by the time of her next appointment. She was surprised how kind and gentle he was with her, explaining exactly what was happening to her body and what they were going to do to combat it. The results showed that she had a Stage 1 cancer, a small tumour, no more than one centimetre in diameter. It sounded so innocent. That was good, Dr Michael explained. The cancer was confined to the one breast and had not had the chance to spread to any lymph nodes. Survival rates were very positive, 88%. He arranged for her to go into hospital the following Tuesday and see the oncologist. Brisk and efficient, he told her that she would need to have the lump removed; a lumpectomy was probably all that was required, no need to remove the whole breast. After that she would have a short course of radiotherapy and medication and everything would be fine again. The oncologist would answer any other questions she had. That was Dr. Michael at his best, practical and straight to the point.

It all happened just as her doctor described. However he had not told her about the waiting, nor given her any advice on how to survive those long drawn-out days and nights before her operation. It was not scheduled for two weeks, not a great deal of time to wait, in the normal course of events but, to Beth, it had seemed like an eternity. She imagined the cancer growing larger and larger inside her and sometimes would wake in the night, sweating with the fear that they would be too late to save her. She longed for Joe to return. She knew she could not handle it on her own but she dreaded telling him and, worse than that, she dreaded telling Luke. It was not because she didn't want to worry them, although she didn't; it was because she could not bear to see them look at her as someone with a terminal illness. She did not want their pity. She did not want them to look at her differently. Silly thoughts invaded her head and kept her awake at night. They were going to remove part of her breast. She would be maimed, scarred at the very least. What would she look like? Would Joe still fancy her afterwards? She had never been particularly vain but the idea of being less than whole upset her equilibrium.

When people heard the word cancer they instinctively thought the worst; she understood that. She had been guilty, on occasion, of the same negative reaction. But she did not want people to react to her like that; she did not want any negative thoughts around her. She had to remain positive. So she told no-one. She would get through this, she told herself. Somehow she would be one of the 88% who survived.

Joe came home on the Sunday morning before her operation. She drove into Barnstaple to collect him from the railway station, her heart pounding. He knew straight away that something was wrong; it was not possible to keep it from him. As soon as she saw him, waiting by the platform, tanned and smiling, she broke down and cried with relief. It was going to be alright, now that Joe was home. He would not let her die.

They decided to tell Luke together; Beth felt she could manage it better if she had Joe with her. It was odd; she was more concerned about upsetting her son than the fact that she might die. But she did not die. She survived the operation, survived the thirty-two sessions of radiotherapy, driving to the hospital every day, Monday to Friday, survived the discomfort, the tiredness, survived the burning, itching skin that the treatment left her with. She had regular check-ups and took her post-op medication religiously. Then, five years later, they told her that she had the 'all clear'. She had survived. She could look forward to a long and happy life, they said; the cancer was gone. But they were wrong.

She stops and sits down by the edge of the path, dropping her rucksack beside her. Her shoulders ache and the straps of the rucksack are cutting into her skin.

There is no-one about, neither in front of her nor behind. She has been so absorbed in her own thoughts that she has not been watching for the waymarks. It is a lonely place, the Meseta and disorientating. She checks the map in her guidebook. Surely the sun should be over her left shoulder but, if anything, it is to her right. Has she taken a wrong turn? Surely not. She is puzzled. She is certain she has kept to the path. She looks around her; it is difficult to get her bearings. Everything looks the same, whichever way she turns; the scorched landscape never changes, it runs out to

77

the horizon in every direction. The heat presses down, flattening her like a smoothing iron. She can hardly breathe; the air is so hot and dry it is searing her lungs. She feels that the blood in her veins is turning to vapour. Any minute now she will desiccate and drift away like the dry husks of corn that surround her. She drinks the last of her water and unlaces her boots. Her feet are swollen and bruised from the hard earth. She rubs them with some cream and replaces her socks but it is hard to get her boots on again. She tugs and tugs at them but her protesting feet refuse to be encased.

'Oh, for God's sake,' she swears aloud in exasperation. 'Why on earth did I come on this God forsaken pilgrimage?'

Tears of self pity trickle down her cheeks. No movement stirs the still air; there is not the whisper of a breeze to relieve the heaviness. She looks up at the sky and sees a buzzard circling far above her. Or is it the vultures again? Maybe Fran was right. Maybe this one is waiting for her to die and then he can swoop down and strip the flesh from her bones. She shudders at the thought. Death seems to be forever present in this land. She should have listened to Dr Michael; she is not strong enough for this. She vows that if she ever makes it back to civilisation, she will get the next bus out of here.

She pulls at the laces until they are completely slack and tries once more to put her boots back on. This time she succeeds. She stands up but her feet are painful. Well, painful or not, she cannot sit here in the middle of nowhere for ever. She has to decide which way to go. She scratches her leg. The bites hurt as well as itch. She wishes she had waited for Fran this morning but she had been in such a hurry to get away. Now she could do with some company, someone to talk to, someone to tell her which way to go.

Ahead of her she can see the crossing of two paths through the field of stubble. Is it just a break in the corn or is it a crossroads? She is not sure. She hesitates. In the distance she can just make out the shape of a tall figure, walking due west. She checks the sun again. Yes, if she follows him the sun will be over her left shoulder again; she should be back on track. She veers right and sets off after the ghostly figure. At first she quickens her pace, hoping to catch up with him, but every time she thinks she has him within shouting distance, he seems to speed up and she is left trailing behind once more.

He does not look like a farmer and there are no sign of sheep, so he cannot be a shepherd. She is sure that he is a pilgrim; she can see his staff, one of the old fashioned kind, long and with a hook at the end, nothing like her own walking poles, of shiny aluminium with their leather loops. He wears a wide brimmed hat and a cloak, or poncho, she cannot get close enough to tell which. Either way it seems unusual in this heat. He must be roasting.

The sight of this strange figure in the distance is oddly comforting. She follows him for an hour and then discovers, to her delight, that she is back on the *Camino*. The usual blue and gold waymarks are there to direct her. She wants to cry with relief. The pilgrim must have quickened his pace because he is no longer in sight. After a while she comes to the Arroyo San Bol and sits down to rest by a stream. Here there is a patch of dense shade made by the overhanging branches of a small grove of poplar trees. It is wonderful to be out of the relentless sun for a while. She pulls out her guidebook and checks how far she has travelled; she cannot believe she has only come six kilometres since she started this morning. It is now obvious to her that she had wandered a long way off track. The burble of running water is cool, refreshing music to her ears and she stretches out in the shade and falls asleep.

The sound of singing wakes her. A group of young pilgrims are crossing the stream, the tramp of their boots reverberating along the bridge. She gathers her things together and tags along behind them. They are all young and enthusiastic and walk at a steady pace but she is determined to keep up with them.

'Beth, is that you?'

It is Helen.

'Hi.'

'Are you coming with us? We're making a short detour to San Anton.'

A detour. Beth feels her heart sink. She just wants to get to the hostel and get out of this unrelenting sun; she does not feel like sightseeing.

'It's not far. It'll be worth it; there's an ancient monastery there, where the hermit, Saint Anthony of Egypt stayed.'

Beth is far from interested in Saint Anthony or any other saint at the moment. She thinks there are too many saints in Spain. There seems to be at least one for every day of the week.

'Alright. If you're sure it's not too far.'

She cannot face walking on her own. It will be better if they all stick together. She does not want to get lost again.

To enter the hamlet of San Anton the group of pilgrims pass under Saint Anthony's Arch.

'Look. Do you see those alcoves in the arch? That's where they used to leave bread for the pilgrims,' Helen tells her. 'Nowadays people leave messages for each other.'

She puts her hand in one of the recesses and takes out an envelope. A name is scribbled across the envelope.

'See.'

Beth wonders who left it there and how long ago. It doesn't seem a very secure way of getting information to someone.

'Wait. I'm going to leave a message,' Helen says.

She returns the envelope to its place and taking a page from her notebook, writes something hurriedly. Then she folds it up and tucks it in one of the alcoves.

'So who's the message for?' Beth asks.

Helen blushes.

'No-one in particular. I just wanted to do it. Come on we'll have a little look at the monastery before we move on.'

'I think I'd prefer to stop and have a cup of tea,' Beth says. 'I don't have the energy for wandering around old buildings.'

'OK. You wait over there and I'll be back in half an hour.'

Beth is just finishing her second cup of iced herbal tea when Helen returns.

'That was wonderful. And look what I bought for myself. I couldn't resist it,' she tells Beth.

She pulls a small, wooden cross in the shape of the letter T out of her pocket. It is carved from ebony and polished until is shines.

'It's called a Tau cross, after the Greek letter 'tau'. It guards against evil and sickness.'

'Does it help with sore feet?' Beth asks.

'I expect so. It was said to be a cure against St Anthony's fire, a fungal disease that people suffered from in the Middle Ages. It must have been highly contagious because thousands of people were struck down by it and often died. Apparently the monks here were particularly successful at curing it.'

'What, just by waving this cross at them?'

Beth is feeling particularly cynical today. She does not believe in all this rubbish, she tells herself. It is probably just made up for the tourists.

'So they say, but I expect faith had a lot to do with it.'

'More likely something in the water.'

She sees the rest of the pilgrims moving back towards the *Camino*.

'Shall we go?'

'Yes, if you're finished your tea.'

Helen wraps her cross in a twist of paper and puts it back in her pocket.

'You obviously enjoy looking around old churches,' Beth says, remembering what Helen said about visiting as many cathedrals as she could.

'I love it. I can't tell you how much I'm enjoying this trip. I've dreamt of getting away on holiday for so many years but there was never an opportunity.'

'With your mother, you mean?'

'Yes, that's right. I couldn't leave her.'

'But your brother and sisters, couldn't they even give you a few weeks break?'

'They were all busy with their own lives. It's OK. That's just how it was. Mammy was bed-ridden for ten years and in that time I had to juggle looking after her with my job at the local secondary school. My brother moved to London and only came home at Christmas and little Martha got married and had twin boys. There was just me and Mammy, left in the family home.'

'What about your father?'

'My father died, knocked down by a bus one evening as he staggered home from the pub.'

'Oh dear, I'm sorry.'

'Yes, Mammy took it very hard. I don't know why; he was never there most of the time, anyway. Then things just got steadily worse. The house grew more and more run-down, the window frames were loose and rattled all night, the walls needed painting and the patches of mould in the bathroom grew worse. It was a struggle to keep the back garden in order and the weeds grew everywhere, pushing up the paving stones of the path and choking the flower beds that Mammy used to love so much. The trouble was that there was no money to pay for any help. I cleaned and cooked and every Sunday afternoon I battled with our ancient lawn mower in a vain attempt to at least keep the lawn in order. My father's death had left us financially unprepared and it was hard to make ends meet. I found I had to give up the few luxuries that I had enjoyed and day by day I did less and less with my life; I stopped visiting my friends and I stopped going to concerts. I didn't have the energy nor the money to enjoy either. I used to be a member of the local history society but I even had to give that up. In truth I became a plain, lonely spinster, whose duty it was to care for my mother.'

'But that's all changed now.'

'Yes. I had resigned myself to thinking that was all I could expect from life. Then one day my mother died. It was in the week leading up to Christmas. She had not been any worse than usual, maybe a bit weaker; the cold weather did not help her bronchitis and we had had some bitterly cold days that year. I kept the heating turned up as high as I dared but the house was draughty and Mammy still complained about feeling cold.

I remember the last few days of term were particularly hectic and the week before Christmas was worse than ever; even the older children were excited about the coming holidays and there were so many things to organise. As I was the teacher in charge of religious studies, it always fell to me to produce the nativity play each year. This took up all my spare time at school and two evenings in the week as well. Then there were the Stage 3 SATS to mark and the end-of-term reports to prepare. I barely had time to draw breath. Maybe it was because I was so busy, that I didn't notice the decline in Mammy's health.

I took her breakfast in to her that morning, as usual: a cup of milky tea, a few Cornflakes, some buttered toast and some home-made marmalade, that one of the women from the church had given us. Mammy lay there, her white hair spread out on the pillow, her face grey and waxy. She did not move. I called her name but she didn't open her eyes. At first I didn't realise. It took a few more moments to understand that Mammy was gone.'

'So you were on your own?'

'Yes. But once the Christmas holidays were over and the funeral passed, I received a letter from my mother's solicitor. Mammy had left the house to me. I couldn't believe it. I thought it would be shared equally amongst us all, but no, she had left it to me in gratitude, she said in her letter, for the years of sacrifice I had given her.'

'What did your brother and sisters say?'

'Oh, they made a few comments, but even they couldn't deny that I'd earned it.'

'So what will you do?'

'Well I've put the house on the market. Before leaving for Spain, I instructed the local estate agent to sell it. After all, what do I need with a ramshackle, draughty house and a garden that needs constant attention? No, a nice modern flat will suit me much better.'

At last they arrive in Castrojeriz and Beth checks into the first *albergue* she can find. By now, she is seriously considering giving up, taking a bus back to civilisation and flying home. Her feet are sore, her back hurts from carrying the rucksack and she is suffering from a surfeit of sun. Somehow it all seems pointless. She cannot understand why she decided to come here in the first place. Why is she putting herself through all this pain and discomfort? What is it for? Is she trying to prove something to herself? Is it to find peace of mind or is it just to spite Joe? She has been hoping for clarity, for answers but all she has are more unanswered questions.

She dumps her rucksack on her bed and goes out in search of a chemist shop. She is in luck; there is one in the next street. She pushes open the carved, wooden door and goes in; a blast of cold air greets her. A woman in a white coat stands behind the blue and white tiled counter. There are old stoneware pots ranged on the shelves behind her, each one glazed in the same blue and white as the counter and with the name of a different herb on each. Everything in the shop is a feast for the eyes. An open cupboard displays a range of fascinating glass bottles: tall thin ones, square ones, fat ones with thin necks, ribbed ones with droppers; some are brown, many are various shades of green and once again there is that incandescent blue.

'*Te ayudo*?' the woman asks.

'I need some ointment for my feet, *mis pieds*,' Beth tells her, using a mixture of sign language and Spanglish.

'Sit down and show me the problem,' she instructs her, in perfect English.

'Oh, wonderful. You're English.'

The woman smiles.

'Yes, born and bred. I know all about sore feet; I did the *Camino* ten years ago.'

'What and just stayed on?'

'No, I went home but I kept thinking about this place and in the end I came back. I met my husband in Oviedo; he's the chemist,' she explains, 'and we opened the shop here.'

'How extraordinary.'

Beth takes off her boots and shows the woman her blistered feet.

'My, you've got a fine case of pilgrims' foot,' she says with a smile. 'Don't worry. I've got just the stuff for you.'

She takes a tub of ointment off the shelf.

'I give this to all the pilgrims. It'll heal your feet in no time. Put it on each night before you go to sleep and then again in the morning before you leave. Wrap your feet up well before you put on your boots and you'll soon see the difference.'

'And something for bed bugs?' Beth asks.

'This'll do the trick,' the woman says, handing her a large tube of cream. 'And take this spray to spray your mattress each night. You can never be too careful.'

Beth decides to take some strong painkillers as well. But still this feeling of hopelessness won't leave her. She thinks it was a mistake to come here; she shouldn't be wasting what time she has left. Maybe she should have asked for some anti-depressants; she has heard that you can get all sorts of things in Spain without a prescription. She takes her purchases back to the *albergue* and showers, administers the ointment to her feet and smoothes the cream into her bites. There is no-one else in the room so she swallows two of the painkillers and lies down on the bed. Perhaps she will feel better after she has had a decent sleep.

But sleep won't come. Her head is swirling. It's no good. She does not know why she has come here. It's not going to solve anything. Before she can stop herself she is sobbing into her pillow. She knows what happens with cancer. It follows a pretty clear pattern. They give you five years after the treatment. If you are clear after that then, probably, you have been cured. But if it comes back, as hers has, then that's it. Your life is over. An end-date is in sight and there is nothing you can do about it. What is the point of fighting it? She wishes there was someone with her. For a moment she wants to be a child again and have her mother there to comfort her and tell her everything will be alright.

CHAPTER 7

Whether it was the hot shower and a sound afternoon's sleep that made the difference or the tablets, she does not know but, when she wakes, her headache is gone and she is feeling more positive. She knows she will go on. She is not a quitter and anyway she cannot abandon the pilgrimage so soon. Beth lies on her back looking at the ceiling; a spider is busily weaving a web around the light fitting. Now there's a creature with perseverance, she thinks. Stubborn as well.

Someone has opened the shutters and a fresh breeze floats across the room, bringing with it the smell of frying garlic. She hears her stomach rumble and realises just how hungry she is. She pulls herself up and looks around her; she is alone. The other beds are obviously taken but their occupants have already left to spend the evening in the town. She examines her feet; they are no longer throbbing, so she spreads some more ointment on them and puts on her sandals.

The concierge is at the reception desk when she goes down.

'Good evening. Did you want dinner?' she asks.

'Yes please.'

'It's nine euros and you have to help clear away,' the woman tells her.

'Fine.'

'Through that door there.'

She can hear the sound of pots clattering and excited chattering coming from the next room.

'By the way,' she says. 'I'd like to send my bag on ahead tomorrow. Can you arrange that?'

She wants to treat herself, to walk unencumbered.

The woman takes up her pen.

'No problem. Where will you be?'

'Frómista. Can they leave it at the *Auberge Romano*?'

She watches her write down the address and then goes into the dining room. At least forty people are sitting at two long trestle tables; some are eating and some are still waiting for their food. She notices that it is the pilgrims themselves who serve the food, which is passed through to them from the kitchen. It smells wonderful. She sits between a young Asian man and a priest in black robes.

'Hello,' the young man says.

He passes her a basket of bread and someone puts a plate of fried green peppers and chicken in front of her.

'You've missed the first course,' the priest tells her. '*Gazpacho*.'

She looks around the room, hoping to see the pilgrim from that morning but it is impossible to say if he is here or not. She does not have enough to go on. Since she began this pilgrimage she has grown used to recognising people from their manner of walking; usually it is the first thing she notices about them. So even though she never got very close to the pilgrim she noticed that he had a slightly stiff gait; this makes her think he is an old man rather than a younger one. She looks at the priest. Could it be him?

'Did I see you this morning?' she asks. 'Somewhere near San Bol?'

He shakes his head.

'No, my child. I arrived here yesterday. I have been helping Father Ramón with his parish duties today. Tomorrow I will continue on my way.'

'Room for a little one?' a man's voice asks.

It is Walter. He puts his plate of food on the table and squeezes himself between Beth and the priest.

'You staying here then?' he asks.

'Yes, I just went to the first place I saw,' she says and explains what a traumatic day she has had.

'It's a tough walk across the Meseta,' he agrees. 'I reckon the temperature must have been 45° today. I thought the blood was boiling in my head.'

The skin on his arms is red and peeling. Walter is a big man, with a square chin and huge hairy arms. His once ginger hair is mostly white now but he still has plenty of it, despite his age. She wonders how he manages; his complexion is not one suited to Spanish sunshine.

She tells him about the pilgrim she followed.

'Did you see anyone like that?'

'No, can't say I noticed. But it sounds as though it was a good job you spotted him. I wouldn't want to get lost out there in that wilderness; you could wander round and round in circles for ages.'

He helps himself to another hunk of bread.

'I was with a group of Australian lads. They never stopped chattering about cricket, all the way.'

He wipes the juice off his plate with the bread and says:

'Coming for a drink afterwards?'

'Of course. I definitely need one tonight.'

'Good.'

'I walked with Helen for a bit today,' she tells him. 'She was telling me what a hard life she had, looking after her mother.'

90

'Yes, she's not had it easy.'

He drinks some of the wine then says:

'She's a nice woman. I think I could become quite fond of her.'

Beth looks at him and smiles.

'A bit of romance in the air is there, Walter?'

'No, of course not. I'm far too old for her.'

'Do you think so? She's in her fifties, you know.'

'I know, but it's not just that. I'd feel a bit awkward, at my age. And then there's my kids. What would they say? Their mother's only be dead a few years.'

'Didn't you say it was five years now; that's a long time. If your wife was as nice a woman as you say she was, I'm sure she wouldn't begrudge you some happiness. I think we should make the most of our lives. After all you never know how much time you have left.'

'Well that sounds serious, Beth. I hope I've got a few more years in me yet.'

'I'm sure you have, but then I expect you thought that about your wife.'

'That's true. I never expected her to die before me. All the statistics say that women live longer than men. And in my job, with the long hours and stress, I thought I'd be in my box long before her.'

Beth eats one of the peppers; it is a bit oily but very tasty. She must try to snap out of this mood. It must be fatigue that is making her so morbid. Maybe she will feel better when she sees Fran again.

They find Fran in the first bar they try. Once again she is with Helen and the young couple from Birmingham. Lucky is curled up at Fran's feet.

'Hey. Had a good day?' she asks.

Beth plumps herself down in the chair opposite and lets out a sigh of exasperation.

'Not really.   I was all for packing it in a few hours ago.'

'And now?'

'Well you know, things don't look so black now.'

'They all say that if you can get through the first two weeks, you'll make it. It's like, you start off on a high, full of excitement but then you realise it's harder than you thought and you lose the enthusiasm.   You think you've made a mistake or that you're useless. If you can just keep going, you start to feel a sense of achievement and that lifts you for a bit, then, as you near the end, there's a final surge of excitement,' Darren tells them. 'Well that's what they say.'

He traces a graph on the table to illustrate his point.

'You're probably right.   I certainly felt I'd made a mistake today. I was somewhere about here.'

She points to the nadir of the curve.

'It wasn't helped by the fact that it was unbearably hot,' Fran adds.

'How did Lucky cope with the heat today?' Beth asks.

'Surprisingly well. I'd have thought she'd want to find a shady spot and curl up all day long but no, she wouldn't leave my side. She trailed behind me all the time.'

'Got to keep an eye on where the next meal's coming from,' Walter says.

He turns to Helen.

'How are you? Did you have a good walk?'

'Excellent. Beth and I stopped at the ruins of the 11th century convent of San Antón. They have a small *albergue* there and it was so beautiful that I was very tempted to stay the night, but then I thought about you all meeting up here.'

Beth thinks she looks at Walter in particular when she says this.

92

'You didn't tell me about the *albergue*,' she says. 'I would have been very tempted to stay.'

'I know the place,' says Fran. 'We stopped there for a rest and some water. They used to leave bread for the pilgrims under the arch.'

'That's right, in the alcoves. Now people leave messages for each other.'

'Did you leave one?' Walter asks.

Helen smiles and nods.

'Did you now? Who for?'

Helen blushes.

'No-one really. It was just a short prayer, a traveller's prayer. I thought someone might open it and read it.'

'How sweet,' Sheri says.

'Yes, and I bought a Tau cross.'

'Oh, that's lovely,' Sheri exclaims, when Helen produces the cross. 'You should get a chain for it and then you can wear it with your other one.'

Helen already wears a silver cross on a silver chain.

'Well we had a nice day,' Fran says, bending down and stroking Lucky. 'I bought Lucky a new collar and a lucky scallop shell.'

Sure enough, the dog has the pilgrim's emblem hanging around his neck.

'So she's a proper pilgrim now,' Walter says.

The dog senses that they are talking about her and thumps her tail on the ground in appreciation. She has been following Fran for a week now. Already she is losing that starved look but, despite the shampoo that Fran gave her, her coat still has a mangy aspect to it. It will take a while for the bare patches to regrow. Beth wonders how long she was scavenging for scraps before she met up with Fran.

'I've got a dog at home,' Sheri tells them. 'He's a giant schnauzer, a beautiful great soft thing. We all love him.'

'Yes, I swear she loves that dog more than me,' Darren adds.

'Are you married?' Helen asks.

'Not officially, but we've been living together for eighteen months now.'

She smiles shyly and takes Darren's hand.

'So what brought you to the *Camino*?' Beth asks.

'Just for a laugh really,' Darren says. 'We had some mates that had done it and they said it was a great experience.'

'We were only going to do the last hundred kilometres,' Sheri says, 'but then we thought why not do it all. It's not as though we don't like walking and Darren had just been made redundant, so we decided to do it before he starts a new job.'

'If I can get one,' Darren mutters.

'We're members of the Solihull Walkers and Ramblers Club,' Sheri tells them.

'That's where we met,' Darren adds. 'Walking the Pennine Way.'

'In the rain and wind. God that was an awful weekend.'

'Thanks. I thought you said it was the best weekend of your life.'

Sheri blushes.

'Well it was, but I was talking about the weather.'

They all laugh at her discomfort and Walter signals for the waiter to bring them another bottle of wine.

Darren bends down and fingers Lucky's new collar.

'So what's this about the scallop shell? Why a scallop shell and not an oyster shell for example?' he asks.

'Good question,' Helen replies. 'As with many other aspects of the pilgrimage the origin of how this symbol became associated with St James is clouded in myth and legend. One version tells how the disciples bringing James' s body back to Spain were shipwrecked off the coast of Galicia, near the town of Padrón and the apostle's body was lost at sea. The disciples managed to scramble ashore but were devastated that they had lost the saint's body and prayed to God for forgiveness. Some days later St James' body was washed ashore, unscathed but covered in scallops.'

'But why scallops?'

'Because there are thousands of them on the Galician coast,' Fran tells him. 'They're ten a penny there. I love them. I have to admit, the seafood was one of the main attractions for doing the *Camino*.'

'A bloody long way to walk for a few scallops,' says Darren. 'Easier to get them in the fish market.'

Fran gets up suddenly and hurries outside. When she does not come back Beth decides to go and look for her. She is sitting on the steps next to Lucky.

'You OK?'

'Not really.'

'What's the matter?'

'I've started to bleed.'

'Oh no.'

'Maybe it's for the best. Maybe it was never meant to be.'

CHAPTER 8
WALTER

Something woke him. He never knew what it was. He rolled over and put his arm out, to touch Nora's neck. That was when he knew. She was cold and still, far too cold and still for a sleeping woman. She was dead. His wife of forty-years had slipped away in the night, without a word.

It was not as though she had been ill, not really. She had complained about feeling tired a lot and not having the energy she used to have, but they both thought that was just a symptom of getting older. Then she collapsed in the road, on her way back from the supermarket. He had told her, many times, not to carry so much shopping.

'I could have picked you up in the car,' he said. 'You just had to ring me.'

But Nora was independent; she was used to doing things on her own, he now realised. She did not like to bother him.

'Angina,' the doctor said when Walter took her to the A and E. 'There's no need to worry. We'll get her on some medication and she'll be as right as rain.'

Nora had smiled at him and nodded in agreement. No need to make a fuss. Nora hated to make a fuss.

But before he could even get the medicine for her, she had gone, melting away in the night without a word.

He had always tried to be a good husband and father, or so he thought. He and Nora had been married for forty years, three months and twelve days, more than half his lifetime and she had never complained once. He knew it could not have been easy for her, married to a policeman; his hours were long and irregular.

The police force took over his life. He could see that now, but at the time it seemed perfectly natural; the police force was his life. Now, when he looked back, he realised that the job always came first, before family, friends, children, even his wife. But that was how it was then. The man went out to work and the wife looked after the kids. After all he was doing it for them, he had told himself on the many occasions when he knew he had disappointed them.

Walter is sitting at a table inside the bar when Helen arrives. He can smell the pungent aroma of fresh coffee as the coffee machine goes through its customary cycle of grinding and hissing before finally, with a huge mechanical sigh, extruding a fine dribble of coffee into the cup.

'Hi, there you are,' he says, getting up and pulling out a chair for her. 'I've just ordered a coffee. What will you have?'

'*Café con leche*, please.'

The bar is doing a good trade. Sleepy pilgrims are ordering provisions for the day, buying bottles of water and hunks of cheese then joining their friends, to breakfast on warm, brown bread and olive oil.

'I thought we might walk part of the way together, today,' he suggests. 'If you don't mind company, that is?'

Helen's face flushes with pleasure.

'That sounds nice.'

'It looks as though we've got rather a steep climb to start off,' he says.

'Yes, I noticed that, but it's flat after that and it's all on country roads, no hard asphalt to walk on.'

The waiter puts a milky coffee on the table in front of her.

'*Gracias*,' she says and smiles at the young man.

She has a lovely smile; it's infectious. He finds himself smiling too.

'What?' she asks.

She seems almost girlish as she put her head on one side and looks at him quizzically.

'Nothing.'

'Do you miss being a policeman?' she asks.

'That's an odd question,' he says. 'I suppose I must do, in a way. After all I joined the force at nineteen, not long after leaving school. I was a right lanky lad in those days, but they liked you tall in the police. I had a shock of red hair, just like my father. He was a policeman too and two of my uncles were special constables. So, you see, it was no great surprise to the family when I told them that that was what I wanted to do.'

'Following in the family footsteps,' she says.

'Yes. I think it was in the blood.'

'Well it's a good career,' Helen says.

'Yes and no. It's hard on the family. I was lucky that Nora was a homebody. She gave me forty hassle-free years of marriage. I was a lucky man; I could get on with climbing the promotion ladder while she looked after the home.'

'I expect she wanted you to do well.'

'Yes, I know she did, but nowadays I ask myself what I gave her in return. My poor kids. I can remember the disappointment on their faces because I couldn't join the other parents at sports' day, or go the the carol concerts. I never even made it to the school parents' evenings. I just left Nora to discuss our kids' progress with their teachers. That all came under the heading of 'Mum's responsibilities'. The only thing I really made an effort for, when I could, was going to watch my son play rugby for the school. Even then I'd miss some of the matches because of work.'

'Well I don't think that's so terrible. Things were like that years ago. I never remember my father doing anything with me and my brother and sisters. It was always Mammy who went to the school.'

He looks at her. She is such an understanding woman but she doesn't realise how selfish he used to be. By the time he met Nora he was already a sergeant but that was not enough for him. He was ambitious; he wanted to be a detective. He had done more than the obligatory two years as a uniformed policeman, he was bright and he was hard working, so the year he met Nora he sent in his application. He was doing it for them, for their future, he told her, but really it was for himself. He was never going to let anything stand in his way, certainly not a wife and family. Now he would give anything to have those years back, to make it up to Nora.

'But you were a policemen when you got married, so Nora must have understood,' Helen says.

'Yes. I was preparing for my detective exams when we got married. But even then the job came first. We had a brief honeymoon in Margate and then it was back to working my usual shift while studying all evening. I have to admit Nora seemed to be happy about my ambitions, although now, looking back, I sometimes wonder if she would have preferred me to have stayed as a humble bobby.'

'I expect she just wanted you to be happy.'

He smiles at her and nods. She is right. All Nora ever wanted was to please him. But it became worse after he had passed all the exams and interviews and was promoted to detective sergeant; DS Jones, he had loved the sound of it.

His days were not clearly laid out; he often had to work unsociable hours and sometimes far more than he was paid for. But he enjoyed the work and, as Nora never questioned him about all the time he spent at the station, he never asked himself how she was coping without him.

'Yes, she was so happy for me when I got promoted first to DS and then to DI. She knew it was what I'd always dreamed about but for her it meant even more sacrifice. The last job, as DI, was in Oxford, over a hundred miles away. I knew that, deep down, she was not happy about the move. It was a lonely time for her. By then the kids had grown up and left home. She missed them and she missed her friends and family. We bought a small house in Kidlington and Nora, still my uncomplaining Nora,' he smiles as he says it, 'tried to make herself a new life, but with no children to smooth the way into new relationships, she found it difficult. I promised to be home more, to spend more time with her but, despite all my efforts, the job, increasingly, took me away from her.'

'I can just imagine what she went through,' Helen says. 'It's not easy making friends when you move to a new area.'

'I kept telling her it was just for a few more years. I wasn't that far off early retirement. The promotion to DI had made a significant difference to my pension,' he explained, 'I was at the top of my grade by the time I retired.'

'When did you retire?'

'Seven, nearly eight years ago. We only had a couple of years together, to do all the things I had been promising her. The first year we went on a cruise around the Mediterranean, Venice, Istanbul and the Greek Islands. Nora had enjoyed that.'

'I've never been on a cruise,' Helen says. 'I've always fancied the idea. Perhaps when I'm older.'

For a moment he thinks she is suggesting that he is old. Well he is, although he doesn't feel it. He may be sixty-eight but inside he still feels twenty.

'I started playing golf; bought myself some golf clubs and joined a local club. I wanted Nora to take it up but she wasn't interested. She was never very sporty. She was only just five foot, you know,' he tells her.

'Didn't that mean leaving her on her own again?' Helen asks.

'Yes, but I had this idea of playing golf in Portugal. I thought Nora would like that. We even flew out to Portugal and looked at some apartments that were for sale. Nora was very keen on that. She liked the idea of spending her winters in the sun.'

'That sounds nice. Whereabouts?'

'Lagos. We had actually decided to go ahead and purchase a small apartment when Nora collapsed. The papers were due to be signed that week. Of course I never did anything about it after that; what use was a holiday apartment without Nora?'

'Well you could still have used it to go out there with your golfing friends.'

'I suppose so but, to be honest, I didn't have the heart. This is the first break I've had in five years.'

'Well I think you should do more with your life,' Helen tells him. 'You have to make the most of your time. We all have.'

He is reminded of Beth's words the previous evening. She is right; they both are. It's best not to waste the time they have left.

She gets up and puts her rucksack on.

'Shall we get going?'

DAY 15

CHAPTER 9
FRAN

Since they first met Fran had always been the one to capitulate, to be swayed by his extensive reasoning skills. Tim was a very persuasive man; she had always recognised that. Too persuasive, in fact sometimes his attitude verged on domineering. Just like her sister. She had dominated Fran all through their childhood; just because she was the eldest she thought she could tell her what to do. But then Fran was always too easily persuaded to do what others wanted; she knew that. She was not sure whether it was because of feelings of her own inadequacy or because she just wanted a quiet life. It probably had something to do with her own childhood. It had been a troubled one. Her father had been a philandering drunk who had stayed in the family home only because he had nowhere else to go. He and her mother had argued and fought constantly; there was barely a night went by without a row about something, usually another woman. As Fran had grown up she became used to going to bed early, switching on her Walkman, putting on the headphones and burying her head under the bedcovers. In that way she both cut out the noise of her parents fighting and managed to get some sleep.

Then, when she was fourteen her parents were killed. They had been driving home from somewhere, she can't even remember where they had been, probably a party or dinner with friends, when the car swerved and hit the central reservation. They had both been killed instantly. Years later her sister told her that their father had been driving whilst under the influence of alcohol; drunk, she had said and it was no surprise to either of them. She could imagine the scene in the car as clearly as if she were there: her father weaving the car across the road, a cigarette in his right hand, barely in control of the wheel and her mother screaming abuse at him for talking to some floozie or other.

She still found it hard to understand the way she had felt that day; shock, disbelief, pain and relief had muddled themselves round and round in her brain. She had loved her parents despite everything but she had spent so long distancing herself from them and their rage that she could no longer reach out to them, even in death. They were dead. She would miss them but she would not miss their constant fighting and the bitterness that permeated the air which they all shared in their small terraced house. She would not miss the noise of the neighbours banging on the wall at three in the morning or their pitying smiles as she passed them on her way to school. She would not miss seeing her mother's tear-stained face as she poured her tea in the morning or the ravages of a sleepless night carved under her father's eyes.

An aunt had looked after them until Fran was eighteen and then she had left for university, determined to build herself a life and have a family of her own.

Well she had built herself a good life: an interesting, well paid job, plenty of friends and a man she loved and hoped one day to marry. But it seemed, after all, that he did not love her, at least not enough to have a baby with her.

Now it looks as though there is not going to be a baby. No baby and no Tim. The blood last night was not heavy but enough to worry her. Beth had wanted her to go to a doctor, but she could not face being pulled about by a stranger, especially one she could not understand. She would let nature take its course. Beth had insisted that, at the very least, she should go and lie down, so she had agreed to go back to the hostel, take a couple of paracetemols and go straight to bed. She promised that if the bleeding did not stop she would let Beth take her to see someone the next day.

She is going to have to move soon; she is dying to have a pee but she is frightened to get up while so many people are still milling around. What if she stands up and the bleeding starts again? No she cannot face it; she will wait a bit. She rolls over onto her side; the pain in her stomach has gone. Maybe it was a false alarm, after all. And if so, how does she feel about it? Last night she had cried herself to sleep. It was her hormones she tells herself, nothing more. But she knows it is something more than that. From the moment she thought that she was going to lose the baby she knew that she wanted it to live. This is her child.

'Hey there. How are you feeling?'

It's Beth.

'OK, I think. I'm pretty sure it was nothing, just a bit of spotting. I'll be alright. Look Beth can you do something for me?'

'Of course.'

'Can you go down and check that Lucky is alright. I left her tied up in some old sheds round the back. Here give her a few of these.'

She passes Beth a handful of dog biscuits.

'Then what?'

'Untie her and tell her I'll be down shortly. She'll look after herself until I get up.'

'You're sure you're OK?'

'Yes, don't fuss. I'll see you down at the bar for breakfast.'

The need to pee is getting desperate now, so she waits until her friend has left then heads for the bathroom.

A man is coming out just as she arrives.

'You OK, love?' he asks. 'You look like death. Had a hard night?'

She brushes past him and goes into the first stall. A violent spasm shakes her and she is sick. Nothing more than morning sickness she hopes, not knowing if this is a good sign or not. At least there is no evidence of fresh bleeding, so she assumes that all is well. She will take it easy today and if she feels unwell she will stop at one of the *albergues* on the way.

She is glad she is walking with Beth and Lucky. She likes the company but also, neither of them walk at a very fast pace, so she can go more slowly than usual. In fact she does not feel unwell; she is an athletic young woman. Regular sessions in the gym and plenty of walking have kept her fit. It is the threat of a miscarriage that has made her nervous. She does not want anything to happen out here in the middle of nowhere.

'You're looking much better,' Beth tells her. 'There's some colour in your cheeks at last.'

'I told you I'd be alright.'

Her mobile is buzzing, so she takes it out, looks at the text message quickly and deletes it. Beth is watching her as she flicks the phone shut, with a snap.

'Who was that?' Beth asks.

'Tim.'

'What does he say?'

'No idea. I've deleted it.'

'Has he been texting you regularly?' Beth asks.

'At least twice a day.'

'And you delete them all?'

107

'Yes.'

'Without reading them?'

'Yes.'

'What if it's important?'

'I told him not to contact me. I need time to think.'

'So why don't you turn it off?'

'Someone else might want to get in touch,' she tells her. 'Anyway you don't keep in touch with your husband. You haven't even brought your mobile with you.'

'That's the whole point of this trip for me, to leave my worries behind.'

'Isn't that a song?'

Fran begins to sing something that sounds vaguely like 'Don't worry, be happy', before collapsing in hysterical giggles.

They continue on their way, singing snatches of the songs they can remember.

After an hour they stop by the roadside to rest and drink some water.

'Are you going to keep the baby?' Beth asks.

'I don't know. I think so. But the thought of being a single mum terrifies me.'

'Plenty of women bring up children on their own these days,' Beth tells her.

'I know. I could probably manage alright, financially. I have a lot of money saved and a good job. There's no way they would get rid of me, just because I was pregnant.'

'Of course not.'

'But it would give my boss a wonderful excuse for refusing me the promotion I was promised.'

She pours some water into Lucky's bowl.

'All things considered, I think I'd be able to manage quite well on my own. But still the thought of bringing a child up without its father worries me. I want my child to have a normal life with both a mother and a father.'

And who're not at each other's throats all the time, she thinks but does not say aloud.

'Tim might change his mind,' Beth says.

'Pigs might fly.'

Suddenly she feels angry with her lover.

'Whatever happens, whether he wants me back or not, there's no way I'm going to let him vacuum this child out of my body and out of my life.'

WEEK 5
DAY 29

CHAPTER 10
BETH

Beth stretches her legs and sighs. This bed is far too comfortable to leave but it is dawn already and time to get up. Silence hangs over the village like a blanket that she knows will soon dissipate and be replaced with a cacophony of bird song from the surrounding woods. She does not move but lies there listening as first one blackbird, then another begin their daily chorus. Soon she will hear the sounds of the local people moving about their business and other eager pilgrims, like herself, preparing for the day ahead. She has no idea of the exact time; for a moment she misses her watch and her mobile phone, still lying on the kitchen table in Bideford.

She should have stayed overnight in Sarria, a small town with plenty of accommodation, but she had felt the need to press on and find somewhere quieter. She arrived in Barbadello too late to get a room in the local *albergue*, a 17th century farm with only thirty beds and decided to treat herself to a night in a small hotel instead, with an individual room and her own bathroom. What luxury. Here there are no smells of stale food, garlic and onions, no stench of other people's sweaty socks, no bodily odours, bad breath or worse, no damp washing hanging out of the windows and cluttering up the bathrooms; here she can sleep in peace and quiet, without the incessant snoring of strangers or the creaking of beds.

It has not been easy to adapt to communal living. She is sure that if it wasn't for the fact that she is dog-tired each night and would sleep on a clothes-line, if necessary, she would not have been able to put up with it.

She had been determined to make the most of her stay in the hotel and had wallowed in the bath for most of the afternoon, soaking away the grime from the road and trying to soothe her protesting feet. She had washed her hair and shaved her legs. She had given her clothes to the chambermaid to be taken away and washed then she had wandered into the town, looking for her friends.

Beth swings her legs out of the bed and sits up. Her feet, battered and bruised, seem to look at her accusingly. A blister runs right across the ball of each foot and her heels are raw, but it is her toes that shock. They look as if they have been hit by a hammer, the nails black and about to part company from her flesh. Will she be able to hold out for another five days? Through the former schoolhouse windows she can see a patch of morning sky, flushed with pink; soon the sun will be flooding the room. She quickly showers, best not to waste the opportunity of a personal shower she tells herself, and dresses. Before pulling on her walking boots she carefully re-tapes her feet, applying plasters to the raw parts and wrapping an elastic bandage around her ankle then pulls on some clean socks. She repacks her rucksack, places a wide sunhat on her head and tucks her walking poles under her arm. She is ready. There are only 115.2 kilometres to go and today she plans to walk at least twenty of them.

The hotel is quiet, no-one is up yet; it is a good job that she has got into the habit of paying for the room the night before. She carefully unlocks the front door and slips out into the cobbled street. A cock is crowing somewhere close by and a couple of stray cats are scavenging in the dustbins; apart from that, she is alone. According to the guide book that she has wrapped in plastic and secured in the pocket of her voluminous shorts, the next stage of her journey is along quiet country roads, not the special tarmac pilgrim ways that now occupy a large part of the *Camino de Santiago*. A prettier prospect but not necessarily so easy on her feet.

It is strange how, after four weeks on the road, her thoughts return again and again to her feet. She promises herself to take better care of them when she returns to England. Then she remembers why she is here and the care of her feet dwindles in importance.

It is a perfect morning. A few mares' tails float across a clear blue sky; there is no wind and she knows that it is not going to be too hot until at least lunchtime. She hitches her rucksack into a more comfortable position and strides on.

There is a crossroads ahead, where the path traverses a main road; a solitary car goes past and the driver lifts his hand in salute. She waves back and smiles. The path dips down again into the woods and she is walking once again under the shade of tall oaks and chestnut trees. After a while she notices a figure ahead of her; he looks familiar. It is the pilgrim. She increases her pace, her interest piqued at the possibility of seeing what he looks like, at last, but somehow she cannot reduce the distance between them.

'Hello,' she calls out to him. '*Hola.*'

But he does not hear her. Or, if he does, he does not acknowledge her.

It is two weeks now since she first time saw him, as she was leaving Castrojeriz and has seen him again on a number of occasions. He is always ahead of her so she can never see his face but the wide hat and poncho he wears, whatever the weather, are unmistakeable, as is the long pilgrim's staff with its shepherd's crook. From a distance he is almost a caricature of a pilgrim, unlike the motley collection of pilgrims she normally encounters, dressed in their lightweight shorts and Pacelite waterproofs.

It is strange that she only ever sees him when she is alone. She has asked many people if they have seen him but the answer is always no. Sometimes she thinks he is a figment of her imagination. She looks for him in the bars and *albergues* where she stays but as she has little to go on, she has had no luck in identifying him. Nevertheless she finds herself giving particular attention to any of the more seasoned pilgrims who carry the traditional pilgrim's staff and observes carefully as they walk away from her.

She trudges along the path, lost in her thoughts. The pilgrim has disappeared from sight now. She passes through the small hamlet of O Brea and sees the next waymark ahead of her. When she reaches it she stops and sits down beside it. She has made a habit of this recently, only allowing herself to rest at the waymarks. This one is about a metre high, pyramidical in shape and the usual pilgrim's symbol, the scallop shell, is engraved into the stone. She feels a thrill of pleasure as she looks at it. Only one hundred kilometres to go, it informs her. That seems nothing after the distance she has already travelled. She lets her fingers move across the weathered stone, tracing the graffiti that tells her that Rocio was there before her, and Juan and Pablo, that Conchita and Alvero are in love. She smiles. It would be nice to see the stone pristine, unmarked in this way, but the graffiti is, after all, just a sign of human nature. Everyone wants to leave their mark on the world in some little way. There is a pile of small stones on top of the waymark. She searches around until she finds a suitable stone, picks it up and adds it to the pile. Her stone, her mark. Time to move on.

Before long she arrives in Ferreiros and there, next to the church, is a café. Apart from the owner, a thin, hollow-cheeked man, who looks at her suspiciously, there are only two other customers, a young Spanish couple, eating large slices of *empanada*.

She orders a coffee and some toast and sits at one of the tables.

'*Hola,*' the young woman says.

'*Hola*,' she replies.

'Oh, you are English,' her companion says. 'We've been to England.'

'To Brighton,' the woman adds. 'We worked in a hotel, to improve our English.'

'Your English is very good,' Beth tells her.

They are keen to practise their command of the language on Beth and take it in turns to tell her about themselves.

'But now we are unemployed,' says the man whose name, she now knows, is Pablo.

They have both finished their university education and cannot find any work.

'I want to work in marketing,' says Laura, 'but I would accept anything.'

'None of our group from university have found any work in marketing,' Pablo adds. 'There are too many people and too few jobs. One of our friends works as a doctor's receptionist; she has a degree in Marketing, a Masters in PR and speaks French and English fluently. And now she's a receptionist.'

He shrugs in disgust.

'At least she has a job,' Laura says.

'So why are you here?' Beth asks.

'It's the cheapest holiday we could find,' Pablo says without hesitation. 'If you have the pilgrim's passport you can stay in the *albergues* for very little money.'

'Sometimes as little as five euros a night.'

'And we eat the 'pilgrim's menu' every day and that's not much more than six euros each.'

'How long have you been looking for work?' Beth asks.

'Two years. The first year we decided to go to England to see if it was any better there, but it was just as bad. All we could find was hotel work and they treated us as though we were complete idiots.'

'Besides which the money was awful. If it hadn't been for the fact that we got one meal a day as part of our pay, we would have starved. Everything is so expensive in England.'

'So, after six months we came back. We thought that if we were going to be poor, it was better to be poor in Spain, with our families close by.'

'And we had to get back to the warmth.'

'Yes, we are from Cadiz. We don't have winters like they have in Brighton.'

'No snow?'

'Only in the mountains and never by the sea.'

Pablo finishes the last piece of *empanada* and counts out some money for the waiter.

'We're off now,' he says and picks up his rucksack. 'Enjoy the rest of your walk.'

'*Buen camino*,' Beth says.

They both smile and repeat:

'*Buen camino*.'

She watches them march away, their poles propelling them forward through the trees. She is enjoying the toast and the coffee is hot. As she sips it slowly, rolling the strong earthy taste around her mouth, she pulls out the guidebook and reads about the next stage of her journey. According to the author, the road she has been walking along becomes a track fairly soon after leaving the village and then begins to rise to 660 metres above sea level to the Peña do Cervo before descending again into the Miño valley. It looks a hard climb; she is glad that she has had her breakfast before starting it.

She would love a cigarette, but she doesn't have any; besides which she gave up smoking six years ago. It had been easy. When the doctor told her she had cancer she stopped, just like that, and she hasn't smoked since. Yet lately the craving has returned. Maybe, when she reaches Santiago, she will reward herself with a packet of cigarettes, she thinks with a smile, knowing full well that she would never do that. Luke would not approve. She will have to make do with an extra glass of wine.

She has thought a lot about her son today; she misses him. It is a strange feeling; it is not as though she sees much of him these days anyway, not since he moved in with Jennifer. She and Luke used to be very close, but since he went to university she has felt a distance growing between them. It is only to be expected, she tells herself. He's a man now and like all sons, his allegiance has moved from his mother to his partner; that's how she has been instructed to refer to his girlfriend.

'We're more than girlfriend and boyfriend,' he told her. 'We may even get married, one day.'

'So, why not fiancé?'

'Don't be so old-fashioned, Mum. She's my partner,' he had told her.

Beth likes Jennifer. Luke had met her at university. He was studying History and she was in the English department; but although they started together, she stayed on a year longer than Luke, in order to do her teaching certificate. Now she's a teacher in an inner-city school, one of the new academies. It's an experimental place, she told them, based on the American model; small in size, big in discipline is their motto. Beth knows that Luke is not happy about his partner working in that environment but she would never mention it to Jennifer. He confided in her one day, just after Jennifer took the job:

'Some of the kids in that area carry knives and almost all of their families have had some sort of run-in with the law. I don't think Jen knows what she's letting herself in for.'

'Oh, I'm sure she can handle it,' Beth said, trying to put his mind at ease. 'And anyway aren't these new academies supposed to be helping these very same children to make something of their lives. Isn't that the point of them, to give something back to the underprivileged?'

'That's the theory, but when have any of these politicians ever been inside an inner-city classroom? They come up with schemes that they think will be vote-catchers but don't think through all the ramifications. Only last week, one of Jen's colleagues was threatened with a knife, by an angry parent.'

'Have you spoken to her about it?' Beth asked.

'Yes, but she's so committed to the children that she can't see the dangers.'

Beth had left it at that; it was not her place to interfere.

The pathway dips down for a while and she walks fairly briskly until it veers back to a steady climb. The guidebook is correct; the views over the reservoir are spectacular. For a moment she wishes she had brought a camera with her; she would like to share some of this experience with Joe. But, she reminds herself, that can never happen now. Anyway sharing is not the point of the exercise; the idea is to be on her own, have her own space, not share it with Joe or anyone else. She scans the landscape but there is no sign of the mysterious pilgrim, nor the couple from the café; there is no sign of anyone. Maybe she will see the pilgrim when she arrives in Portomarín. She has already decided where she will stay tonight. She can't afford another night in a hotel, so it will have to be an *albergue*. The first one listed looks promising; there are only five people to a dormitory and it has all the usual facilities. It is only five euros a night.

The path is downhill all the way into Portomarín. She enters the wide, green basin of the river Miño, its banks lined with trees and crosses the new road bridge that has been built next to an old medieval crossing. Halfway across, she stops to look around her; the river has been widened here to accommodate the Belesar Reservoir. She realises it must be almost noon as the sun is high in the sky. Its rays fall on the fast flowing river, causing the water to glisten and glitter as it tumbles over the rocks. Two men sit on the towpath, fishing rods in the water, their catch by their side. She sees fish, swimming to and fro in the eddies around the pillars of the bridge, just out of the men's reach, while a cormorant perches on a ruined wall and watches them, hungrily. It is a peaceful place, with little traffic. A boy on a bicycle passes her, ringing his bell in greeting to the pilgrim.

She continues across the bridge and stops at the bottom of an ancient staircase that leads up into the town. It is formidable but the alternative is an extra half-kilometre's walk up an equally steep slope. She adjusts her rucksack and begins the climb. The staircase, called, according to the sign, the steps of *Nuestra Señora de las Nieves*, Our Lady of the Snows, is actually all that remains of the original medieval bridge that once crossed the Miño. She has read that the town was originally spread over both sides of the river and for many years this bridge was the only place the pilgrims could cross without a boat. On one side of the bridge the church of San Pedro, which had close ties to the Knights of Santiago, used to stand and on the other, where she is now, there was the church of San Nicolás, which was linked to the Knights of St. John. All pretty standard stuff, she thinks until she reads about the reservoir. Portomarín is a new town, built in the sixties after they flooded the old town in order to build the Belesar Reservoir. Even the Church of San Nicolás was demolished and then rebuilt, brick by brick, in the new town.

She stops, out of breath from the climb and looks out over the valley, trying to imagine the houses that would have nestled there and what it looked like before the waters of the reservoir took over. She wonders what the people of the town thought about having their homes destroyed like that. Had they complained? Did they demand compensation? Did they welcome the move to a new, modern town or did they just want their old way of life to go on? It was in 1962; Franco was still in power. She has read enough about dictatorships to know that it is unlikely that much of a protest was made, no matter what the townspeople thought. She feels strangely moved looking at the beautiful lake spread out below her and yet aware of the distress that it most certainly caused. The cormorant, tired of waiting for the fish, flaps lazily away.

By the time she reaches the town, she is hot and sticky and glad to book herself into the *albergue* recommended by her guidebook. It is a modest looking establishment and she is welcomed by a homely woman in her forties, who goes through the usual routine of stamping her *credencial* as proof she has been there and then shows her straight to her room. Setting off early has meant that she is one of the first to arrive and there is no difficulty in finding a bed. The room is small, only five beds as promised and a cupboard to store her luggage. The bathroom is down the hall but looks adequate and, most importantly, is spotlessly clean; a strong smell of ammonia and bleach waft up from the toilet. She unpacks her bag and heads for the shower.

CHAPTER 11

She is been dreaming about the pilgrim. He is bending over her and smiling; his eyes are kind. He stretches his hands out towards her, encouraging her to take them in her own. He wants her to trust him. She is anxious. He wants her to do something but she does not know what it is.

The sound of someone dumping their stuff on the bed next to hers wakes her. She opens her eyes to see who it is. A young girl, no more than twenty, she guesses, is unpacking her rucksack.

'Hello,' Beth says.

'Oh, I hope I didn't wake you,' the girl replies.

She is a pretty girl. Her white-blonde hair is cut short, in an almost boyish style. She is wearing a green and grey camouflage jacket.

'No, not really. Well yes, but it doesn't matter; it's time I got up anyway. I was just sleeping off my lunch,' she adds.

'I brought mine with me,' the girl tells her, opening a carrier bag and taking out a loaf of bread and a packet of strong smelling cheese.

'There's a fridge in the kitchen,' Beth tells her.

'Thanks.'

She sits on the edge of her bed and breaks off a piece of the bread. Then she unwraps the cheese; it smells foul.

'Would you like some?' she asks.

'No thanks.'

She makes herself a rough cheese sandwich and bites into it with relish.

'I'm starving,' she says. 'I could have eaten on the way but I made myself wait until I got here.'

She seems pleased with her restraint.

'Where were you last night?' Beth asks her.

'I stayed in Samos. We took the alternative route so that we could visit the Benedictine monastery.'

'We?'

'My boyfriend and I. Well, he's not exactly my boyfriend, more a friend that I made on the way. We've walked the last three hundred kilometres together, so I feel I know him quite well.'

Beth thinks she can detect an Australian accent.

'So you've walked all the way from Samos today?'

'Yes. I usually try to stick to the recommended stages but we were having such a good time in Samos that we stayed longer than we intended.'

'And your friend?'

'He stayed in Saria. He's waiting for someone, he said. We'll meet up later on.'

She brushes the crumbs from her jacket and lies down on the bed.

'What are the showers like?'

'OK. There was plenty of hot water when I arrived, but I'm not sure about now.'

'It doesn't matter. I'll shower later. Right now I too tired to do anything. It was quite a trek.'

'Why didn't you stay in Saria with your friend?'

'I can't afford the time. I need to get back on schedule or I'll miss my flight. I'm going to England next.'

Beth would like to ask her more questions but she can see the girl is tired; her eyes are already closing.

'My name's Roxanne, by the way,' she mumbles and turns on her side.

'Hello, I'm Beth.'

But the girl is already asleep.

As quietly as she can, Beth gets up and pulls on her sandals. She is already wearing a clean tee-shirt and a cotton sarong tied around her waist. She is as presentable as she is ever going to be so she pushes her rucksack under the bed and creeps out of the room.

She glances at the girl as she squeezes past her bed; she is sound asleep, her head thrown back and her lips parted. The sound of tiny snores float up, reminding her of the rhythmical purring of a cat she once had. Well if her snoring is no worse than that she will have a good night after all; she hopes the others are quiet sleepers. There are two beds opposite and a further one under the window at the end of the room. All are taken now, although Roxanne is the only person she has met so far. Perhaps the others came in while she was sleeping.

Portomarín is a quiet town but people are already stirring, waking up after their siestas and preparing for the evening. She decides to have a look around the town before finding a bar. Maybe she will find the church that was saved from the depths of the reservoir.

The church is unimpressive, despite its strange history; it is an austere rectangular building with none of the charm of the English churches that she is used to. In fact the town as a whole is unimpressive. It is clean, modern yet not modern and well set up for the pilgrim trade. A few of the more important buildings, like the church, have been saved and reconstructed on this higher ground and the rest is post-1960.

It does not take long for Beth to do what she terms her 'cultural bit' and then she makes for the main square, the Praza Condes de Fenosa and begins to check out the bars. Almost immediately she sees Fran, sitting across the other side of the square, opposite the church. She is at a table with some others; her leg is propped up on a chair and Beth notices she has a bandage on her knee. Lucky is lying at her feet, as usual.

'Hi,' she calls, waving as she approaches.

'Beth. I wondered when you'd get here. Sit down.'

She moves her foot from the chair so that Beth can sit down.

'So what happened to you?' she asks.

'Oh, it's just a sprain. Twisted my knee coming down the hill from Peña do Cervo. I thought I ought to wrap it up, if only to get a bit of sympathy.'

'You should be careful, in your condition,' Beth says.

'It's nothing.'

'Even so.'

'Don't fuss Beth, you sound like my Gran.'

'Ooops. Sorry.'

'It's an old injury actually. That knee has been giving me gip for years, ever since I fell, running the London Marathon.'

She is impressed.

'I didn't know you'd done the marathon.'

'Only that once. The guys at work were doing it for charity and I decided to join them. I didn't do enough preparation, that was the problem. I thought because I went to the gym every week that I was fit enough to do it. I should have done more running, built up to it slowly.'

'Did you prepare for this?'

She waves vaguely around, indicating that by 'this', she means the *Camino*.

'Yes, in a way. I was walking every weekend for weeks before I set off. You know, each time increasing the mileage until I was doing twenty to thirty miles at a time. Walking's much easier on my knee that running. And I did that charity walk last year to raise money for St Bart's Hospital, but that was only fifteen miles.'

Fran is very athletic and looks it; she has walked further along the *Camino* than Beth. She started in France, the other side of the Pyrenees, at Somport.

'What time did you get here today?' Beth asks.

'Sometime mid-afternoon. I managed to get a bed in that new *albergue* overlooking the river. What about you?'

'Midday.'

The couple opposite have finished their conversation and turn to Beth, expectantly.

'Hi.'

The woman nods and smiles at them. Beth recognises her; it is María.

'*Encantada*,' she says, getting up and kissing Beth on both cheeks.

As she smiles the skin around her eyes crinkles and dimples appear in her rather plump cheeks. Her black hair, which Beth remembers was pulled back into a pony-tail and half-hidden under a flowered headscarf, is now neatly scraped back into a bun. She is a pretty woman.

The waiter comes across to their table.

'Red wine,' Fran tells him.

She looks at Beth. Beth nods.

'Yes, I'll have red wine too,' says a man's voice. 'What about you Helen?'

It is Walter; she notices Helen sitting by his side. She nods. Beth has not seen them for a few days now.

'Better make it a bottle then,' Fran says. 'And a bottle of water, a large one.'

'Anything to eat?' the waiter asks.

'Not for me,' Beth says.

Fran turns to him and orders some *tapas*.

'I'm always so hungry,' she confides. 'And I just can't resist those *empanadas*.'

Fran is in a talkative mood this evening; Beth thinks she is feeling better. She wonders if she has spoken to Tim yet.

The waiter returns and they fall silent while he pours out the wine and sets the dishes of tapas in the centre of the table. There are three dishes: one of olives, another of broad beans and chopped smoked ham, covered in olive oil and a third, a plate of tiny pastries filled with tuna and garlic. These are the e*mpanadas* that Fran covets.

'So María, what brings you to the *Camino*?' Walter asks, pouring her a glass of wine.

There is a slight pause while the group help themselves to some of the food and taste their wine, then María says:

'I have come to ask God to help me.'

She says it in such a simple, matter-of-fact way that Beth believes her.

María sips her wine and looks at them sadly. She tells them what she has already told Fran and Beth. It is no easier hearing it for a second time and Beth feels immensely sorry for this fragile Spanish woman. As before, she does not know how to respond. She cannot think of anything more horrible than losing your child.

Her thoughts immediately turn to Luke. Luke, her only child, who she loves more than life itself, she realises with a pang. What would she have done if this had happened to him? It had been bad enough that time he disappeared at the fun-fair. One moment he had been holding her hand and the next he had pulled away and disappeared into the crowd.

127

She never wanted to experience again the mind-numbing fear that had descended on her, paralysing her until, only seconds later, Joe had suddenly appeared with Luke on his shoulders.

'Lost something?' he had said, with a laugh.

She had not felt like laughing.

'Did the police find out anything?' Walter asks.

María stares at him with angry eyes.

'No, nothing. They found nothing. Four years and they have found nothing. No sign of him anywhere.'

'Not even his bike?' Walter asks.

'Nothing.'

'That's awful,' Fran says.

Beth notices her hand move instinctively to her stomach in a protective gesture.

'Because he was so small they started looking for him straight away; there was none of the usual rubbish about waiting to see if he had run away from home. The mayor even closed the airport and the ports for twenty-four hours; there were no boats, no taxis, nothing was allowed in or out. They put up posters and leaflets about him everywhere on the island, on billboards and walls; it must have cost a fortune. The mayor paid for everything; he is a good man,' she adds.

'And they found nothing?' Fran asks.

'No, not a trace of him. It was as if he had never existed.'

'That's awful. I can't even begin to understand how you must feel, not knowing if your child is alive or dead,' Beth says.

'Four years,' Walter murmurs. 'My God.'

Beth remembers watching a TV programme about missing children; it was frightening how easily a child could disappear.

'Thousands of children disappear every year,' María tells them. 'Most of them turn up. They're often from broken homes and have been abducted by one of their parents.'

'Usually the father,' Walter adds.

María continues:

'In Gran Canaria, at the moment, there are two other families with missing children. I talk to the mothers and we try to support each other, but it's hard. We have had posters printed and distributed all over Spain but it has been no good.'

Beth thinks she saw a poster about missing children when she got off the bus in Roncesvalles. She wishes she had taken more notice of it now.

'I read on the internet that there are over two hundred children missing in Spain,' Walter tells them. 'Right now, at this very moment.'

'Two hundred? That's incredible,' Fran says. 'Why don't we hear more about them?'

'People aren't really interested,' he tells them. 'Yes, at first. But then after a while, when there're no developments and nobody has found anything, people lose interest. It's natural. It's no longer news. Once the police stop searching for them they're as good as dead.'

María's eyes fill with tears at this comment.

'My husband and I have been on the television and the radio, appealing for people to come forward with information, but it has all come to nothing. We have done so much. My husband even went to talk to some gangsters about it; to see if they knew anything.'

'Really? What here in Spain?' Fran asks.

'No, in Gran Canaria. We wanted to get a private investigator but we just didn't have the money. Then one of the local police suggested we speak to a man in Las Palmas, who has links to the Mafia.'

'The police suggested that?'

'Yes, they said that the gangsters could do things that the police couldn't and maybe they would have heard something.'

'So what happened?'

'My husband went to see this man. I didn't go. Pepe wanted to do it on his own. He said the man was very sympathetic and promised to make some enquiries but in the end he couldn't find out any more than the police.'

She sounds defeated. Beth wishes there was something she could do or say; she feels helpless in the face of this woman's suffering.

'At first I was very ill,' María tells them. 'I couldn't eat; I couldn't sleep. I just used to sit at home and cry all the time. My poor husband didn't know what to do to help me. And he was suffering as well. In the end the doctor told me I had to get a hold of myself for the sake of the family.'

She takes a photo from her pocket and hands it to Beth. It is crumpled and creased but Beth can make out two figures, a younger María and her husband. The man is holding the hand of a small boy and María has a tiny baby in her arms.

'That is Ana; she was just six weeks when Manuel disappeared. So you see I have to do something for her sake.'

'Where is she now?' Fran asks.

'She's with her father.'

Walter picks up the bottle and tops up their glasses.

'I think we need another,' he says and signals to the waiter.

'The worst part is the feeling of utter helplessness,' María continues. 'I want to do something to find him but there is nothing we can do. We don't know where to start looking. Once the police had searched the island and found nothing, what was there we could do? It is hopeless. Gran

Canaria is only a small island; if he is not there, then where is he?'

'Could he have been taken to Spain?' Walter asks.

'The police think it is possible but nobody has reported seeing him in Spain either. We have the priest say a special Mass for him every month but sometimes I feel even God has deserted me. That's why I am doing this pilgrimage,' she adds. 'I want to prove to God that if he returns my son to me, I will be a better mother and a better Catholic.'

She crosses herself and whispers something in Spanish.

'His room is just as he left it,' she tells them. 'When he returns I want him to know that we have never stopped thinking of him, never stopped praying for his return.'

Beth does not know what to say. Surely it is impossible that her son will return after all this time.

'He knows I am here,' she continues. 'Every day I tell him what I am doing; I tell him I am doing this so that God will help me find him.'

So it is her son that she talks to as she walks the *Camino*.

'What do the police say?' Fran asks. 'Do they think they will ever find him?'

María shrugs sadly.

'I think they have given up on him. They won't say that the case is closed but I know they've shelved it. As far as the police are concerned, my Manu is dead. Even my husband wants me to stop looking for him. He says that I must move on with my life, for little Ana's sake.'

Nobody speaks. There is nothing they can say to help this woman.

'What about you Walter? You've never said why you decided to walk the *Camino*,' Beth asks.

131

'It was our local vicar who put the idea into my head. After my wife's funeral, a few close friends and the local vicar came back to the house for the customary tea and sandwiches.'

He smiles ruefully.

'I'd have liked something stronger but they all said tea was fine. The vicar wanted to know what my plans were. I told him I didn't really know, that life was going to be very strange without my Nora. He told me that he was going with a group of his parishioners on a pilgrimage to Santiago de Compostela. He said there was a spare place, if I wanted it.'

Walter drinks some of his wine.

'I didn't think it was for me, and said so. It was kind of him to think of me, but I couldn't see myself doing that. I didn't even go to his church; it was Nora who went.'

He laughs.

'She said the prayers for both of us.'

'So?'

'Well, it was strange; the idea didn't go away. It hung around in the back of my mind until one day I decided I'd do it anyway. It was nothing sentimental, you know. I wasn't asking Nora for forgiveness or anything like that. I didn't need to ask her for forgiveness. She had loved me and she accepted me for what I was. There had never been any recrimination about my work from her. But I knew the toll that a policeman's life took on his family. I only had to look at some of my colleagues: Frank Smith, twice divorced, Ben Richie, divorced, even young Dickie Jones was separated from his wife and they had only been married for three years.'

He counts them off on his fingers.

'The list is as long as my arm. No I wasn't going to do it for forgiveness; I just wanted to give something back to her. I suppose I'm doing this walk for Nora.'

Helen smiles at him and touches his hand.

Walter drinks down the last of his wine.

'Well folks, I'm off to bed. I want to get an early start tomorrow. See you again in Palas de Rei.'

'Right. Goodnight then.'

'Me too,' says Helen. 'They're pretty strict at my *albergue*. The doors are locked at ten o'clock.'

'Yes, I'm going as well. Thank you for your company,' María says and gets up to leave.

Beth watches Fran push her long, dark hair back from her face. How is it that her friend can look so elegant after walking twenty-odd miles and with a crepe bandage on her leg? But she does. She is one of those lucky women who always seem to have immaculate make-up, whose hair just naturally falls into place and who can wear any clothes as though they have been tailor-made for her. She feels a tinge of envy; even in her younger days she never managed to achieve this ease of dressing.

'What about you?' Beth asks Fran.

'Let's just have one more, shall we?'

'OK, just one for the *Camino*.'

They laugh. This is their joke. .

'Just a spot for me,' Fran says stretching out her hand.

Beth drains the last of the wine into their glasses and they finish it off.

'Maybe we should go to bed as well,' Fran says. 'What do you say Lucky? Shall we call it a day?'

The dog looks up at her with adoring eyes and thumps the ground with her tail.

CHAPTER 12
MARÍA

María poured herself a glass of water and swallowed two paracetamols. She had to do something; her head was splitting. It was lack of sleep. The baby had been particularly restless last night and she had got up four times to feed her. Pepe was very good about it; he would have taken it in turns getting up with her but she was still breastfeeding and Ana was only interested in her mother's attentions.

She was quiet now, sleeping like an angel in her pram. María bent over her and pulled the sheet back from her face. Her skin felt a little warm; maybe she would take her up to the bedroom later, where it was cooler and she could put the air conditioning on.

She opened the door to the washing machine and pulled out the latest batch of wet nappies.

'Mama when are we going to the beach?' her six-year old asked.

'Later Manu, when Mama's finished her work.'

'But you keep saying that. I want to go now.'

She sighed; Manuel was becoming so demanding. She knew it was because of the new baby; he was jealous. It was natural enough, she thought; she did not have so much time for him now, nor energy. All her time was taken up with the baby. It was killing her. She did not remember being so exhausted after Manu was born. This time she could hardly drag herself out of bed in the mornings and her head ached all the time. Perhaps she should speak to the doctor about it. No, what was the point? She shook her head sadly. No, he would just tell her that it was normal, that it was just a question of getting into a routine. A routine. Everyone kept telling her that. How could she get into a routine when her head was hurting so much and she couldn't think straight. It wasn't a routine she needed, it was a good night's sleep.

If only her mother lived near by but she had moved back to Spain not long after María and Pepe had got married. She knew she could ask Pepe's mother to help but she was reluctant to do that. Although well-meaning, her mother-in-law was a domineering woman who considered that caring for her grandchildren was not only her responsibility, it was her duty. María had seen the devastating effect she had had on Pepe's brother's marriage, sidelining her sister-in-law at every turn. She had swept into their house the day their baby was born and taken control. No wonder the marriage had broken up. But Pepe was different to his brother; he was stronger, more independent. He managed to keep his mother at bay. They visited her regularly but she rarely came to their house; it worked much better that way. If María asked for her help now, she would never be free of her.

'Mama, Mama.'

'Go and find something to play with, Manuel and leave me in peace. I'm busy.'

She opened the back door and went into the yard to hang out the nappies. It was a nice sunny day and a fresh breeze was blowing across from Africa. They would be dry in no time.

'Mama, when are we going to the beach?' the boy asked yet again. 'You said we could go.'

'Soon.'

'But when, Mama?'

The baby started to cry, little snuffly cries at first that María knew, if ignored, would build and build until she was bawling her head off.

'Look what you've done now. You've woken your little sister,' she snapped at him.

She went back into the kitchen and picked up the crying baby.

'Hush now, shhh,' she whispered, gently bouncing her against her shoulder. 'Shhhh.'

'Mama.'

'Why don't you play on your bike for a bit, then I'll take you to the beach later on, after lunch,' she said, moving the baby to her other shoulder and patting her back.

'Alright.'

Manuel seemed happy with that. The bicycle was new and, usually, he was only allowed to ride it when his father was there to keep an eye on him.

'You must be very careful now and don't go too fast.'

'No Mama.'

'I'll go and put Ana in her cot and then I'll come down and watch you.'

'OK, Mama.'

He ran round to the side of the house to get his bicycle. As she went upstairs with the baby she could hear him riding around the yard, singing to himself. Poor little chap, she must try to find more time for him; it was not fair that the baby took up every moment of her day. Still Pepe had his holidays next month, that would make things easier; they would have all of July together and she would take Manu to the beach every day.

The baby was quieter now, but not asleep. María switched on the air conditioning and lay down on the bed, with Ana in the crook of her arm. The baby would be asleep in no time, already her eyes were closing, and then she would go down to see to Manu. She continued humming to her and before she knew it her eyes were closing too.

The sun streaming through the bedroom window woke her. She looked at the bedside clock; it was past eleven. Ana was fast asleep, her tiny fists clenched and held up in front of her. Carefully María extricated herself from the child and sat up. The baby continued to sleep. Not wishing to wake her, María laid her in her cot and pulled a sheet over her. The room was cool now so she turned the air conditioning off and that was when she noticed it, the silence. There was no sound coming from below. She hurried downstairs and into the kitchen. The back door was open.

'Manu,' she called. 'Manu. Where are you?'

She went into the yard. The nappies flapped gently in the breeze. The gate to the lane stood open.

'Manu. Manu,' she called, running out into the lane.

There was no sign of him. She ran to the corner but still she could not see him. What could she do? She couldn't leave the baby.

'Manu, Manu, Manu,' she called repeatedly, but Manu did not answer.

'What is it María?' her neighbour asked, putting her head out of the bedroom window.

'It's Manu, I can't find him. Have you seen him anywhere?'

'He was right there a little while ago, on his bike. Maybe he's at Antonio's house,' she suggested.

'Yes, of course.'

María ran down the lane and knocked on the gate of one of the houses.

'What is it?' an old man's voice asked.

'Antonio, is your grandson in?'

'Little Antonio, you mean?'

'Yes, is he in? Is Manu with him?'

'No, he's gone shopping with his mother.'

'And you haven't seen Manu?'

'Why would I have seen your son? I've been in the house all morning.'

'He's disappeared. I can't find him,' she said, tears starting to flood her throat.

She ran back to her house, hoping he would be there, hiding in the shed, waiting to jump out and scare her, like he used to do. He loved hide-and-seek. How many times had she opened the hall cupboard to get out something and he had leapt out at her, squealing with delight at her surprise. It was his favourite game until he got his new bicycle. But there was no one at home and now the baby had woken up; her angry cries were like tiny daggers of pain, digging into her brain. She ran upstairs and lifted her out of the cot.

'Shss, now, Mama is here,' she crooned, rocking her back and forth before laying her down in her pram. 'We'll go and look for your big brother, shall we? He's gone off on his bike, the naughty boy, worrying his Mama like this.'

She popped a dummy into the baby's mouth and together they went out the back gate and walked down the lane. She wanted to phone Pepe but she thought he would say she was being silly, over anxious. He always said she fussed over the children too much. Manu would turn up, she told herself; he could not be far away.

The lane was deserted, as it usually was at that time of day. Most of the men were at work and the women were inside, preparing the mid-day meal. There was no-one to tell her what had become of her son.

How long had she been sleeping? She tried to work it out, an hour, maybe a little bit longer. She realised her headache had gone, instead she had this pain in her chest, like a stone, tucked there under her ribs. This was her fault. How could she have been so neglectful of her son? He seemed so grown-up but, she reminded herself, he was only six, not much more than a baby himself, despite going to school. He loved school, he had been so disappointed when the holidays had started and he could no longer go. Most of his new friends lived in a different part of the town, too far for Manuel to go on his own. There were few children of his age in their street, only Antonio and Antonio's mother was not keen on her son playing outside. She began to cry. What was she going to do? She had come to the main road now and still there was no sign of him. She saw a police car parked further down and hurried towards it. Maybe they had found him.

'Officer, can you help me?' she said.

Two Guardia Civil officers were coming out of a bar; she guessed they had just had their breakfast. One of them was brushing some crumbs off his uniform.

'What is it? What's the problem?' they asked.

She could barely speak for the tears.

'Come, come. We can't help you unless you tell us the problem,' one of them said kindly.

She swallowed hard and said:

'My son is missing. I can't find him.'

They sat her down at a pavement table and asked her to explain. She told them all she knew, but left out the fact that she fell asleep when she should have been watching him.

'Well, don't fret. I expect he's gone to a friend's to play. You know what kids are like; they just don't think.'

'But I've asked his friends that live close by. Nobody's seen him.'

'Look, the best thing you can do is go home, in case he shows up. We'll take over from here,' one of the policemen said.

'Where's your husband?' the other asked.

'He's at work.'

'Does he know what's happened?'

'No, I wanted to be sure that Manu wasn't hiding somewhere first, before I worried him.'

'Is that something your son does? Hide?'

'It's a game,' she explained.

'Has he run away before?' the other asked.

'No.'

She feels indignant.

'No. He's only six, after all. We're not talking about a wayward teenager, you know. He's just a normal little boy.'

'Yes, yes, we understand.'

'We have to ask.'

She walked back to the house and telephoned Pepe.

'What do you mean he's missing?' he asked. 'How can he be missing?'

She explained what had happened, how she had only left him for a minute and he had vanished.

'Have you looked in the shed? You know he likes hiding in there.'

'Yes, he's not there. I've looked everywhere.'

'Have you telephoned his friends?'

'Yes, some of them.'

'What about the park? Have you been along to the park?'

'No, I'll go there now.'

'Yes, do that. What about the police?'

'I've spoken to the police; they told me to go home and wait for him.'

'Good God, where has he got to? The little devil.'

'Pepe, I'm so frightened. What if something has happened to him?'

'Look, I'll have a word with my boss and I'll be straight home. Don't worry María, he can't be far away. You stay put, in case he turns up; I'll drive by the park and see if he's there then I'll come home. OK?'

'OK.'

Then she telephoned her mother-in-law, her brother-in-law, her friends, Manu's teacher, the parents of Manu's little friends; she steadily worked her way through the address book until she had told them all.   Someone had to know where he was. Someone had to help her find him.

DAY 30

CHAPTER 13
BETH

The next day Beth eats a hurried breakfast in the bar opposite the *albergue* before setting off. The town is stirring and some of the pilgrims are already on their way. The *Camino* is becoming more crowded now, the closer she gets to Santiago. Like the tributaries of a river, various paths are linking into the main *Camino* as it approaches its destination.

The day is overcast; she hopes that it will not rain. She descends the steps of *Nuestra Señora de las Nieves* and follows the path skirting the reservoir. In the early morning light the Embalse de Belesar looks eerie. She walks beside the dark water thinking of the people who once lived there, their lives, their homes now hidden from view. Centuries of history drowned beneath the water. It has been a long hot summer and the level of the reservoir is low; she can make out the ruins of some of the houses and imagines she can hear the lamentations of the villagers as their market-gardens, their homes, their vineyards are destroyed for ever. They will never herd their animals down the cobbled streets again, never hear the rumble of the ox carts passing their doors; children will never play outside those houses, nor old women sit in the doorways, chatting to their neighbours. The old men will never walk down to the river's edge and sit and smoke, watching the boys scramble over the rocks looking for crayfish and the women washing their clothes in the river. All the small details of their lives were changed or taken away that day in 1962 when the construction of a huge hydro-electric dam meant more than the homes of the people of Portomarín. What ghosts haunt this pathway she asks herself. What silent screams protest against this injustice? She is tempted to stop and sit by the water's edge for a while but the *Camino* is calling her and she continues on her way. Her feet are particularly painful this morning but she tries not to think about them as she climbs up through the trees and leaves the reservoir and its past behind her.

Beth stops and prises a stone out of the sole of her boot. She is in the tiny hamlet of Castromaior. Time to stop for a coffee and maybe a second breakfast; she feels hungry today. There is a small café next to the church and she sits down eagerly, glad to rest her feet.

'*Café por favor*,' she tells the woman who comes out to serve her, '*y pan tostado.*'

She can hear the contented clucking of chickens in the yard; if she moves her chair, she can see them through the open back door. She puts her rucksack on the ground and stretches her legs in front of her; her feet are throbbing. A couple of people whom she vaguely recognises are crossing the square; they are not stopping. One looks across and waves. She waves back. Yes, she saw them last night in Portomarín.

The coffee is hot when it arrives and the toast is made from dark home-made bread, typical of the area. The woman has brought her a small dish of chopped tomato and some olive oil. She dribbles the oil on the hot toast then spreads it with the tomato. It is delicious. So different from breakfast at home: cereal for Luke, toast and marmalade for Joe and the usual yoghurt for her.

It should have been easy to tell her friends the bad news but it wasn't; it had been very difficult. Her closest friend, Anne, with whom she plays golf every Tuesday, rain or shine, had been widowed the year before. She was taking a long time to get used to her new life as a single woman after twenty years of marriage and the slightest thing reduced her to tears. Even now, she had trouble coming to terms with the death of her husband, who had had an unexpected heart attack one Sunday morning, after a round of golf with his friends. So when Beth at last plucked up the courage to tell Anne about the cancer, she saw the distress in her friend's eyes, straight away. In fact it was Beth who ended up having to comfort Anne. The thought of having to go through that again was too much; Beth could not face telling the others one by one and repeating the same dire news, so she rang Penny, the most pragmatic of them and asked her to tell everyone else. That had worked. Her friends approached her one at a time, discreetly mentioning that they had heard her news and offering their help. They gave her sympathy but not too much. They were marvellous, visiting her in hospital, offering to accompany her to the radiotherapy sessions, doing her shopping when Joe was away and most of all being there to listen to her when she felt too depressed even to speak to her husband. Yes, they had been good, solid, practical friends and she had been glad of their support.

Luke was only seventeen at the time, still doing his A levels. When she and Joe told him that she had cancer the look of horror on his face stayed with her for days. She could see that he had difficulty believing that this was happening to his family but he rallied and pretended it was no big deal. Breast cancer was no longer the killer it used to be, he said and there had been wonderful developments in the treatment available; she would be better in no time. He rambled on like

146

an old man, not the frightened kid he was. She had felt proud of him, trying to comfort her with the sort of platitudes he heard others use. She had hugged him and said yes, they had caught it in time. She talked him through the treatment that the doctor had outlined and swore to him she was not worried. She promised she would not die.

Beth takes a sip of her coffee and places her tablets on the table in front of her. Their colours are bright, like Smarties, but there are no chocolate centres. She pops the largest one into her mouth and washes it down with the coffee; this is the new anti-cancer drug that the specialist insisted she take with her. When the results of her last check-up had revealed that the cancer had returned, he had wanted to keep her in hospital and start treatment but she refused.

'No, I'm not going through that again,' she told him. 'Not now. I need to get away on my own for a bit.'

Reluctantly he agreed to let her go, but only if she, in turn, agreed to take the tablets.

'You will be miles from the nearest hospital,' he told her when she admitted where she was going. 'You will need specialist medicine.'

The others are a mixture of vitamins and minerals: vitamin C, vitamin D, calcium, magnesium, potassium and caesium. She read about their efficacy in a woman's magazine and one by one she dutifully swallows them down.

She sees another small group of pilgrims walk by and waits until they have passed before setting off. She is not unsociable but she likes walking on her own; it gives her time to reflect on her life. Usually it was Joe and her, walking side by side, sometimes in silence, sometimes chatting about little incidents, the weather, the scenery, a recollection of someone or somewhere. They never had serious discussions while they were walking; those they saved for later, at home or in the bar after they had showered and eaten. Walking the Ridgeway or across the Pennine Way was not the place to discuss international events or political differences; it was not the place to discuss whether they should paint the outside of the house this year or employ a gardener now that Luke was no longer around to help mow the lawn. It was an opportunity to let that world drop away and enjoy just being together, in the open air. Or so she had thought. Now she realises that she never really knew what Joe was thinking.

He could not understand why she needed to do this trip; he thinks she is trying to punish him. But this is something she needs to do on her own, although she hasn't told him why. She can't. She can't go through it all again.

The sky has grown very dark and just as she is wondering whether to put on her waterproof poncho, there is a sharp crack of thunder and the rain begins. It falls in a heavy curtain, straight down, soaking the pathway in minutes. There is nothing for it, she has to go on; there is no shelter nearby. Besides which there is still a long way to walk to reach Palas de Rei and, before that, there is a steady climb ahead of her to the Sierra Ligonde. She shrugs her way into the poncho, and trudges along, head down, watching the rain run off her hat and drip down the khaki cape. She tugs at her hat. She is glad she brought it; its brim is wide enough to shade her from the sun and it is made from a lightweight, waterproof material, so protects whatever the weather. The path takes her through the wood where the trees hold back the full force of the rain for a while; instead it drips noisily down from wet leaves and forms a small stream along the path before her. Her boots splash through the puddles, sending muddy streaks up her bare legs. In another couple of kilometres, according to the guidebook, there is a *venta* where she can stop and shelter for a while.

The *venta* is crowded with dripping, wet pilgrims. She edges her way to the bar and orders a coffee. The heat from the bar is causing the pilgrims' soaked clothes to steam and the air is heavy and humid. Even the windows have steamed up and someone has drawn the wobbly outline of a scallop shell on one of them. The owner of the *venta* is obviously delighted to have so much passing trade and beams at her as he passes her the coffee. She spots a spare chair at a table near the door and heads towards it.

'Hi there,' says a young man, wearing a green camouflage jacket and matching hat. 'Bit wet out there. My name's Dave, by the way.'

'Hi Dave. I'm Beth,' she says, sitting down opposite him.

She looks at him carefully.

'I don't think we've come across each other before, have we?'

This is unusual because she keeps seeing the same people over and over again, sometimes in the bars, sometimes in the distance.

'No, that's right. Probably because I'm on my bike.'

She notices that he has hung an orange, plastic cape over the chair behind him and there is a helmet on the floor, next to his rucksack; water is dripping off the cape and pooling on the floor around him.

'You're cycling?'

He nods.

'In this rain?'

'Well, it's been OK most of the time. I keep to the asphalt path where I can.'

'The path through the wood was getting flooded when I came by,' she tells him. 'It must've been hard going on a bike. I had to make more than one detour.'

'Yes, it was. I had to carry the bike for a bit. Still it's pretty straight forward from here on. If the rain eases up I should make it to Ribadiso tonight and then on to Santiago tomorrow.'

The door opens to let in some more bedraggled travellers; the rain is still bouncing off the cobbles in the courtyard and shows no sign of abating.

'What a day,' one of them laughs, taking off his wet poncho and shaking it vigorously.

'You doing the *Camino* on your own?' Dave asks Beth.

'Yes. And you?'

'Yes. I hoped a mate was coming with me, but his girlfriend made such a fuss that he ducked out.'

'Well I suppose it does take quite a long time. I've been on the road a month now. I imagine his girlfriend would have missed him.'

'Frightened what he'd get up to, more like. She's a right possessive cow. He's even stopped coming to the cycling club now because Julie doesn't like cycling. I couldn't believe it when he told me. We've been members since we were sixteen. Cycling's what we do. We've always had bikes; we bought our first BMXs together. Now he says he hasn't got time for it.'

He seems astonished that his friend would forsake him and cycling for a woman.

'I take it you don't think much of her.'

'Well, she's pretty enough but she's so jealous; he isn't allowed to do anything without her. He used to be such a laugh in the old days. We went to school together and hung out all the time. That was until Julie got her claws into him.'

'I take it your girlfriend doesn't mind you being here?'

'Don't have one. I was going out with a girl for two years but then she started talking about marriage and babies and I thought, no, that's not for me.'

She wonders how old he is, maybe thirty, tops.

'So you decided to come on your own?'

'Yes, it's been OK. You meet lots of people. Of course it would have been more fun if Steve had come, but then he'd probably have been on the phone to her all day long, so I guess it's for the best. I'm having a good time actually.'

He looks at the rain beating on the windows and adds:

'Despite the weather.'

'It doesn't seem to be letting up,' Beth agrees. 'I think I'm going to have to brave it.'

'You're not waiting for it to stop?'

'No, I think I'd better move on,' Beth says, finishing her coffee.

'You'll get soaked.'

'I'm already pretty wet and anyway, the sooner I get there, the sooner I get a hot shower.'

'A hot shower, what a lovely thought,' Dave says. 'Well, best of luck.'

'Thanks.'

Reluctantly she puts on her wet poncho and leaves the warmth of the *venta*. If she can get back into a rhythm, she should be in Palas de Rei in a couple of hours, maybe a bit more because of the climb ahead of her. She sets off through the dripping woods and wonders, not for the first time since she came to Spain, if it is all worth while. With each step the water squelches from her boots and her feet feel numb. She plods on, head down, willing herself to keep going, unable to think about anything other than finding refuge and getting herself warm and dry.

She reaches the top of the ridge and there he is; her pilgrim is ahead of her, striding along through the puddles, the rain running off his cape. She feels elated at seeing him but, once again, she cannot get close enough to speak to him.

No matter how much she quickens her pace he is always the same distance away from her. Maybe, he too, likes his own company. She stops trying to catch him up and returns to walking at her own pace. She is content just to keep him in sight. It is surprising how he always seems to appear whenever she is feeling lost or lonely.

The rain has turned the pathways to mud and it is hard going, so it is not until three hours later that she arrives in the town, wet, cold and tired. The rain has fallen persistently since she left the *venta* and the sky is black, the rainclouds blocking out all the light. Her pilgrim has disappeared, melting into the misty air as they approached the town. Palas de Rei is a quiet, unremarkable town. Its inhabitants, those who have dared to venture outside today, dart from doorway to doorway, their umbrellas held aloft; cars rush past, their drivers tense and anxious, dirty spray shooting up from their wheels. She sees a small, white painted building with the sign '*Albergue*' outside and prepares to cross the road to see if they have any room. At that moment the bus from Lugo passes, its nearside wheels skimming the gutter and sending up a glistening spray of water that drenches her from head to foot. If it were possible to get any wetter, then this would have done it. She wants to shout at the bus driver but the angry words die in her throat; it is too late, the bus has already rounded the corner and disappeared from sight. Instead she laughs. It is as bad as the time when she played the final of the Batsby Golf Cup and it had rained from start to finish. That day, a strong westerly wind had driven the rain in horizontal sheets across the golf course while she and her opponent battled it out. They were on the final green when the club secretary came running out to tell them that they were closing the course due to bad weather so the competition was cancelled. She had looked at her opponent in amazement and they had both collapsed in hysterical giggles.

Now the water is running off her poncho in rivulets and fat drops of rain drip off the rim of her hat and run down her face. Her rucksack is waterproof, according to the salesman who sold it to her in Bideford, but she doubts that it can withstand this heavy downpour. Everything will be soaked, she is sure. Cold, wet and miserable, she checks into the *Albergue del Sol* and heads straight for the shower.

The rain has stopped by the time Beth leaves the *albergue*. Her wet shorts are hanging up in the room, her boots are stuffed with newspaper and she has left her poncho dripping into the bath alongside two others. Wearing her universal sarong and a warm fleece because the downpour has left the temperature cool and damp, she heads for the nearest bar. Palas de Rei is a disappointment; there is nothing much to attract one's attention. In fact, with its wet, shiny pavements it has a sad, sombre air. Its name promised so much more: King's Palace. In fact it hasn't been the residence of a king since the Visigoths, over a thousand years previously. There are one or two faded buildings that boast of a once, forgotten glory but most of the town resembles a modern, administrative centre with clean office blocks and wide streets. The main interest, as far as she can see, is that everywhere she looks the symbol of the *Camino* is visible. It is even carved on the doorway to the bar she is entering.

'Hi, over here. Beth.'

She looks round. The girl from the *albergue* in Portomarín is waving at her; she is sitting at a table with half a dozen others. The bar is crowded with people, most of whom seem to be locals, drinking beer and eating an early evening tapas, while the long trestle tables are taken up by the pilgrims. The atmosphere is lively, all the pilgrims happy to be sitting, at last, in a warm, dry, convivial place where they can exchange stories about their day.

'Come and join us, Beth,' she calls. 'There's bags of room.'

They all move up a bit so that there is a space for Beth to sit down.

'Hi,' she says, looking round hoping to see a face she recognises.

'We were in the same *albergue*, last night.' Roxanne tells the others.

They take it in turn to introduce themselves and shake Beth's hand. They are a motley group: a bearded giant of a man, wearing glasses and an intense look, a young, athletic boy in a Barcelona football shirt, a thin-faced man who is smoking something that smells like marijuana, a tall Australian with piercing blue eyes and Roxanne with her wide open smile and dazzling, blonde hair.

The Australian passes her a glass.

'Beer?' he asks.

'No, but I'll have some wine if there's any.'

'That's never a problem in this country,' says the man smoking weed.

He pours some Rioja into her glass.

'Hey there you are. We've been looking all over for you.'

It's Fran; she and Walter sit down opposite her.

'Hi. I've only just got here,' Beth explains.

'God, what a day. I got drenched. They said Galicia was the wettest place in Spain and I can believe it.'

'How's the knee?'

'It hurts like shit.'

'Probably the damp atmosphere,' Walter says. 'My rheumatism's playing me up tonight. I haven't noticed it

154

hardly at all for weeks, but since we entered Galicia it's started.'

Walter is probably nearer to seventy than sixty and, like many men his age, he talks a lot about his aches and pains. She murmurs, sympathetically and says:

'Hello, Walter. Where's Helen? She not with you this evening?'

He gives her an embarrassed smile and says:

'She'll be along later.'

'Good, I want to ask her what she knows about James the Moor-slayer,' she says. 'By the way, this is Roxanne; we met yesterday.'

'Hello,' he says, shaking her hand in his old-fashioned way. 'So, Beth, where are you staying? *Casa Concello*?'

'No, that was full by the time I got here. I'm in a little place near the market place, *Albergue del Sol*.'

'Hey, so am I. Maybe we're roommates again,' Roxanne says.

'They like a bit of irony around here, do they?' Fran asks. '*Albergue del Sol*, when did they last see the sun in this town?'

'I'm sure it doesn't rain like this all the time.'

'So what's this Hostel of the Sun like then? Is it OK?' Fran asks.

'Oh, it's just like all the others, six bunk beds to a room and only two showers. But there's plenty of hot water, though,' she adds.

'Here help yourself to some wine; we can always order more,' Roxanne says passing them the bottle.

'Where's Lucky?' Beth asks.

'Outside, she's a bit too muddy to bring in. I'll take her something to eat in a minute.'

The door opens letting in a gust of cold air and Helen joins them.

155

'Hello. I'm sorry I'm late. Wanted to pop in the church and have a look around before it got too dark.'

'Oh, you're wearing your new cross,' Fran says. 'It looks lovely.'

The cross of Tau that Helen bought in San Antón hangs around her neck on a shiny silver chain.

'Thanks, Walter bought me the chain. He said it was a shame to wait until I got home to wear it.'

She smiles across at her new friend and tugs at the chain, a little self-consciously.

'It's just a little thing I saw in one of the local shops,' he mutters, obviously embarrassed that it has been mentioned.

Beth sees that Roxanne is deep in conversation with the weasel-faced man; he seems to be annoyed with her about something. His head bobs up and down with each word he speaks as though to emphasise the gravity of what he is saying.

'I'll go to the money machine on my way back to the *albergue*,' she tells him.

The man shrugs and passes her a small packet. She slips it into her pocket and gives him a kiss on the cheek.

'Helps me sleep,' she tells Beth.

'I don't think I'll have any trouble sleeping tonight,' Beth says. 'It was hard work walking in that rain today.'

She notices the Australian whisper something to Roxanne but she pulls away from him and turns to Fran, who is cutting up some chicken scraps that someone has left on their plate.

'Who's that for?' she asks.

'The dog. I'll put this in with her biscuits,' she says. 'She likes a bit of chicken.'

'So did you have a good day?' Beth asks.

'Apart from the rain, my knee hurting like shit and Lucky not wanting to walk in the rain? Yes, great, thanks.'

'That's what a pilgrimage is about,' Helen says, seriously. 'Today was a challenge and we all had to face up to it.'

'Well I can do without many more challenges like that,' Roxanne says. 'I thought Spain was going to be hot and sunny.'

'How far have you come?' Walter asks.

'Brisbane.'

He laughs.

'No, on the *Camino*, I mean.'

'From Roncevalles. I've travelled with these guys, on and off, for most of the way.'

She gestures at her companions. One of them, the man with the thick sandy beard, is busily typing something into his computer. She sees Beth staring at him.

'This is Rob, he's a writer. Say "hello" Rob.'

He looks up and smiles.

'And blogger. Writer and blogger extraordinaire, that's me. Hello there.'

He gives them an airy wave with his hand and returns to his blog.

'Rob is chronicling his travels. He blogs what he's been up to, every day,' Roxanne explains.

'Not everything, I hope,' the boy in the football shirt chips in.

'Only what will get past the censors,' Rob says, without looking up from the screen.

'What do you write?' Beth asks. 'Apart from your blog, that is?'

'Travel books.'

'He's written three books,' Roxanne says proudly. 'One when he was in Brazil, one about Italy and one about walking across northern Queensland. That's where we met.'

'Beth's a writer,' Fran says.

Beth looks up, startled; she has never heard herself referred to in this way before.

'I used to be a journalist,' she tells them. 'Just the local rag.'

'What do you mean, used to be? Once a writer always a writer,' Rob retorts.

She smiles. He is right. She has spent so many years thinking of herself in relation to others, Luke's mother, Joe's wife, her parents' daughter, the Ladies' Captain of her golf club, that she has forgotten that she is first and foremost Beth. And Beth is a journalist; Beth is someone who writes.

'So are you doing a piece about the *Camino*?' Rob asks.

'Well no, actually I never even thought about it.'

'Why ever not? I'm sure your paper would love a couple of articles.'

'Maybe. I'll think about it. Right now I'm too busy worrying if I'm going to make it to Santiago.'

'Of course you will,' Walter says. 'If an old codger, like me, can do it then sure as hell you can.'

Beth smiles. He may be older than her but Walter is fit for his age. He was probably a very handsome man when he was younger.

'So it was Rob's idea to come on the *Camino*?' Fran asks Roxanne.

'Yes. I'd never even heard of it before I met him. But I'd always wanted to come to Europe, so I jumped at the chance. I'm going to England next, to visit my aunt.'

She looks at the Australian as she says it.

'Mike's thinking about coming with me. He's never been to England, so it's a great opportunity. My aunt has a flat in London; we'll be able to see all the sights.'

Beth thinks that Roxanne seems a lot more enthusiastic about her intended trip than Mike.

'Seems strange doesn't it, meeting up with another Aussie when there are all these other people about,' she adds.

'I don't know. Look at us, we're all from England. I suppose you just gravitate towards your own countrymen.'

'And women.'

'Well it helps when you have a language in common,' says Rob.   'I'd love to tag along with some of those Spaniards, but I can hardly speak a word of the language.'

'So are you all from down under?' Fran asks.

The thin-faced man, who is called Bruce, nods his head.

'Almost.   I'm from New Zealand,' he says.   'And Mike here is from Sydney.   Only Rob and Grant are Pommies.'

'And what's brought you to the *Camino*?' Beth asks.

'I'm trying to give up smoking,' Bruce says with a laugh, stubbing out his dog-end on the sole of his boot.

'Well you're not doing very well at it,' Fran tells him.

'Oh that's nothing, that's for medicinal purposes. It's the fags that are the problem. I used to smoke forty a day.'

He gives a short, sharp cough as if to emphasise the dangers of smoking.

'Will you write another book, about your travels along the *Camino*?' Walter asks Rob.

'Probably. Depends if my publisher thinks it will sell.'

He finishes whatever he is typing and closes his laptop.

'Any wine left in that bottle?' he asks.

Roxanne turns it upside down.

'Sorry all gone. We'd better order another.'

'Make it two,' Rob says.   'It's early yet.   I take it nobody is planning to give up drinking wine?'

'You've got to be kidding.'

'Have you been collecting stories about the *Camino*?'
Helen asks Rob.

'Stories? What kind of stories?'

'Well you know there are all sorts of myths linked to
the *Camino de Santiago*?'

'I know there's one about how the city got its name.
Are there more?'

'Plenty. I've been writing them down. I can go
through some of them with you, if you like.'

'Sounds a great idea.'

He pulls out a notebook and pencil.

'Helen knows all about the local legends.' Fran says.

'That reminds me, Helen. I wanted to ask you about
The Moor-slayer. I saw a reference to it in the guidebook but
it didn't give many details.'

'Oh yes, that's a well known story about St James. It
refers to the time, in the ninth century when Spain was
occupied by the Moors.'

'I've heard of that,' says Rob. 'The Arabs were
fighting against the Christians.'

'Yes, in a way. The Moors were from north Africa:
Berbers, Arabs and negroes, who sailed across the straits of
Gibraltar to find new land. They established their court in
Córdoba and gradually expanded their territory northwards
until they reached Clavijo in the north of Spain. There, in 844
AD, the forces of the Emir of Córdoba, Abd ar-Rahman II,
came up against the Christian troops of King Ramiro I of
Asturias.'

'So they conquered all of Spain?' Rob asks.

'Not quite. They got as far as Clavijo. Anyway,
because the Christian army was greatly outnumbered and the
troops were disheartened, it looked as though the Moors were
going to win the battle. That was when the people of the area
decided to make a vow before God that, if the Moors were

driven from their land, they would give a portion of their income to the Church of St James, for evermore.'

She takes a sip of wine and continues:

'The story goes, and who are we to deny it, that Saint James appeared to King Ramiro in a dream and promised him victory. The next day the saint, dressed as a soldier, riding a white horse and carrying a white banner with a red cross on it, appeared before them. He rode to the front of the battle field, his sword raised in his hand and told the soldiers to take heart, because God was on their side. The sight of the warrior saint, fighting alongside them, rallied the soldiers and they charged into battle. They say that the saint killed 60,000 of the enemy single-handed, that day. The Moors were vanquished and the Christian soldiers were victorious.'

'So that's how he became known as the Moor-slayer?'

'Exactly. No-one doubted that the victory was due to St James' intervention and the towns-people happily paid the tribute to his church.'

'I wonder if the local people still pay it?'

'Now that I don't know. But that's why the cross of St James is shaped like a sword.'

'So it is; I never noticed that before,' Rob says.

He seems delighted with the story; Beth can imagine him adding it to his blog. She sips her wine slowly and watches him. He is so full of life, questioning everyone, interested in what people are saying, constantly jotting things in his notebook. She used to be like that before she stopped being Beth. Perhaps she will buy herself a notebook, just in case she decides to take his advice.

CHAPTER 14
MARÍA

Pepe suffered too. Maybe as much as her, maybe even more because Pepe had lost not only a son but also his wife. She knew that, but there was nothing she could do about it. He was a good man; he had stood by her as they searched for Manu week after week, month after month, when one year ran into two, then three and now finally four. Maybe there was something about the number four that said it had gone on long enough, but that was when he told her, on the fourth anniversary of Manuel's disappearance.

'You have to let it go, María,' he said. 'You have to accept he is not coming back. I know it's hard my love, but you have to accept it.'

He spoke quietly, kindly and he stroked her hair as he spoke. But she leapt up, pulling away from him.

'No,' she had screamed. 'No. I can't do that. He's out there somewhere, I know. They aren't looking for him. They've given up but he's alive. I know he is.'

'No, María, you don't know. We know nothing. It's been four years and there's been no sign of him anywhere, not even any sightings. He's dead. We have to face it.'

She had cried, inconsolable. Nothing Pepe said or did made any difference. She knew she had become a slut; she hardly washed and her hair was uncared for. She could not get up in the morning and lay in bed all day, weeping. When she did rise she walked for hours, all the time calling Manu's name and then, exhausted, returned to her dirty, neglected house. All these things she knew but she could do nothing to change them. She was sunk so far in her grief that she could not lift her head even for the sake of little Ana.

'Let us bury him and let him lie in peace,' Pepe urged her.

'How can we bury him? We have no body,' she screamed. 'How can he lie in peace when we don't know where he is? Are you mad? Our son is missing, not dead.'

'María, this has got to stop. You have a daughter to think of as well. Manu wasn't our only child, you know. How can I look after Ana when I'm at work all day? You have to be a mother again.'

He sat there, his head in his hands and wept.

'Oh María, my María. I want you back, I want my wife back and Ana wants her mother.'

But she had ignored him. How could she give up? It was not possible. Manu was her little boy and he was out there somewhere. Maybe he was crying for her, maybe he was in pain. He needed her. If it took her the rest of her life, she would find him.

In the end Pepe had taken Ana and moved into his mother's house. He had left her to suffer alone. That was when she knew she needed to get God on her side again; that was when she decided to walk the *Camino*.

DAY 31

CHAPTER 15
BETH

It is not until she swings her legs over the side of the top bunk and tries to jump down that Beth realises that something is wrong. Her legs buckle under her and she has to grab onto the bed frame to steady herself.

'Are you OK?' asks Roxanne from the next bunk.

'I'm not sure. I feel a bit funny. Maybe I'll just lie down a while longer,' Beth tells her.

'Let me help you back up.'

Roxanne hauls her back onto her bunk.

'Thanks. I'm fine now,' she says, feeling anything but fine.

Why does she feel so weak? She stretches down for her rucksack that is wedged at the foot of the bed and pulls out the canvas bag that holds all her tablets.

'Are you sure you're OK? What about some water?'

'That'd be good.'

She points to a bottle on the floor.

'You probably got a chill in that rain yesterday,' Roxanne suggests.

'Yes, I expect that's it. I'll just take an aspirin and shut my eyes for a while.'

'OK. I'm off to get some breakfast. Want me to bring you anything?'

'No, really, I'm fine.'

'OK, well maybe see you in Ribadiso, then.'

Roxanne picks up her bag and leaves.   Once she has gone Beth takes out the tablets the doctor prescribed her and swallows one. She can feel the panic starting; surely it can't be happening so quickly. He told her she had at least another year left, maybe even two.

Dr. Michael had not been happy when she told him what she was planning to do.

'Now Beth, this is ridiculous,' he said, tapping the table, impatiently, with his gold fountain pen. 'We need to get you into hospital again as soon as possible.'

'I'm going away,' she told him, looking out the window at the harbour and wishing she was on one of the sailing boats heading down the estuary.

'Away? For how long?'

'Six weeks, more or less.'

'No, that's impossible.   You need to start your treatment right away. You should be getting a letter from Exeter General any day now.   I'm surprised that your specialist has agreed to it.'

'He wasn't too happy,' she replied.

'Neither am I.'

'It's all arranged. It's been planned for months. I'm going on a pilgrimage.'

He had looked at her as if she were mad.

'What does Joe say about it?'

'It's nothing to do with Joe. It's my life.'

She could see his frustration mounting. He was, after all, a good man, even if he was rather pedantic.

'Now Beth,' he said, 'we've known each other a long time. I wouldn't be saying this if it were not important. You do understand, don't you?'

'Yes, the cancer has come back, I understand that.'

'Exactly. This is your life we're talking about. The results of your tests show that the cancer has metastasised. It's vital that you start a course of chemotherapy as soon as possible. There's still a chance we can catch it in time and give you another few years.'

'But you can't guarantee it, can you?'

'There are no guarantees with things like this,' he said, pushing his greying hair back from his face, almost in a gesture of despair.

She had noticed him do that before when he was frustrated; she wondered if he realised that he did it.

'Have you even discussed it with your husband?' he asked.

She shook her head.

'Why not? Doesn't he have the right to know?'

'Maybe he does, but I'm not ready to tell him just yet. I'll tell him when I get back from Spain.'

'Isn't he going with you?'

'No, I'm going on my own. I told you; it's a pilgrimage. I want to be on my own for a while.'

He had said nothing more to persuade her. She did not even have to ask him to keep the news to himself; she knew she could rely on his integrity. He wrote her a handful of prescriptions and told her to come and see him as soon as she returned.

She waits until everyone has gone then tries once again to get up. This time her legs hold and the dizziness has left her. It was probably just as Roxanne said, a chill from the rain, yesterday. She goes along to the deserted showers but the water is cold so she just splashes some on her face and gets dressed. If it is a chill there's no point in exacerbating it by having a cold shower.

The town is quiet; most of the pilgrims have left and there are few people in the streets. It is like a ghost town after last night. She imagines this is how it is in these little villages along the *Camino*, an influx of people from midday onwards and then a mass exodus first thing in the morning. This must be the brief period when the village returns to normal, when it is left to the villagers. She has a cup of coffee and some toast in a bar then sets off, past the *Campo dos Romeiros*, the field where, in the Middle Ages, the pilgrims gathered to pray before leaving for Santiago. *Romeiro* is the Portuguese word for pilgrim and used also in Galicia, the woman at the *albergue* told her. Luckily she has no steep climbs today, the journey is through a series of river valleys, reasonably flat but probably rather muddy after yesterday's rain.

She is deep in the Galician countryside now, the sky is dark with heavy rain-filled clouds, the fields are lush with thick, green grass and she has twenty-five point eight kilometres to go to Ribadiso. Her clothes are dry although she can feel that her boots are still damp from the previous day and her feet continue to hurt. She rubbed them all over with vaseline this morning and added the zinc oxide tape, that Darren recommended, to the other dressings she has been using. And still they hurt. She is glad of the walking poles; they take some of the strain off her legs and feet. Well she is not going to give up now, not when she is so close to her goal; not dizziness, sore feet nor aching legs are going to stop her.

The road ahead is deserted and for the first time since she began this journey she feels nervous; today she would like to have some company. But everyone has gone; they left hours ago. If she had her mobile, she thinks wistfully, she could have phoned Fran and asked her where she was and to wait for her.

The Galician countryside is distinctive. It reminds her a little of her own West Country, with its small fields and dry-stone walls. The change was obvious as soon as she reached O'Cebreiro, set in the green, rolling hills across the border from León, and saw the round stone houses of the area, with their straw roofs and Iron Age design. She has even passed Celtic crosses at the roadside, so like the ones in Cornwall, and fields of fat, contented brown and white cattle. Just like the west coast of Britain and Ireland, Galicia receives its fair share of Atlantic wind and rain and this is evident in the verdure of its countryside. No, she is no longer walking through the dry Meseta; this part of Spain is very different and, to her, feels more like home.

The path takes her across a main road, where the roadsigns are in both Spanish and Galega, a language still spoken by many in the area, and on into the tiny hamlet of Carballal. A woman is feeding her chickens, her arm making huge sweeping arcs in the air as she scatters the corn and the excited birds flap about, chasing and pecking at the seeds. Two of them wander into the lane and peck at Beth's legs as she goes past. The woman lifts her hands in apology and smiles. The air is rank with the smell of chicken manure and pig swill.

As she rounds the bend she sees the pilgrim again. She cannot believe it. Once more he is there when she needs him. Today she does not bother to try to catch up with him; she knows it is useless. She wonders if he's a ghost, maybe the ghost of a pilgrim who walks the *Camino* looking for other pilgrims in distress. Then she laughs at her own silliness. Beth does not believe in ghosts or spirits and she does not believe in witches and hobgoblins either, despite the myths that haunt this road. The pilgrim seems to have stopped next to a *hórreo*, one of those carved, wooden granaries that are set on stone stilts to protect the grain from rats. They are ubiquitous in Galicia and each village or farm has its own design: some have lattice-work sides, others have

170

crosses on their tiled roofs, while some are made of stone, with wooden panels engraved with intricate designs. All have a sturdy, sloping roof to take away the rain and all are raised above ground level. She will see what he looks like now she tells herself but as she approaches the *hórreo* the pilgrim is nowhere to be seen. He has vanished. But she can hear the sound of someone singing. She makes herself walk more quickly, eager to see who is ahead, around the bend. She expects to see the pilgrim but it is not him; it's Roxanne. She is sitting by the roadside, leaning against her rucksack and singing to herself.

'Ah, good, you made it,' she says, as though she has been waiting for her.

'Roxanne, what are you doing here? I thought you left ages before me. Weren't you going to meet up with your friends?'

'Yes, I did. They've gone on ahead. I thought I'd just have a bit of a rest.'

'Are you alright?'

'Fine.'

This seems strange; she must have been sitting there for at least an hour in order for Beth to have caught her up.

'OK. I was worried about you. I shouldn't have left you back there in the *albergue*. It was obvious you weren't well. I should have stayed with you.'

'No, I'm fine now. Really.'

'Anyway, as I said I was worried, so I thought I'd just sit here for a bit and see if you came along. And here you are.'

Beth is more pleased than she could ever have imagined. It must be telepathy. She wishes for company and then suddenly there it is.

'I heard you singing,' she says.

'Yes, it makes the time pass quicker.'

Beth is not sure she wants the time to pass any quicker. She sits down beside her and rubs her ankle.

'Been bitten?'

'No, pecked.   Some damn chickens pecked me as I walked past.'

Roxanne laughs.

'Well it all happens here: dog bites, bed bugs, chased by cows, now chickens.'

'Who was chased by a cow?'

'Darren. He was walking through Castromaíor, yesterday and these long horn cattle were coming down the street. One of them took a fancy to him and he had to jump over a wall and hide in someone's front garden until they'd gone.'

Beth smiles. She hasn't seen Darren and Sheri for a couple days.   Darren is a rather macho young man; it must have been quite humiliating for him to be chased by the cow.

'I'm surprised he told you about it.'

'He didn't. It was his girlfriend who told me.'

She stands up and swings her rucksack onto her back.

'So, shall we get on?'

'Yes, of course.'

'Do you sing?' Roxanne asks.

'Not really.'

'Well you can just hum along.'

She begins:

'Onward Christian soldiers, marching as to war ....'

It is not what she expected Roxanne to sing but it is stirring stuff and good to march to. She finds herself falling in step with the young woman and soon they are walking side by side and singing together.

After a while she finds the pace a bit tiring but at least she has no time to dwell on her own problems; she is too busy trying to keep up and remember the words to this long-forgotten hymn.

'Which part of Australia are you from?' Beth asks when they come to the end of the hymn.

'Born and bred in a small town, east of Brisbane,' she tells her. 'It's a quiet town; we never get many tourists. Hordes of holiday makers arrive in the area every summer with their cameras, their surfboards and their binoculars ready to explore our beautiful coastline, but they usually pass us by. Cars and caravans speed through our sleepy town but hardly ever stop; the tourists prefer to go to Jacob's Well or Southport or into Brisbane itself.'

'Well that's nice isn't it?'

'Not if you're young. I've got plenty of years ahead of me for peace and quiet. I wanted some life and that place was dead.'

'What do your parents do?'

'They run a boarding house but, even in high summer, they're rarely very full. We had hardly any guests. When I was a teenager I used to help my mother clean the bedrooms and serve breakfast. Then on Sundays I had to accompany them to church; my parents are really strict church-goers. I used to sing in the choir,' she adds.

'So that's how you know the words of all those hymns.'

'Yes, I liked that bit. I love singing. I was in a local group for a while until my father decided it wasn't good for me.'

'A group? What sort?'

'A girls' band, sort of mix between classical and pop. Classical cross-over they call it. There were three of us, a violinist, a guitarist and me as the singer. We called ourselves "Melbarreto".'

'Strange name.'

'Yes, it was a bit naff. After Dame Nellie.'

Beth shakes her head in puzzlement.

'Dame Nellie Melba, the famous opera singer.'

'Oh, of course.'

'Anyway, my father made such a fuss that I dropped out.'

'What happened to the others?'

'They're still together. They just play as part of a regular quartet in Brisbane now.'

'Do you keep in touch?'

'Not really.'

They cross another small river, the fourth since they left Palas de Rei, and begin a short climb up to Melide.

'I told the others I'd meet them here for lunch,' Roxanne tells her. 'The town is famous for its octopus stew.'

'How will you know where to find them?'

Roxanne holds up her mobile.

'Technology.'

'Of course.'

'I just can't understand how you could leave home without your mobile. I'd die without mine. I'm in a blue funk if the battery dies.'

'I didn't want anyone to ring me,' Beth says.

Roxanne looks at her in disbelief.

With that her mobile rings and she flicks it open.

'Hi. Yes, we've just arrived. Where? *El Molin*o? OK, see you.'

'Your friends?'

'Yes, they're in the bar *Molino*; it's in the centre somewhere.'

'Is your boyfriend there? Mike?'

'Oh Mike isn't my boyfriend; I told you, he's just a mate.'

'He seemed to be behaving like a boyfriend the other night.'

'Oh that. He doesn't like me smoking pot; he says it's the start of the slippery slope. Mike's a sports freak. He doesn't like anything that messes up the body.'

'He doesn't seem to mind putting away a few pints.'

'True, but I don't think he puts that in the same class as marijuana. Anyway it's only a bit; it helps me sleep. But he can get a bit boring about it. He says he won't go to my aunt's with me unless I give it up.'

'Why's he going to your aunt's? If he's not your boyfriend then why does it matter?'

'Well, it's complicated.'

She sighs then continues:

'I want him to pretend that he's my boyfriend, so that my aunt will ring my parents and tell them.'

'You're right; it does sound complicated.'

'They're always on about me getting a boyfriend.'

'Well most parents want their children to meet someone and settle down.'

'I know, but I'm not ready for settling down yet.'

'So, Mike is to pretend to be your boyfriend just to get your parents off your back, is that it?' Beth asks.

'Sort of. Oh, what the hell, I might as well tell you; everyone seems to tell people everything on this pilgrimage. It's... Well, I'm gay. That is, I think I'm gay. I had this girlfriend back in Australia but my parents went ape-shit about it so I left.'

'Where's your girlfriend now?'

'She's still there. I wanted to come here on my own to sort out my head. You see she's definitely gay, but I'm not sure if I am or not. I wanted to come on the pilgrimage to see if it was all just a mistake. I mean, I'm from such a boring little town, maybe I was just looking for some excitement.'

'Well it sounds as though you found it.'

Roxanne smiles.

'So, have you decided what you want to do?' Beth asks.

'No, not really. I like Mike and I like the other guys, but they're just good mates. I don't feel anything else for them. And we've been in some pretty close situations together,' she adds with a wink.

'Even if you are gay, it doesn't mean that this girlfriend is the right one for you,' Beth tells her.

'I think she is.'

'Whichever way it goes, there doesn't seem much point in complicating things by lying to your aunt, does there.'

'No, that's true.'

They are at the entrance to the small town now.

'Look Roxanne, I think I'll just keep going. You go and meet up with your friends.'

'No way. You can come with me for a bit and have something to eat.'

Reluctantly Beth follows the girl through the town. It seems a busy place and, like many others she has passed through, has a mixture of modern and medieval architecture. Although she has never been here before, Roxanne seems to have a clear idea of where they are going and very soon they are standing outside a gaily decorated bar with the words *El Molino* etched above the door.

'Hey, Roxanne, over here.'

A group of young people are sitting at one of the tables, empty beer jugs on the table in front of them.

'Good God, where on earth have you been? We've got through two of these and Rob's just asked for a third.'

'Have you ordered any food yet?' she asks, sitting down beside them and throwing her rucksack on the ground. 'You remember Beth?'

They all look at Beth, acknowledging her in their own individual ways; Rob nods, one gets up and gives her a kiss on her cheek, another grunts and Mike says:

'Nice to see ya again. Roxie says you weren't feeling so good this morning.'

'That's true, but I'm OK now.'

'Glad to hear it.'

He turns to Roxanne and asks:

'Right, we going have some of this octopussy stew then?'

The *pulpo Gallego* was delicious. She pays her share of the bill and tells them that she is leaving. She wants to walk on her own now; she has enjoyed Roxanne's company but she cannot keep up the pace of the others.

'Well I can hang back and walk with you,' Roxanne says.

She looks back at the others.

'We can meet up in Ribadiso.'

'No, really Roxanne, it's very sweet of you but I'm OK, really,' Beth says.

'It's probably your singing Roxie. I bet she was singing that god-damn awful hymn?'

Beth smiles and nods at him.

'I knew it. She was a choir-girl, you know. Well you just give us a ring if you feel bad and one of us'll come and look for you.'

'Thanks, but I'm sure I'll be fine.'

She waves goodbye to the group, who are now ordering another jug of beer and sets off, back to the *Camino*. A group of old men are sitting in the shade of a chestnut tree, playing dominoes; she hears the clack, clack of the tiles as they hit the table. They look up at her, disinterested and return to their game.

Once she has left the town the path takes her through leafy woodlands; oak and chestnut and even a few pine trees line the way; the sound of blackbirds calling to each other fills the afternoon air and, looking about her, she notices a magpie sitting in a tree. In vain she looks for a second. One for sorrow, two for joy, she repeats in her head. Suddenly a second magpie lands on the path in front of her. Her sigh is audible and she curses herself for being so silly. It is peaceful here, without the chatter of the others. It was nice of them to be so hospitable but she is glad to be on her own again; her journey is nearly over and still she does not know what she hopes to achieve.

Her mother had died of cancer. It was the year that Luke was born. They had kept the news from Beth for six months, not wanting to upset her in her condition, her mother explained at the end, when it was not longer possible to conceal it from her. By then Luke was a month old and her mother had lost all her hair. Beth did not know what to feel. It was as though God was giving her something with one hand and taking away something else with the other.

Her mother had suffered and they all knew it. She was never one to suffer in silence; and why should she? She was angry that her life was being taken away from her so soon. The doctors did what they could for her but, in the end, the chemotherapy, the radiotherapy and a whole cocktail of drugs did nothing to stem its relentless progress. She knew it and they knew it. Beth was angry that the doctors had put her mother through it all for nothing. She always felt that the chemotherapy her mother had endured was far worse than the cancer itself; she remembered how sick she had been after each dose and how she dreaded going into the hospital for her next session. Her mother, a strong feisty woman who never took any nonsense from anyone, was reduced to a frail, angry woman with no hair. There had been little hope right from the start the doctors confided afterwards; the cancer was widespread and it was incurable, some rare strain that had, as yet, not attracted enough funding to eradicate it.

Beth had visited her mother every day, taking her tiny baby with her. But the grandmother was too ill to really appreciate this little bundle of new life; she was too busy, desperately trying to hang on to her own life. When she died, in a clinically clean hospice, accompanied by two caring nurses, her estranged husband and Beth, she was only fifty-five. Whenever Beth thinks about her death she shivers, as though anticipating her own.

By the time she reaches Ribadiso she is exhausted and heads for the first *albergue* she sees. It is full and the owner, a rather jolly man with a beer drinker's paunch, directs her to another at the far end of the town.

'We're always the first to get full,' he says. 'That's why we're going to build onto the barn. Put in another twenty beds for next year.'

'Thanks, I'll try it. *La Casa de Juan* you said?'

'Yes, that's right. You can't miss it; it's just past the main square.'

The walk through the town is pleasant: everything is clean and sparkling in the late afternoon sun, as though the previous day's downpour has washed the town clean. *La Casa de Juan* is a tiny *albergue*, next to the chapel. As she is about to go in, she notices María.

'Hello María,' she calls and waits while the Spaniard crosses the road to speak to her.

'*Hola* Beth. How are you today?'

179

'A bit tired, to be honest. I've just arrived. Are you staying here?'

'Yes, I checked in a while ago. It's fine,' she whispers. 'Very clean.'

'Have you been to eat?'

'No I just wanted to sit in the church for a while. I'll eat tonight.'

They go into the *albergue* together. The owner greets them with a warm smile.

'*Buenos días señoras,*' he says.

'Do you have a bed?' Beth asks.

'Yes, of course.'

He takes her *credencial,* checks it and stamps it and then directs her to an empty bunk.

'I'm going to lie down for a bit,' she tells María. 'I'll see you later perhaps.'

'Yes, perhaps when I go for dinner.'

Beth takes off her boots and lies down on the bed. It is hard but the room is, as María said, spotlessly clean.

Poor María. What does she hope to achieve by this pilgrimage? Does she really believe in miracles? Does she really think that God will give her back her son? And what about her, does she think walking this pilgrimage is going to cure her of cancer? A feeling of hopelessness envelopes her. Is it really worth all the effort? Everyone has to die at some time. Why fight it?

She closes her eyes and drifts off into a restless sleep.

CHAPTER 16

It is after nine o'clock by the time she finds the bar where they have arranged to meet. She recognises Lucky first; she is sitting outside the bar, looking wistfully at the door. A couple of bicycles are leaning against the wall and something that looks like a hand-cycle.

'Hi there Lucky,' she says, bending down and patting the dog's head.

Lucky does not move but her tail bangs up and down on the ground in greeting. There is a plastic bowl of water next to her and a plate of dried dog food, mixed with what look like scraps of *pulpo*. Beth pushes the door open and is at once met with the pungent smell of fried fish. She spots Fran at once, sitting in the far corner with Walter and Helen and some others.

'Hi there,' she says, sitting down at the only vacant place.

'We thought you weren't coming,' Fran says.

'I fell asleep. I've only just woken up,' she says, looking round at the others.

One of the newcomers is Dave, the cyclist she met at the *venta*. He has a huge plate of stew and potatoes in front of him.

'Hello there. I thought you'd be in Santiago by now,' she says to him.

'Oh, hi. You're Beth aren't you? We met yesterday in the rain,' he says, mopping up the gravy with a hunk of bread.

'Yes, I didn't expect to run into you again.'

'Had a puncture. I've been stuck here ever since.'

'Is it fixed now?'

'Yes, I'll be on my way in the morning. We're going to travel together,' he adds, indicating the two men on his right.

They are both young men, probably in their twenties and look pretty fit, which is why she doesn't notice at first that one of them is in a wheelchair.

'Hello,' she says, holding out her hand.

'Hi, I'm Andrew and this is Eric.'

'So those are your bikes outside?'

'Certainly are.'

She turns to Fran.

'Had a good day?'

'So so. That bloody morning sickness won't go away. I find I can't eat anything until lunchtime, can't even face a fag.'

'Good job. You shouldn't be smoking anyway in your condition.'

'OK, Gran.'

Beth feels herself blushing and decides to change the subject.

'So you're feeding that pooch on octopus now?'

'The owner offered. Just some scraps left over from lunch, he asked if Lucky wanted them.'

'And she said yes, naturally.'

'Naturally. I don't think she's a dog who's had much opportunity to pick and choose her food. Not by the state of her when I found her.'

'I thought she found you?'

'Well yes, technically. She is, after all, an intelligent dog.'

'You mean she knows a soft touch when she sees one.'

'You could see all her ribs. I know these dogs aren't designed to be fat but honestly, she was nothing but skin and bone; she was filthy dirty, she could hardly stand and she was covered in ticks. When I took her to a local vet, in Lograno, he said that the kindest thing was to put her down. But I couldn't do that. She looked at me with those big brown eyes and I knew she was not ready to die. So he gave her some vitamin injections, bathed her and got rid of the ticks. After a few good meals she rallied and here we are.'

She beams at the dog and tickles her behind her ears.

'You're such a softy.'

Fran laughs and pours some wine into Beth's glass. Beth notices she has a large glass of water. So, despite her bravado, she is taking her pregnancy seriously.

'Are you going to eat?'

Beth shakes her head.

'Not hungry; I'll just have some wine.'

The men on her right are arguing about something; she turns to listen and Dave tells her:

'I had to wait until six o'clock this evening to check into the hostel. I was just saying to the guys that it's wrong to discriminate against cyclists. Walkers can check in as soon as they arrive but cyclists have to wait. I tried explaining that I had to stay another night because of the puncture but the stupid bitch in charge said I'd have to move to another hostel. What a load of bollocks.'

He pulls out his pilgrim's passport, opens it and adds with a grin:

'But the good news is that I got my *credencial* stamped twice.'

'So where are you tonight?' Beth asks.

'Right next door. That's where I met these guys.'

'Is that your hand-cycle?' Beth asks Andrew.

'Yes, that's right.'

'So how do you manage?'

She thinks of the uneven state of some of the paths she has traversed since she started.

'With difficulty,' he says, with a laugh. 'But it's a great machine. I had special high-duty mountain-bike tyres fitted and it gets over almost any terrain. It's lightweight - only twenty kilos, so if I get somewhere that's impassable Eric gives me a hand and carries the Hike across.'

'Hike?'

'That's what I call it. Bicycle - bike, hand-cycle - hike. It has a rack on the back where I can put my wheelchair and rucksack, pretty neat really.'

'Have you travelled all the way together then?'

'No, I met Eric just after Estella, at the wine fountain in Irache. Free wine for pilgrims, seemed too good an offer to miss.'

'Except he didn't have anything to put his wine in,' chips in Eric. 'So I gave him one of my scallop shells and we made a toast.'

'Scallop shell? Not exactly a suitable shape for wine,' Dave says.

'On the contrary, it's an excellent shape for food or drink. It was multi-purpose utensil. Pilgrims used to use it as a bowl for eating or a cup to drink water from,' Helen tells them.

'It served its purpose well because we made quite a few toasts, actually: to St James, to King and Country, to Spanish señoritas.'

'Yes, it got a bit silly in the end.'

'I wasn't the only one who was legless by the time we left,' Andrew says with a laugh.

He sees her looking at him and says:

'Afghanistan. Took a sniper's bullet in the spine when I was on patrol. Didn't feel a thing, just dropped like a stone. Next thing I knew I was in the field hospital at Camp Bastion.'

'I'm sorry,' Beth says.

Her words sound feeble but she can't think of anything else to say. Of course, she should have realised he was a soldier; his black hair is cut close to his head and is shaved up the back of his neck, leaving a distinct line which probably coincided with his regimental cap. His upper body is square and muscular, as though he has worked out on a regular basis. He must have had an impressive physique before he was injured. Without really meaning to, she compares him to her son. They are a similar age but Luke is slight by comparison, although he is over six foot tall and you would never mistake him for a soldier. There is something almost effeminate about Luke, maybe it is the long hair he favours, even though it is not really the fashion.

'There wasn't a lot they could do for me. Patched me up and sent me back to England, to Stoke Mandeville. I'm not going to walk again, that's for sure, but the rest of me works OK. And I'll say one thing for the people at Stoke Mandeville, they did give me the will to carry on.'

'It's very brave of you to do the pilgrimage,' Walter says. 'It can't be easy on a hand-cycle.'

'It's not, but then, what is easy in this life? At least I'm still here to complain about it. Not like some of the mates I lost in Afghanistan.'

Beth wonders if he is hoping for a miracle. Many people do the pilgrimage for that reason, even if they don't admit it.

'So how did you manage before you met up with Eric?' Fran asks.

'I'm not sure really. There always seemed to be someone around when I needed them. The most difficult parts were when the path went downhill, especially when it was that awful loose slate and gravel, or places where the path seemed to give out altogether. If I had a problem I just sat and waited until someone came along and they gave me and the Hike a lift across whatever was in the way. Pilgrims believe in helping each other,' he adds.

'We're hoping to make it to Santiago tomorrow. It's only forty-odd kilometres after all; we should do it easily,' Dave says.

'With two of us to help get the Hike over the difficult parts, it should be a doddle,' Eric agrees.

'When I arrived in Roncevalles, I saw a priest with a group of disabled people. They were from some parish in Madrid and they had at least a dozen helpers with them. Why didn't you consider doing something like that? They even had a coach that took their luggage from one *albergue* to the next. Surely it would have been a lot easier than doing it on your own?' Walter asks.

'Actually, it was suggested that I take part in a wheelchair relay to raise money for Spinal Research; there were eighty of them, from all parts of Britain. They set off from Paris back in August and will arrive in Santiago sometime in October.'

'So why didn't you?'

He shrugs.

'It wasn't what I wanted to do.'

'It would have been a lot easier.'

'Maybe, but I wanted to do it my way, do the whole pilgrimage, not just part of it. And anyway I wanted to go on the Hike, not in my bloody wheelchair. I'm not just doing this for me. This is for my mates; the ones who didn't make it. It's for my parents, who think my life is over. It's for my

186

girlfriend, who's stood by me through it all,' he adds passionately.

He looks away from them and adds:

'But if I'm honest, it's most of all for me, to prove I'm still a man.'

Beth feels her eyes fill with tears at these words. She drinks some wine and says:

'I think we all have something to prove to ourselves, maybe not as fundamental as that, but most people on this pilgrimage have a reason for being here.'

Fran nods.

'Like María.'

Dave looks at her.

'María?'

'She's looking for her lost son.'

'I saw her earlier. She said she was going to eat this evening, so she might join us,' Beth says.

'Isn't that her, over there?' Helen says. 'Look, sitting at the bar on her own.'

'Yes. Shall I go over and ask her to join us?' Beth suggests.

'Good idea.'

María looks pleased to see her. She has just finished eating and was about to leave, she explains.

'Don't go yet. Come and have a night-cap with us, first.'

She follows Beth back to their table.

'I saw you here but I didn't want to interrupt,' she explains.

'You're not interrupting anything,' Walter says. 'We were just hearing how these lads met up.'

He picks up the wine bottle and pours out some wine for María, then tops up Helen's glass. He looks at Andrew.

'Wine?'

'Just a spot. I shouldn't overdo it because of the pain killers. They don't really mix.'

He pours Andrew half a glass and then says, tipping the bottle upside down:

'Time to order another bottle; this one's dead.'

He waves across at the waiter.

'You're very quiet Helen. Everything alright?' Beth asks.

'Yes, I'm just a bit tired.'

'I know what you mean. I'm beginning to wonder if I'm going to make these last few miles,' Beth says.

'It´s not far now,' Dave says. 'You can't give up after coming all this way.'

'It's alright for you, you're on a bike,' she says with a laugh. 'You've got a pair of wheels to take the strain. My poor feet have been complaining for weeks now.'

'My feet may be better than yours but I'm getting a bit saddle sore and that's worse.'

'Still as you say, not much further.'

She feels a thrill of excitement as she says it. They are coming to the end of their journey. What will it mean for everybody? Will they all just return to their old lives as if nothing has changed? Will she?

'So how are you María?' Fran asks.

'I am alright, thank you. My husband phoned me today. He says my daughter is missing me.'

'I expect she is. You've been away a long time.'

'I spoke to her,' she says. 'She was crying. She's only four, you know. She wanted to know if I'd be home for her birthday.'

'Well, as Dave says, we're almost there. Your journey will soon be over and then you can go home to her,' Beth says.

She reaches across and squeezes María's hand.

'Anyone got a story for us tonight then?' Fran asks.

'I heard one about a bird who comes every day and washes the face of a statue of the saint? It was in one of those little villages at the beginning of the *Camino*, near Estella, or somewhere like that.'

'That sounds rather sweet,' says Helen.

'Do you know any stories about ghosts?' Beth asks.

'Ghosts? There are hundreds of ghost stories. In what connection?'

'Well you know, the ghosts of pilgrims, wandering the *Camino*.'

'Nothing comes to mind. If I hear of one I'll tell you. Why are you interested?'

'Have you seen a ghost then?" Fran asks with a laugh. I'd never have thought you'd believe in such things.'

'I don't. I just wondered.'

CHAPTER 17
ANDREW

At first his mother said nothing when he told her. He knew she had not wanted him to join up.

'Haven't we got enough soldiers in this family,' she eventually snapped and went into the kitchen to resume whatever she had been doing when he arrived.

His father had been a regular soldier and now worked as a security guard for a big insurance company. His mother was a soldier's wife and a soldier's daughter; it was in her blood so she should have understood. But Andrew was her youngest and he knew that she favoured him over the others. Tom and Rick, both regular soldiers, were twelve and fifteen years older than him, respectively; they had joined up while he was still at primary school. It was no wonder that she treated him like her baby.

She wanted him to go to college and learn a trade, become an electrician or a plumber.

'You'll always have work then, no matter what happens to the economy. People always need a plumber and getting a decent electrician is harder than gold dust,' she added. 'Why don't you apply for a place at Bristol Tech?'

'It's not called that anymore,' he told her.

'Well, it still does courses, doesn't it?'

'The army will train me,' he said. 'I'll get a trade there.'

She did not argue with him. Maybe she had had that particular argument with his brothers and he had been too young to realise. At any rate his mother was realistic; she knew how stubborn he could be. But that did not stop her switching the television off every time there was a report of soldiers being killed in Afghanistan.

'They probably won't even send me there,' he told her. 'It's usually the more seasoned troops that get sent into action.'

She knew he was lying but she was, after all, a soldier's wife; she knew when to hold her tongue. Why make it worse? He had made his choice.

He did not want to join his brothers' regiment but the recruiting officer seemed to think it was a good idea.

'Makes it a family tradition,' he said.

He had protested that he was not a real Welshman, having been born in Bristol, but the fact that his father, grandfather and uncles were all Welsh and his brothers were already serving with the 1st Battalion The Royal Welsh, was enough to be accepted. So he ended up being the only Englishman in a regiment of Taffies.

The Royal Welsh Regiment had three battalions: the 1st was stationed at Chester, where he was duly sent to do his basic training, the 2nd was at Tidworth and there was also a third battalion of Territorial Army recruits. It was a new regiment, formed in 2006 from three other Welsh regiments, one of which dated back to the seventeenth century; before the merger, his brothers had served in The Royal Welch Fusiliers.

He enjoyed it from the first. The army was in his blood; he could feel it. The first time he put on his uniform he felt different; this was what he had been born for, to be a soldier. When he was at school he excelled at any physical activity, played football for the school, cycled with the local cycling club and took part in as many sports as he could. At fifteen he joined the Army Cadet Force and learnt a whole range of new skills: how to abseil, archery and rock climbing; he devoted two evenings a week to the Cadets and most of his weekends. His father, at times, had to remonstrate with him because, if it was a choice between studying and playing sport, there was never any question which would win. His bedroom was littered with cups, medals, pennants and certificates for everything from cross-country running to hockey. No wonder he was attracted to the army; where else could he have such an active life and be paid for it? So, by the time he had finished his A-Levels, he already had his future career planned out. He joined up.

The whole world lay before him. When the news came that his battalion was being shipped to Helmand Province in the southern part of Afghanistan he was not worried; he was excited, high on the adrenalin that flowed through his body. It all seemed so simple. They would go there, do their tour of duty and then return home. He came home sooner than he expected.

He wakes early. It's best to get up before the rush. Most of the hostels where he has stayed have been great, with wheelchair access and disabled toilets. Sometimes it takes him a while to find a hostel where there is an available bed on the ground floor, but most of the time people have been very helpful and keen to accommodate his needs.

He swings himself out of bed and into his wheelchair, grabs his things and sets off for the toilet. It's easier to get dressed in there than messing about on the bed.

They were a nice crowd last night. Didn't ask too many questions and treated him like a normal person. If only.

He was never going to recover from his injuries; that had been made quite plain.

'Hi, you're up already,' says Eric. 'Need a hand?'

'No, I'm fine. I'll see you outside in half an hour.'

'OK. I'm going to brew up some tea in the kitchen. Do you want any?'

'Please. Two sugars.'

'I'll leave it in the kitchen for you.'

'The regiment's being posted to Afghanistan,' their CO told them. 'We ship out tomorrow.'

It was not news to them; they had been training for it for months. The preparation had been very thorough, all that were missing were the heat and the snow. Everything else had been thought of and simulated in a corner of Norfolk that the MOD had converted into Afghanistan. Here they had replicated the sights and sounds of Afghan life; they had built a Middle Eastern village of narrow, winding streets and square, stone houses. They had added the smells and colour of the village, its markets, its cafés and, with the help of Afghan nationals in the UK, its people: women, children, old men and Taliban fighters. The call of the muezzin, summoning the faithful to prayer, interrupted their days at prescribed times. Except for the lack of sunshine and the fact that no-one died, they could have been in Afghanistan. He did not think it would work. He thought once they were actually there, in a hostile theatre of war, it would be different, he would act differently. The training would be revealed as mere play-acting. But no, he responded just the same. By then it was instinctive; he knew how to approach a hostile situation, how to protect his back and those of his comrades. He moved around the terrain as though he had been there before and, in a way, he had. There was no time to think 'well this must be different because this time it's for real', his training took over and he acted on instinct. They all did.

At first it was as though they were going on holiday. They packed up their kit and were taken to RAF South Cerney for processing, then on to RAF Brize Norton to check in for their flight.

Andrew was used to flying. He and his family had moved a lot with his father's postings; they had lived in Cyprus, Germany and even had a spell in Kenya. He was no stranger to airports; when he was twelve his parents sent him to a boarding school for army kids, in Sussex and he flew back to visit them every Christmas, at Easter and for a couple of months in the summer holidays. He clocked up thousands of flying miles. This was not so very different.

But his mate Jeff was not relaxed. It was his first time on an aeroplane and everything, from the roar of the engines to the turbulence they encountered over the mountains made him nervous. He was more worried about dying in a plane crash than being shot in the heat of battle.

An RAF Tri-Star flew them directly to Kandahar where, after seven hours in the air, they landed in the dead of night. That was when it changed. That was when he knew this was going to be no holiday. The heat hit him straight away, a dry searing heat that could have cooked a steak on the barbecue. And the smell, the air was filled with an indescribable smell that he would forever associate with Afghanistan. Later, when he had been there some time, he knew it came from the fetid pools of water, the rank and putrid piles of rubbish lining the streets, from the lack of sanitation, from piles of rotting vegetables, from the smell of cordite and weapons, from the fragrant fields of opium poppies, from the herbs and spices that flavoured the food, from the goats and horses that cohabited with their owners, from the crumbling buildings and the dusty roads. All that was Afghanistan combined to make this unique smell.

As they lined up on the tarmac he felt disorientated; it was so dark there was no way they could see anything or tell how big an area they were in. His uniform began to stick to his shoulders and he could feel the sweat running down his back. Every fibre of his being was alert. There was over an hour to wait for the Hercules that was due to take them on to Camp Bastion and everyone was starting to get edgy; they wanted to get there, they wanted to get on with it. Their platoon commander came over and told them to put on their body armour and helmets; they were about to fly through Afghan airspace and, he warned, anything could happen.

They arrived at Camp Bastion without mishap, although diversionary tactics on the part of the pilot of the Hercules had given them all a scare when they suddenly found themselves dropping abruptly through the black night.

They were out on patrol immediately, replacing a battalion of the Yorkshire Regiment that were due some recuperation leave.

'Our mission here is to provide security to the country. We are the face of law and order here. Remember that. Our job is to protect civilians from Taliban insurgents,' the officer in command told them. 'Remember what you've learned and watch your backs. Don't trust anyone.'

He let his gaze wander along the ranks then said:

'Above everything else, be vigilant. For the first few days everything will be very strange to you and therefore you will naturally be extremely alert. The danger comes when you become more relaxed with your surroundings. You may feel that you can drop your guard a little. But you can't. That is the time you will start to make mistakes. That is the time when you must be even more vigilant. I want you to remember my words: you must be alert at all times.'

He emphasised the 'all times' and glared at his men.

'At all times,' he repeated. 'You can never drop your guard out here. You never know who is the enemy or where he is lurking. He could be just around the next corner.'

Their mission was to patrol the area. It seemed straightforward; their presence was all that was required. As far as he could make out, the local people seemed reasonably pleased to see them. There was little actual contact with the Afghans; occasionally he would speak to someone in the markets or greet someone as he passed them in the street but, by and large, they kept to themselves. Many of the nationals were wary of the soldiers.

He quickly settled in. His years at boarding school had accustomed him to being away from his family. That was how it was with army families, the job came first and everyone got used to living their lives at a distance. His mother, although she rarely complained in front of her children, had spent many hours, weeks, months waiting for his father to come home from an operation. It seemed as if most of her life she was waiting for someone, at first her husband and then her sons. She had often said, usually in exasperation when they were getting on her nerves, that she wished she had had daughters. But they had laughed at her and told her it was equal opportunities now in the Army; having a daughter was no guarantee she would not be a soldier.

His mother wrote him long, rambling, chatty letters telling him all the news from home and Louise emailed him and sent him text messages, most of which he could only pick up when he was back at HQ. For a while he followed his mates on Facebook, but that world seemed so remote from his present life that he gave it up. His real mates were here with him, in B company.

That was the most frustrating, being out of range of the communication satellites when they were on patrol, but he got used to it. It was surprising what he got used to. The job took up all their time and energy. They were focussed twenty-four hours a day. There was time to eat and sleep and clean his weapon, even, some days, time to relax and kick a football around, but the focus never wavered. They were on their guard always; they had to be.

Their first action was only a few days after they arrived. They had received news that some Taliban soldiers were holed up in a deserted farm; their section was told to check it out. There were ten of them and their sergeant. But when they arrived at the farm there was no sign of any activity. They waited in the cover of a ruined stone barn, while the sergeant sent someone ahead to check for land mines. The ground between them and the farmhouse was declared clear, so in they went. At first it seemed to be going well. Two fusiliers went into the building first while the rest of the section waited. They checked the first room, then the second. The building appeared to be empty. Suddenly there was a tremendous explosion and clouds of dust and debris flew into the air. One of the doors had been booby-trapped. The two fusiliers were buried under the debris but uninjured. Andrew followed the others into the farmhouse and helped to pull them to safety. Nobody seemed to know how they had survived the blast. They were lucky to be alive. Their sergeant said it was a bloody miracle. By now the adrenalin was pumping through Andrew's blood and he was ready for anything. He realised that he was not frightened. All the nervous thoughts about what could happen, all the fears that they might be attacked, had vanished, washed away on a tide of adrenalin. It was not until later, lying in his bunk, that he felt the relief; he was OK. He had survived, for now.

Eric was already outside by the time he emerged, washed, shaved, dressed and having drunk the mug of sweet tea that his friend had prepared. It was still dark but a glimmer of light was on the horizon and it would not be long before the sun was up. They would probably make it to Santiago today.

'Ready?'

'As ready as I'll ever be.'

'Where's Dave?'

'I'm here,' he says, cycling round the corner and stopping beside them.

'OK, let's get off then.'

He can hear Dave and Eric chatting for a bit but he cannot make out what they are saying. It's difficult to talk when you're pedalling a hand-cycle. Your companions are too far away to hear you properly, so the journey is usually made in a companionable silence until one or other decides to stop. He doesn't mind this although it means it is harder to stop his thoughts drifting back to Afghanistan.

The patrol were going to a village in the southern-most part of the province. Suspected drug smugglers had been spotted in the area and they were to check it out and apprehend them if possible. It was routine procedure. The sort of patrol they had been on dozens of time. But Jeff wasn't with them this time; he was having two days off, recovering from diarrhoea and sickness. They had all had bouts of it by then.

The village was quiet, nobody on the streets. If there had been any Taliban there they would have seen the soldiers arrive; it was impossible to disguise the dust thrown up by their armoured vehicles on those dirt roads. They were told to proceed with caution and the section walked slowly down the main street, their rifles at the ready. A dog startled him, running out from an alley with a scrap of something that looked like a dead rat in its mouth but, apart from that, there was nothing. He should have known that something was not right. Maybe the silence should have alerted them. It was really far too quiet for the middle of the day. The heat was intense and he wished he could just take his helmet off for a moment and pour some water over his head but he kept his eyes on the alleyways and the dark spaces inside the buildings and he walked on. Every nerve in his body was taut and he could feel the same tension in his companions. Something was going to happen.

Just as they turned the corner a covered truck appeared from nowhere. The driver slewed it across their path, scattering them. Two Taliban insurgents, in the back of the truck, sprayed them with gunshots. The fusilier next to Andrew dropped to the ground. He was dead, a bullet straight through the head. Andrew had never seen a dead man before. Nothing they had done in Norfolk had prepared him for this. The dead fusilier was called Ken. This was his third tour in Afghanistan and his last. Andrew had hardly spoken to him. He knew next to nothing about him and yet he was one of theirs. The image of his staring eyes and the blood trickling down his face had haunted him for weeks as he lay in his hospital bed wondering how he had survived and Ken had not.

They let off a few rounds at the truck as it sped away and out of sight, but did little damage.

'Everyone OK?' their sergeant asked.

Andrew did not hear the reply. At that moment he felt a sharp pain in his lower back and knew nothing more.

They medevacked him to Camp Bastion and then flew him back to the Queen Elizabeth Hospital in the UK, where they operated to remove the bullet that was lodged against his spine.   Once he knew he was not going to die the only question on his mind was whether he would walk again. No-one could answer it. They patched him up as best they could and sent him to the rehabilitation centre at Stoke Mandeville Hospital.

That was tough.   If he thought it was hard in Afghanistan, it was nothing to the discipline he needed in the hospital; he had to reach deep inside himself and find the strength to go on with his life. Despite what his parents said and Louise's promises to be there always for him, he knew his life was over. Only his brothers understood. They knew how hard it was for him to face the prospect of life as a paraplegic. Maybe it was their sympathetic but realistic attitude to his injury that helped him, eventually, to see a way out. Life was never going to be the same again, but at least he was still here to tell the tale. And he thought once again about Ken, lying on the ground beside him with a bullet in his head.

But that was on the good days. The other days, the bad days, his bitterness overflowed into everything he said or did. He was only twenty, barely started with his life and here he was a cripple, confined to a wheelchair. He could not bear to watch any sport on the television; football matches were particularly hard and, with the 2012 Olympics fast approaching, the programmers seemed determined that all viewers should watch were young athletic men and women competing in their elected sport. He had to get away. He had to try to regain something of his old life. That was why he had come here, to the *Camino*.

Dave signals for him to pull over. There is a small café by the roadside.

'Time for a break,' he says. 'Eric fancies a smoke.'
'OK by me. I could do with some breakfast.'

He pulls himself up and unlatches the wheelchair from the back of the hand-cycle.

'Want a hand?'

'Just hold it steady for me, would you,' he says and pulls himself into the chair.

The café looks rather small and the doorway is low and narrow.

'I'll sit out here,' he tells them.

'OK. What do you want?'

'A bacon and tomato baguette and a coffee.'

'The usual then?'

'That's right.'

A few minutes later they return and join him at the table.

'We're in great time,' Dave tells them. 'If nothing goes wrong we'll be in Santiago by lunchtime.'

'In time for the crazy Mass that everyone goes on about?' Eric asks.

'I doubt it. It starts at twelve. But we can always go tomorrow.'

The waiter comes out with their food. The bacon smells wonderful.

'Did you know a perfume company did some research on which smells were the most popular with men? Do you know what came out top?' Eric asks.

The others shook their heads.

'Bacon.'

'I can just see my ex-girlfriend going out smelling like a bacon sandwich,' says Andrew.

'Ex-girlfriend? Asks Eric

'Louise.'

'But I thought you two were OK.'

'Well we haven't had a fight or anything but she's gone to Madrid to live. She wants to do some course in

Travel and Tourism.   She could have done that in England, but no, she wants to do it in Spain, she says.'

'Well what's wrong with that?'

'Nothing. I just think it's an excuse to get away from me. I can't blame her. Why would she want to spend the rest of her life looking after a cripple? She's only nineteen after all. She has her whole life before her. Why let a sniper's bullet ruin two young lives? No, it's best this way.'

He struggles to keep the bitterness out of his voice.

'You said she was what kept you going,' says Eric.

'She was. She was wonderful, coming round every evening after work, taking me shopping for whatever I needed, sitting with me in front of the telly. My parents idolised her. They kept telling me how lucky I was to have her. They were right. But it wasn't fair on Louise to be constantly at my beck and call. I don't want a relationship based on sympathy. I've got my mother for that.'

He takes a bite of his bacon baguette, before continuing:

'I suppose it wasn't really a surprise when one day she came round and she said she needed to talk. We waited until my mother had gone to the shops and then she told me. She said the usual things, you know, how much she loved me, that she hoped we'd always be friends then she said she was going to Madrid. I mean, why Madrid? Why on earth did she have to go to Spain? Did she really need to go so far away to break up with me?'

'I'm sorry, mate,' Dave says.

'No, it's good,' he says and he means it. 'I'm happy for her.'

It is good for her. How can he expect her to spend all her time looking after him?   She needs to get on with her own life.

She promised to come home in the holidays. She said she would visit him and write and let him know what she was doing. But in the weeks after she left he missed her; he wanted to ring her and beg her to come back to England. He wanted to tell her that things could be the same, that they loved each other and love could conquer everything. But he knew it was not true. His short time in Afghanistan had aged him. He was no longer the innocent, naive young man that had set out from Brize Norton. He was harder, more cynical and definitely more realistic. Life was what you made of it. No, he was not going to deny her the opportunity of doing something with her life just because his was buggered up.

'Are we fit?' asks Eric. 'Shall we get on?'

'Ready when you are.'

They pay for the breakfast and leave. It is warmer now, the sun has banished the early morning mist and falls in dappled pools across the tree lined path. They cycle for another two hours then stop at a *venta* outside Santa Irene.

'Want anything?' Dave asks.

'Just some water. Give me a hand with the chair before you go. I need to find a loo,' Andrew says.

By the time he comes back the others are sitting outside in the sunshine. Dave and Eric are drinking beer and his water is on the table.

'Thanks.'

'What made you buy the hand-cycle?' Dave asks.

'I used to belong to a cycling club,' he replies.

'Yes, what was it? The Rusty Wheels?' asks Eric, with a laugh.

'That's it. We used to meet every Sunday morning at the Lemon Tree, a greasy spoon café on the road from Bristol to Bath. One Sunday morning, not long after I'd been discharged from Stoke Mandeville, my mate Gerry came round. I remember him sitting there, in my parents' front room, in his bright green cycling shorts. Green and white, they were the RWCC's colours,' he added. 'He looked really uncomfortable. Anyway he told me that the other lads sent their best and that he was due to meet them at the Lemon Tree, later. They were off to the Somerset Levels. That's a nice run, fairly flat.'

'Yes, I've done that a few times,' says Dave.

'Anyway we chatted for a bit and then he left. The next week he came round again, on the Saturday. He and the lads had been chatting about how I could get back into cycling. He'd brought me a catalogue of hand-cycles. Now I'd never looked at hand-cycles before. After all, what reason was there to do so? But I knew they existed; I saw some guy on the telly once, riding one in a marathon for the disabled. I have to admit it didn't make much of an impression.'

'Yes, I've seen a few people using them. There's a bloke that lives somewhere near me that has one. They can be a bit of a menace on the roads because you can't always see them. He's got one of the ones that are completely flat, not like yours. When you're in a car you can miss them altogether,' Eric says.

'Well he got me interested. I downloaded all I could find on the internet and arranged for my father to take me to the nearest dealers to see one for myself. I knew as soon as I sat in it that this could be my salvation. There was a staggering range to choose from. I really fancied one of the racing models but it was impractical, so I went for the big wheel version instead. I needed something that would take me anywhere and across any terrain. They adjusted it to my specific weight and height and delivered it within two weeks.'

'Was it expensive?' Dave asks.

'I suppose so, but then a good cycle can cost quite a bit, as you know.'

The others nodded.

'Actually the family clubbed together and bought it for me'.

'It must have been strange at first,' Eric says.

'It was but I soon got used to it. It wasn't the same sensation as cycling but it was as near as damn it. I could get about and I could get up some speed. It was as manoeuvrable going down the high street with my mother as it was riding across the playing fields. It took a while to get used to being in a semi-reclining position and, as my arms and shoulders did all the work, my upper body ached like hell for the first two weeks. But I soon had it under control.'

'So it didn't take long?'

'Not really, I had a couple of mishaps, of course. Like the time I tried to swerve it around the corner and into our drive. I misjudged the position of the kerb, hit the kerbstone, flew into the air and landed in the rose bed.'

'Were you hurt?'

'No. Just a scratched face and injured pride. More importantly the Hike wasn't damaged. Then another time I was bombing down the lane and, because of my angle of vision, I didn't see an enormous puddle in front of me. I went straight through it and was soaked. Anyway, I eventually felt that I had mastered it well enough to phone Gerry and tell him that I was ready to join them.'

'How did it go?' asks Dave.

'OK. At first the others were a bit too concerned for my welfare and I got annoyed that they were trying to mollycoddle me but gradually they all became used to me and my new contraption. It was great. For the first time in a long while I felt I'd got my independence back. I was mobile again and I was having fun.'

'Talking about being mobile, I think we should get on. Next stop Santiago.'

DAY 32

CHAPTER 18
BETH

The next morning Beth is up early. She is only two days away from her destination and the excitement is bubbling at the prospect of arriving in Santiago de Compostela at last. She is tempted to hurry this last stage of the walk and feels envious of Andrew and Dave who will most certainly arrive there today.

She slips out of the *albergue* without disturbing any of her sleeping companions and breathes in the fresh, morning air. It is clean and cold, smelling of cut grass and wet woodlands, a welcome respite from the warm fug of bodily smells that she has endured all night. The cobbled street is deserted, gleaming wetly from the rain that fell during the night and she makes her way along it until she reaches the under-pass. The sky is overcast and gloomy; it is too early for the sun to make any impression on the forbidding clouds. She hesitates; it looks rather dark inside the tunnel but she has to enter it if she is to pick up the *Camino* again. Cautiously she sidesteps the puddles that have settled on the uneven ground and, once through, she turns right and is back on track, following the route of the N547. A hum of traffic accompanies her, hanging in the air like the background to a melody. The route today runs parallel to the main road all the way to Arca do Pino, where she will stay for the night.

There was no sign of Andrew and Dave when she left the village; their bikes are no longer chained up outside the *albergue*. She wonders if she will see them later; it's possible that, in the interest of speed, they will take the main road. Sadly, she realises that it is unlikely that their paths will cross again.

The walk is pleasant and soft underfoot, the ground squelching with every step. She is in a thick grove of sweet smelling eucalyptus trees which would normally provide welcome shade but, today, just help to reduce the daylight even further.

As she trudges on, she cannot help thinking about the soldier she met the night before. Despite their physical differences he reminds her so much of Luke. Is this just because of their shared youth or is it that vulnerability that all young people seem to have these days? She wonders how she would react if Luke came home and told her he was going to join the army. Would she try to stop him?

She sees a figure disappearing through the trees ahead of her; it is the pilgrim, she is sure. She quickens her pace but he is gone. Maybe it was just a shadow, or an animal flitting through the dappled patches of pale sunlight that are struggling to reach the woodland floor.

She is approaching the hamlet of A Calle and decides to stop for breakfast. It is a pretty little place and she spots a café right by the river. A woodpecker is busy hammering away at a nearby trunk and the sounds echo through the trees.

There are a few people sitting inside, but only two of them look like pilgrims; of the others one is a nun and two are obviously farmers who have stopped for a coffee and a dram of the local *aguardente*. Despite the latest no-smoking laws the small room is heavy with cigarette smoke. Beth takes a seat opposite the nun.

'Do you mind?' she asks her in her best Spanish.

'*Con mucho gusto*,' the nun replies.

Beth notices that her black habit is very grubby, especially around the hem, which is pulled up slightly, exposing rather muddy, sandalled feet. It suddenly dawns on her that the woman is a pilgrim too. Although how she can walk so far in sandals is a mystery to Beth. She does not seem to have anything with her, no rucksack, no bed-roll; all she has are a large silver cross that hangs round her neck and a scallop shell attached to the cord around her waist. There is a glass of water on the table in front of her. She takes a sip from it and smiles at Beth.

'Are you walking the *Camino*?' Beth asks in English and to her delight the woman can understand her.

'Yes. I am doing a penance,' she replies. 'I 'ave come from Arles in the south of France, from the convent there.'

There is a soft buzzing sound to her accent.

'So you're French?'

'I am Swiss but I 'ave lived in the convent in Arles for many years.'

'Have you walked all the way?' Beth asks, looking down at the nun's feet.

'Of course.'

'Where are your things? Your rucksack? Your bedding?'

'I do not carry a rucksack. I 'ave no need of one.'

'But how do you manage? Where do you sleep?'

She wonders if the nun stays in a hotel each night, but it seems unlikely, she looks too poor for that. It is not only her clothes that are dirty, her hair and face look as though they have not seen hot, soapy water in a long time.

'Under the stars,' she replies.

'But the weather has been awful the last couple of nights, surely you didn't sleep out in that?'

The nun smiles; she looks weary.

'Our Lord slept in a manger,' she tells her.

'Why don't you stay in the *albergues*? They're very cheap.'

'We do not carry money,' she explains. 'We do not need it.'

'But what about food?'

'God provides,' she replies.

Each time she mentions God's name she crosses herself and kisses the cross around her neck.

'They have some rooms here,' Beth tells her. 'I am happy to pay for you to stay here, if you like. A good night's rest and a hot meal will be good for the soul. God won't mind.'

The nun shakes her head.

'I am not allowed to accept any charity on this pilgrimage, only food,' she explains.

'Well let me treat you to a coffee and something to eat,' Beth says. 'I'm about to have some breakfast myself. Please join me.'

'Some bread and oil would be very nice.'

'Coffee?'

'No, I 'ave water.'

Beth attracts the waitress's attention and orders the food. She is hungry; she asks for a large slice of Galician bread, with butter and strawberry jam and a piece of cold *empanada*. Then she changes her mind about the coffee and orders a cup of steaming hot chocolate instead.

Within minutes the food is served but, before they eat, the nun bows her head and whispers a short prayer. Beth looks at the feast in front of her; comfort food, she thinks as she begins to eat.

'Have you seen a tall pilgrim, with an old-fashioned staff?' she asks the nun.

'Today?'

'Yes, this morning. I thought I saw him ahead of me.'

She explains how she has seen this figure many times but never been able to catch up to speak to him.

'They talk of many pilgrims who wander the *Camino*, 'elping those in distress,' the nun says. 'But I 'ave never seen one.'

'But I wasn't in distress,' Beth protests.

She swallows down the last of the *empanada* and starts buttering her bread.

'God sends 'is angels to 'elp those in need,' the nun continues. 'Sometimes we don't always know when we need the 'elp.'

'No, I wasn't in need of help. I was just being curious, trying to see who he was. That's all.'

She is beginning to wish she had not mentioned the pilgrim.

'I must be on my way now,' the nun says. 'Thank you for the bread. May God bless and keep you, my child.'

'*Buen camino*,' Beth replies.

She watches the nun walk towards the door; she looks frail, as though a puff of wind would blow her away and yet she has already walked more than a thousand kilometres. She wonders how long it has taken her but sees no point in asking. The nun has not been counting the days, nor measuring the kilometres; she has not been interested in the *albergues* or the bars. She has just been walking, each day getting closer to her destination and closer to God.

Beth finishes her breakfast and leaves. There is no sign of the nun. As she goes down the lane she is forced to let a herd of Fresian cattle come lumbering by, their hooves churning up the path into a morass of muddy hollows. The cows look as though they are due to be milked; their swollen udders swing heavily from side to side. A burly cowherd tips his hat at her and mutters something unintelligible. 'Mind how you go,' maybe? Ahead of her she can see some walkers, most likely the ones who were outside the café, but they are walking too fast for her to catch them. Once the cows have passed, she walks steadily on, picking her way round the cow-pats and wrinkling her nose at the rich farmyard smells. She starts humming to herself and tries not to think about the nun. Why did she think Beth needed help? Could she tell that she was ill? Could she see her future? Or was Beth just reading too much into chance remarks? Whatever it was, it gave her an uncomfortable feeling and she had been pleased when the nun resumed her journey.

She reaches the tiny hamlet of Salceda, then she veers right, preparing to cross the main road. Ahead of her is a monument. She stops and reads the inscription: *Guillermo Watt*. Who was he? William Watt? Spanish? English? All she knows is what Helen told them last night, when she said to look out for it. Guillermo Watt was a pilgrim who died in 1993, only a day away from Santiago. His monument is simple but typifies the man's pilgrimage; beside the plaque, which is set into a low, stone wall, someone has built a niche in which there is a pair of bronze hiking boots. She takes a small pebble from her pocket and lays it on the pile of offerings that other pilgrims have left beside the boots: stones, crosses, scallop shells. She looks around her. It is a quiet, leafy spot although the drone of traffic is never far away. As good a spot as anywhere to die, she thinks. She wonders if he knew he was going to die. Was he ill? Had he, like her, been told his life span was now about to be curtailed? Or had it been sudden? Of one thing she felt sure, he had expected to reach his destination. It seemed sad that he had died just one day before he got there. Sad for those he left behind who, no doubt, would like to believe that he had completed what he had set out to do, but for him? No, not sad for him. Death subsumes everything. Our achievements, our hopes, our dreams are all as nothing when faced with death.

She walks on, feeling depressed. Even the sky is grey now; the watery sun has given up and disappeared behind a blanket of cloud. A glass of wine, that's what she needs. She walks another couple of kilometres and arrives at a crossroads; there is a restaurant tucked away in the shade of some tall eucalyptus trees.

To her surprise Fran and Roxanne are there. They each have a dish of chickpea soup in front of them.

'Well, what a surprise. Didn't expect to see you. I thought you set off ages before us,' says Fran, getting up and giving Beth a kiss on her cheek.

Roxanne smiles but does not move. Beth wonders if she is shy of her now that she has confessed to being gay.

'I probably did. I just seem to have been taking a lot of rests on the way. Smelling the flowers you know.'

As she says it she thinks back to Jill, the woman she met in the Pyrenees. She seemed to know how to let go and enjoy life.

'Smelling the cow pats more like. I've never had to jump over so many cow pats in my life,' says Roxanne.

'Order yourself a bowl of this,' says Fran. 'It'll put some hairs on your chest.'

'Thanks but that's not what I'm looking for in a meal. Although it does smell good, I admit.'

She nods across at the waitress and orders a bowl for herself.

It's nice to have company again. She sits down and tells them about the nun she met earlier.

'God, I couldn't cut myself off like that. No phone, no hot water. Ugh,' says Fran. 'If this pilgrimage has taught me anything, it's that I'm a city girl. Yes, I like the countryside but I need to get back to civilisation after a while.'

'Too true. Imagine a life with no telly, no films, no music. I couldn't bear it,' agrees Roxanne.

'Well I expect she's happy. After all I don't expect anyone is forcing her to be a nun. She probably feels fulfilled.'

'Well I feel fulfilled now,' says Fran, patting her stomach. 'That soup was very fulfilling.'

'Isn't that María?' Roxanne asks, looking out of the window. 'Hey, María.'

She waves. María stops, puzzled and then when she recognises them comes into the restaurant.

'Hello,' she says.

She still looks sad but Beth thinks she looks less distraught than before.

'Hello María, how's it going?' Fran asks.

She sits down and says:

'*Bien.* I was talking with my husband again today. They are going to fly to Santiago and meet me.'

'That's lovely. Your little girl too?'

'Yes, my Ana is coming to get me.'

'So you're going home?' asks Roxanne.

'As soon as I have been to the cathedral and prayed to God. I know he has forgiven me now,' she adds. 'Last night, for the first time since Manu disappeared, I dreamt of my Ana. When I woke I knew that I had made my peace with God. Now I can go home. It is time to let go. I must think of my little girl now.'

'That's wonderful news. I'm sure she has been missing you,' Beth says.

'Yes, she is too young to understand what I have been going through. Now I must spend some time with her,' she says then adds: 'and my husband. Poor Pepe, it has been doubly hard on him because I have been far away. But I'm back now. I will make it up to him.'

'Will you join us for lunch?' Beth asks.

'No thank you. I want to get on. I want to get to Santiago as soon as I can. They arrive on Saturday.'

Today is Wednesday; she should make it in good time.

They get up and kiss and hug María, wishing her well. Beth can hardly hold back the tears. María had not found her son but she has found her family again. That is some kind of miracle of its own.

'I'm so pleased for her,' Roxanne says, as they watch the receding figure of María, disappear down the lane. 'She'll be much better when she's with her daughter again.'

'She has obviously been very depressed if she has wanted nothing to do with the little girl for four years,' adds Fran. 'Let's hope that she'll be able to pick up with her life again now.'

'Do you think it would have happened if she hadn't come on the *Camino*?' Beth asks.

'Who knows. She's very religious. She must believe in all that guff about miracles,' Roxanne says. 'Maybe it was just being away from where it all happened that helped.'

'Yes, maybe. How are you, anyway?' Beth asks, turning to Fran.

'OK. I'm OK.'

The smile disappears from her eyes.

'Actually I'm not. I tried to ring Tim but there was no answer. I think his phone was off.'

'Did you leave a message?'

'No, what's the point. He's probably decided that it's over between us.'

'You don't know that.'

216

'Well I have made it pretty impossible for him to contact me for the last six weeks. Now when I want to speak to him it's no wonder he won't answer.'

'That's the trouble with men, they're not very good at communicating,' says Roxanne.

'I don't think it's just men,' Beth says thinking about her own sorry situation. 'Women are good at keeping secrets too. I'm sure life would be much more uncomplicated if we all spoke the truth and let our loved ones know our true feelings.'

'You're probably right,' Roxanne replies. 'But sometimes it's too hard to tell people the truth. I don't want to hurt my parents and I know they'll be devastated if I tell them I'm gay.'

'But do you really know that or is that what you assume? I expect they might be disappointed if they think they will never have any grandchildren, but you are their daughter. I'm sure they only want you to be happy.'

'Lots of gay couple have babies these days,' Fran adds. 'That's no problem.'

'And nobody pays any attention to gay couples; it's generally accepted.'

'Not in my family, it isn't. A couple of years ago my Dad caused an enormous stink over a couple that wanted to stay in our B and B. Two middle-aged guys they were. They told him they were married and wanted a double room. My Dad went ballistic. There was no way a God-fearing family like ours was going to allow two men to sleep together under our roof. That's what he said.'

'What happened?'

'Well they were perfectly within their rights to report him for discrimination but they were nice blokes. They just said: "No sweat, mate" and they went somewhere else.'

'What a shame. You'd have thought he would have liked the business.'

'That's my Dad all over. If the Church says it's wrong then there's no way you can persuade him otherwise.'

'What about your mother?' asks Fran.

'She just goes along with whatever Dad says. That's why I wanted to get away before they found out.'

'Are you sure they don't already know?' asks Beth.

'I think they have their suspicions but they don't want to face up to it. That's why I jumped at the chance to tag along with Rob. It was an ideal solution. I'd always dreamed of going to Europe. Now I had the opportunity to see all these countries, Spain, France, England, maybe even Italy and to escape from my parents' constant questioning at the same time.'

'But what about your girlfriend?' Beth asks. 'Aren't you running away from her as well?'

'I suppose so.'

'More to the point,' says Fran in her direct manner, 'aren't you running away from yourself?'

Roxanne does not reply but Beth can see that Fran's words have hit home. Is this what they are all doing? Running away from the truth? Hoping to hide from reality on the *Camino*? Well, if she had thought she could do that, she was wrong. It seemed that above all else the *Camino* demanded the truth from people.

CHAPTER 19
ROXANNE

She met Jan at a tennis match. Jan was a brilliant tennis player; she had rangy long legs that enabled her to reach every corner of the court with ease and her serves left her opponents dazed. They played tennis three times a week and gradually a friendship grew between them. She and Roxanne soon became inseparable. At first Roxanne's parents welcomed Jan into their home; she was the sort of girl of whom they could approve: quiet, sporty and wholesome. Unlike some of Roxanne's other friends she did not wear makeup and skimpy tops that showed her cleavage; her hair was not dyed some shocking pink colour and she was not constantly giggling about boys. They loved her.

'She's a sensible girl, that Jan,' Roxanne's mother said. 'You'd do well to take a leaf out of her book. No young man is going to turn her head.'

And they were right. Initially Roxanne did not realise that Jan was gay; they never talked about such things. But she heard some of the lads at the tennis club make a few snide remarks about Jan playing for the other side and even heard one of them call her a rug-muncher, something her friend Vivienne had to explain to her. She paid no attention to the comments, putting it all down to jealousy on the boys' part as

Jan was the best tennis player in their group. She and Jan listened to the other girls discussing the boys that they knew and neither had much to add. Roxanne had never had a boyfriend. She had never felt attracted to any of the boys at school and although there were some undeniably handsome young men at the tennis club, she had little to do with them. She was sure that her parents would not have approved anyway.

But they did approve of Jan, until, that was, Roxanne's brother told them he had seen them kissing in her car. Then all hell let loose. You would not have believed how quickly their opinions could change.

It had taken them both by surprise. It was Christmas, the time when people did silly things: got too drunk, stayed out half the night, smoked some weed. Everyone was having a great time at Billy's party. Roxanne had drunk at least a bottle of wine and maybe a few rum and cokes; she could not remember what Jan had had but it was probably something similar. They were sitting on the stairs laughing at some inane joke when suddenly Jan leaned across and kissed her on the lips. Roxanne's first reaction was to spring back and look around to see if anyone had seen them but everyone was well out of it by then, far too stoned to notice an innocent kiss. Then she realised that she liked it, a warmth was spreading through her body that was not just due to the alcohol and so, she kissed her back. Somehow they managed to push their way through the dancers and get outside without anyone asking them where they were going. They climbed into the back of Jan's car and that's where they were when Rodney came out to look for her.

After that her parents made life impossible for them. They constantly quizzed her about where she was going and who she was seeing; they forbade her to bring Jan into their house again and although they could not stop her going out with her, she was after all nineteen, they contrived to make her feel guilty about it afterwards. Worst of all, they would look at her with such a profound sadness that you would have thought there had been a death in the family. Only Rodney treated her as normal. Once he realised what damage his indiscretion had caused he did everything he could to make it up to her.

And where was Jan in all this? Jan made it clear. She loved Roxanne but she was not going to creep around, hiding in corners and avoiding people just because they were homophobic. It was their problem, she said, not hers. She understood Roxanne's difficulty with the situation; after all, they were her parents but, as she told her again and again, they could not live her life for her. She would wait for Roxanne to make up her mind but she would not live a lie.

So Roxanne tried to put it behind her. She even tried going out with Vivienne's older brother but, when he tried to put his tongue in her mouth as they cuddled up in the back row of the cinema, she thought she would be sick and refused to go on a second date with him. She did not fancy any of the young men that she met. She knew she was getting a reputation for being frigid yet she still could not convince herself that she was a lesbian. Maybe it was partly because of her parents' insistence that it had been the alcohol that had caused her aberration, that all young girls liked to experiment, that it didn't really mean anything and that one day Mr Right would come along and all would be well. She really wanted to believe them but deep down she knew it just was not true. She thought about Jan all the time and, although she knew that her indecision was causing her friend pain, there was nothing she could do about it.

When Rodney told her he had met this English guy called Rob, who was writing a travel book and invited her to join them for a beer, she had been, at first, reluctant to go.

She liked Rob straight away; he was intense but fun and so full of enthusiasm for his work that it was infectious. When he said that he was going to walk the *Camino de Santiago* she knew she had to go with him. Only there would she be able to see things clearly, she told herself. She needed to put some distance between herself and her parents and between herself and Jan if she was ever going to sort out the conflicting emotions that were dragging her down into this morass of uncertainty. Maybe, amongst strangers, in a foreign land, she would be able to find out the truth about her own sexuality.

Needless to say, her parents were delighted that she was going on a pilgrimage. She even let them think that Rob could be a possible boyfriend.

'He's a nice young man,' her mother said. 'I'm sure he'll look after you.'

He could have been Jack the Ripper, but he would still have been a 'nice young man' as far as her mother was concerned. Any young man was better than Jan in her eyes.

'We will pray for you every day,' her father told her. 'We will pray that you find salvation.'

She did not reply to that; that was the very reason she needed to get away. They believed that a simple kiss between her and Jan was evil; she could never accept that. How could love be evil?

CHAPTER 20
BETH

Arca do Pino is a modern, busy town and the streets are crowded with pilgrims. Even though Beth is tired she can feel the excitement in the air as she trudges along, looking for somewhere to stay. The anticipation, the expectations of these travellers, now so close to their goal, is palpable. They come from many countries. Spanish, French, English, Americans, Australians, Italians, Portuguese, she has met them all since she began. Their paths are converging as they approach St James's final resting place, only a day away. She is reminded of the grooves of the scallop shell. There is a feeling of impatience in the air; they are approaching the finishing line and no-one wants to stumble and fall. Everyone wants to rest up and make that final dash to their destination.

She has two choices and so far, has not decided which is best: to rise very early and hope that she can walk fast enough to reach Santiago before midday or to head for Monte del Gozo, spend the night there and arrive in Santiago one day later. The latter is the most sensible; it would give her ample time to arrive for the special pilgrims' Mass in the cathedral at noon, plus the opportunity to enjoy a leisurely walk into the city. But the fever of those around her is to move on, to hurry, to get there as soon as they can.

She passes a shop selling postcards and, caught up in the exhilaration of being so close, she goes in and buys one to send to Luke. It is the usual kind of postcard, a kaleidoscope of images: the cathedral itself, the inescapable scallop shell, pilgrims walking along leafy lanes. It is enough to give him an idea of where his mother has been these last weeks. She scribbles a short message on the back and signs it, *'lots of love, Mum xx'* then pops it into the postbox on the corner. She feels strange; it is the first contact she has tried to make with her family in five weeks. It is as though she has been asleep and is now in that dreamy stage between sleeping and waking.

The first two *albergues* are full and she is directed to one at the far end of the town. It is a shabby building and she hesitates before entering, but she is tired and her feet are sore so she pushes open the door and goes in. The concierge greets her rather brusquely; there are only two beds left. The price is twice the usual rate but she has the feeling that here it is a case of take it or leave it and decides to take it.

Her passport is filling up with *credencial* stamps and she flicks through it proudly. She has never been a collector of things. Luke, she remembers, used to collect sports cards, mostly of footballers and racing drivers; then the fashion was to collect Action Men. He collected both the dolls, although he hated it when she referred to them as such, and the stickers that portrayed them. The stickers usually came in packets of cereal and for weeks they would all have to eat Sugar Puffs or something similar until he had the complete set. Even Joe had a collection of cards, the old fashioned cigarette cards that his forty-a-day father passed on to him; they were, naturally enough, mostly of early cricketers and he kept them in an old Rowntree's chocolate tin. When she suggested he throw them out, along with a lot of other clutter that had accumulated in their loft, he had been most indignant; they were going to be worth some money one day he reckoned. As far as she knew they were still there, alongside Luke's Action Men.

'Hi,' a young man said, throwing his bag onto the bunk above hers. 'Jim.'

'Hi, I'm Beth.'

Their bunk beds were tucked into the corner of the room, right by a window that refused to close. She watched the man struggle with the catch for a while then he turned and said:

'It won't shut; it's broken. That's the trouble with arriving late, you always get the worst bunk.'

'There's going to be quite a draught through there tonight,' Beth replies.

'I'll plug it up with this,' he says, taking a dirty towel out of his bag. 'Look I'm just going to get some grub. Want to tag along?'

Jim's company proves to be disappointing. He cannot stop complaining and he eats like a pig. She watches him dip his spoon into a plate of shellfish stew and transfer the contents to his mouth as though he has not eaten in days. He leans forward, lowering his face towards the plate and slurps up the juice. She cringes, fascinated, as he shovels spoonful after spoonful into his eager mouth. Beth forces herself to look away and drinks some of her wine.

'Great food,' he grunts, displaying a mouthful of *calamari* as he does so.

She nods. Her own *tapa* of prawns is still only half-eaten.

'So the *Camino* has not been what you hoped for?' she asks.

'A commercial con-trick, that's what it is. Too many people for a start. You can't call it a real pilgrimage, now can you?'

'Well, what would you call a real pilgrimage? People walking barefoot, in sackcloth and ashes? That's a bit old-fashioned these days.'

She tells him about the nun she met that morning.

'She wasn't barefoot, but she sleeps out in the open and she has nothing with her, no money, no phone, nothing. Would you say that was a real pilgrimage?'

'She sounds mad.'

'I don't think she's mad, she's just very religious. She believes God will provide for everything.'

'Maybe she is a real pilgrim, but what about the others? It's too easy for them. People need to be stretched. Look at the bus loads of tourist-pilgrims that turn up. How is that walking the *Camino*, going by bus? And the paths themselves, so easy and so boring. You're never very far from civilisation. Take today, for example, we were never out of sight of the main road. Cars and lorries whizzing by all the time. No, there's nothing to stretch you on this walk; it's not demanding enough. That's why there are so many people. I've seen them walking along, three abreast and as many as twenty in a group. You might as well be in Brighton. I have to admit, I'm pretty disappointed with it.'

Beth thinks of her raw and bleeding feet and is grateful that the *Camino* is not more demanding. She remembers the quiet solitude as she walked through the dripping woods that morning; she remembers how she trudged across the Meseta, in the blazing heat with no-one to direct her except the ghostly figure of the pilgrim, always ahead of her, always just out of reach; how she had slithered down the scree strewn paths in the mist, leaving Roncevalles, wondering what she would do if she slipped and broke her leg. She has come here looking for solitude and she has found it; she wanted a challenge and it was here.

'Have you been on other pilgrimages?' she asks, wishing he would finish his stew and they could pay the bill and leave.

'Not as such, but I walked through Nepal last summer. That was awesome. Two months and hardly saw anyone except a few goatherds and some villagers. Now, that was demanding. You couldn't just pop into the chemist and buy a few aspirins when you had a headache. You had to plan and take everything with you, on your back.'

He mops up the last of his stew with a piece of bread and sits back with a sigh.

'Been up the Amazon too. That was pretty scary, what with the snakes and the insects.'

'But that's hardly the same as walking in Spain, is it?' she protests. 'Maybe this pilgrimage was not what you really wanted to do.'

'I had plans to go to Africa,' he admits. 'Was going to walk across the Sahara with my cousin.'

So she is right; he is not really a pilgrim. He is just a young man looking for adventure.

'So why didn't you?'

'My cousin died; he was bungee-jumping in France and something went wrong with the harness. Broke his neck.'

'Oh, I am sorry,' she says.

'So I decided to do this for him instead.'

She does not know what to say.

She has been in almost every bar in the town and can't see any sign of Fran and Lucky, so she decides to check out some of the *albergues*. She is in luck and, in the first one she tries, the concierge confirms that Fran checked in at lunch-time.

'Is she in her room?' she asks.

'Possibly. Go up and have a look. Third floor, door on the right.'

The hotel is an enormous barn of a place and smells of damp wood and poor sanitation. She climbs the rickety stairs and finds the door to Fran's room. She knocks gingerly.

'Fran?' she calls.

The door is flung open by a boisterous middle-aged woman in a flowery raincoat. She is on her way out.

'Yes?'

'I'm looking for Fran?'

'Anyone here called Fran?' the woman asks, turning back into the room.

'Beth, is that you?'

Fran is lying on one of the bunks and Lucky is curled up at her feet.

'There you are. I've been in every bar in town looking for you,' Beth says, sitting on the end of the bed and stroking Lucky.

'I just didn't feel like it tonight,' Fran says.

Beth looks around her; there are twelve beds packed into the room and there is hardly any space to move. A strong stench of smelly feet makes her grimace.

'Bit of a dump, this place,' she says, looking at the muddy footprints on the floor.

'It's OK. They let me bring Lucky in, that's good enough for me.'

She pushes the dog with her foot to give them some more room.

'It's stopped raining,' Beth tells her. 'Look, why don't we go for a walk?'

At the word 'walk', Lucky begins to wag her tail.

'You shouldn't have said that. Now I've got no option. Come on then, let's get ourselves a drink.'

Fran is a lot quieter than usual. As they walk along Beth tells her about meeting Jim.

'He sounds a bit of a pain,' Fran says.

'He was rather. So what about you? Good walk?'

'It was fine. After we left you, we met up with Helen and Walter and walked with them for a bit then they stopped for coffee and we carried on with a couple of Australian girls who took a shine to Lucky.'

She bends down and gives the dog an affectionate pat on her head.

'So what's the problem then? Why so down?'

At first Fran does not reply then she says:

'I just don't know what to do, Beth. We're almost there. Another day and we'll be in Santiago.'

'So? Is it Tim?'

Fran hesitates. Beth can see the gleam of tears in her eyes.

'I suppose it is. I still love him. I don't want to lose him just because I'm being stubborn about the baby. Maybe he's right, maybe we are too young to have a family. He says it's not that he doesn't want to have children, it's just that it's too soon. After all we've got years ahead of us; there'll be plenty of time for babies later on.'

Beth thinks he sounds a selfish young man but does not say so.

'But as you said, the baby's happening now, not in the future. I thought you'd made your decision?'

'I have. I won't have an abortion. I couldn't be that cruel but ..'

'Well you need to talk to him about it and you can't do that if you keep deleting his texts.'

'He's stopped texting me. I haven't heard from him in days. That's why I tried to phone him.'

'Well he's probably got the message then. Try texting him.'

'I've tried. He doesn't reply to that either. I even tried ringing him again this evening but it went straight to voice mail.'

'Did you leave a message?'

'No, how could I? I don't know what I want to say to him.'

'So, why ring him?'

Fran wipes her eyes with her sleeve and mutters:

'I don't know, I just wanted to hear his voice, I suppose.'

'You sound pretty mixed-up to me. Come on, a nice glass of Rioja is what you need. That'll straighten you out.'

'Do you think I should?'

'One won't hurt you either way.'

They tie Lucky up to a lamp-post and go into the bar. Straight away she hears someone call her name; she looks round and sees Walter and Helen.

'We wondered if you were going to make it,' Walter says. 'Thought you might have decided to push on to Santiago.'

'No way, in my condition? I'm taking it easy now. Doctor's orders,' says Fran.

She smiles at Beth as she says it. Everyone knows that Fran is pregnant; she can hardly keep it a secret any more. Her constant peeing and the regular bouts of sickness are a dead give-away.

'Do you know what it is?' Helen asks. 'The baby, a boy or a girl?'

Beth thinks Fran is going to cry again but instead she just shakes her head.

'I think that's best, keep the surprise until it's born. What does it matter anyway. I'm sure you'll be just as happy

230

with a boy or a girl. I don't know why people are so impatient these days. Just so that they can buy baby clothes in the right colours and decide on the paint for the nursery,' Helen rattles on.

Beth thinks she has changed since they first met; she is much more talkative and there is a pleasing flush to her cheeks. She is sure it has something to do with Walter. They seem to be together all the time now.

'Can we talk about something else please, or I shall have to go and pee again,' Fran says with a rather strained smile. 'What did you two get up to after I left you?'

Helen's cheeks turn an even deeper shade of pink and she slips a sidewise glance at Walter.

'We got here about two,' he tells them 'and had a nice lunch in a little restaurant up by the church. Thought we'd celebrate a bit as our journey is nearly over.'

'That sounds nice.'

'Yes and we've booked into a hotel tonight. All the *albergues* were booked by the time we'd finished lunch and tried to get a room, so we decided to treat ourselves.'

By now Helen's cheeks are scarlet and to save her further embarrassment Beth asks:

'What are your plans for tomorrow?'

'We're going to go straight to Santiago and maybe have a couple of nights there,' says Walter.

'Hey, I wondered where you'd got to?'

It is Jim. He stands next to her chair, looking down the table at the others.

'Hello. I'm Jim,' he says.

'Jim and I had lunch earlier,' Beth says.

She sees Fran give her a quizzical look and wants to laugh.

'Sit down Jim,' says Walter. 'You look like a man in need of a drink.'

He offers him a glass of wine.

'No thanks; I'll have a beer.'

'Jim's one of these extreme sports' fanatics,' Beth tells them.

'Not any more. Not since I had my car accident.'

'Really. What happened?' Walter asks.

'It wasn't really my fault, although I may have been driving a bit too fast, I suppose. Anyway this cyclist came out from nowhere and, in order to avoid him, I swerved and ended up in a ditch with a fractured vertebrae. After six months of treatment the doctor made it quite plain that I could no longer sky dive, rock climbing was out and even scuba diving had to be approached with care. No impact sports and definitely no extreme sports were allowed.'

'That must have been devastating for someone like you,' Fran says.

'It was. All the doc could suggest was hiking. So that's how I became interested in walking.'

'Jim's been all over,' Beth volunteers.

The others look at him expectantly.

'Down the Amazon, walking in Nepal.'

'Adventurous trips,' Walter says.

'Yes and expensive but I earn good money.'

'Do you always go on your own?' Beth asks.

'No, I used to go with my cousin, Barry, the one I told you about. We'd known each other since we were kids. We were inseparable. At first, we were going to join the army, but Barry failed his eye test. At least that's what he said; I think he messed up the psychological test. He was a real wild kid. They wouldn't have wanted a loose cannon in the regiment. Anyway, if Barry wasn't going to be a soldier, then neither was I. So that was the army out. Instead we knuckled down, passed our exams and landed jobs in the insurance business.'

'Sounds a long way from walking up the Amazon,' says Fran.

'Yes, but the money was good. Those were the years when young executives like us earned big salaries. We drove fast cars and went on expensive holidays. At least twice a year Barry and I would go somewhere together: one year we went scuba diving off the coast of Mexico, another time we learnt to sky dive, once we climbed a glacier. We looked for adventure wherever it was and didn't count the cost.'

'Extreme sportsmen,' Walter says, with a touch of envy in his voice.

'Yeah, in a way. But as I said, after the accident I had to give it up. So that's when Barry and I decided to go climbing in the Himalayas. I found I quite enjoyed my new pastime but gradually Barry got bored with it. By then he was a real adrenalin junkie and although trekking through the Himalayas was a physical and mental challenge for me, it was too drawn-out for him. He wanted to have the buzz of falling out of an aircraft or diving off a hundred-foot cliff. In fact it was after that trip that he decided to go bungee-jumping. He went with some mates from work, half-a-dozen of them. I knew one or two of them, myself; they were as wild as he was.'

He stops and takes a swig of his beer.

'His cousin died,' Beth tells them. 'He broke his neck bungee-jumping.'

'That's terrible,' says Fran.

'Yes, it was quite a shock. I always expected him to be around, you know,' Jim says. 'We were very close.'

'So now you're here,' Helen says. 'You must find this rather tame after all that you've done?'

Beth expects him to start ranting again about the limitations of the *Camino* but instead he says:

'It's different, that's all.'

DAY 33

CHAPTER 21

The *albergue* is a hive of activity; Beth can hear doors
banging and boots clattering down the stairs, shouts of
farewell and cries of encouragement. Everyone, bar her, is on
the move. She and Fran have agreed to leave a little later
today and head for Monte del Gozo, so she is taking
advantage of this opportunity to have a few extra minutes in
bed. The rules say she has to be out by nine o'clock; out
before nine and in bed before ten, that's what the owners of
the *albergues* like. She will gone before that; she is meeting
Fran in the bar for a coffee at nine and then they will set off
together.

She snuggles down into her sleeping bag; the towel
that Jim used to block up the gap in the window frame last
night was not much use. All night long the wind rattled and
tugged at the shutters, its cold breath creeping across her bed
and down her neck. It is like being back in the West Country,
with dark clouds scudding across the sky and the constant
threat of rain. She thinks of Bideford with a tinge of
homesickness; it's time she went back. She misses the
narrow streets that lead down to the harbour; she misses the
early morning light on the water and the sight of the fishing
boats returning with the day's catch; she misses the way the
sunlight reflects off the white-washed fishermen's cottages of
Appledore, how it glints and winks at her from across the

estuary. She misses the surge of the tide as it races in from the sea and the pungent smell of seaweed and dead fish when it leaves again, exposing the black mud flats to scavenging gulls. She misses scrambling over the rocks, looking for crabs, with Luke splashing through the rock pools behind her. She needs to breathe in once more that fresh salty air and hear the gentle burr of Devon voices; she needs to be home.

Jim has already left and all the beds are empty except for hers. He wasn't so bad after all. She even felt a bit sorry for him. They had walked back to the hostel together last night and he had told her about the girl that he loved, Janice. She had been Barry's girl. It was a typical romantic triangle: two men in love with the same woman. Now that his cousin is dead, Janice is available again. That's how he sees it but he can't tell her how he feels. It's the same old story. She told him what she had told Roxanne. There was no point in keeping his feelings hidden; he should speak to the girl. But his conscience won't let him. He feels guilty for loving his best friend's girlfriend.

She wants to sleep but her mind is racing. Beth finds it easy to give advice to others but she can't find the solution to her own problems. Maybe there are no solutions. She understands just how Fran feels. Beth's journey, too, is almost done and what has she accomplished? It would be easier to answer that question if she had a clearer picture of why she has come here in the first place. It is almost as if she were drawn here, hoping for a miracle, hoping that something in the rigours of the walk would purge her and make her well again. But she is a modern woman; she does not believe in miracles. So why is she here? She does not want to die. Of that she is now certain but does she have the strength to fight this latest attack on her body?

She turns over restlessly, angrily. She has to face it. She has been running away, not from the cancer, but from Joe.

The ugly truth faces her down; she cannot avoid it, no matter how much she tries. She can close her eyes, think of other things, but it will not go away. He is leaving her. He doesn't know that the cancer has come back. He thinks she is still in remission. He congratulates himself that he did not tell her while she was ill; he waited five years. Five years until the doctors told her she was clear of it, that she was well again. He was not so unkind as to spoil her joy, no, even then he did not tell her right away, he waited a little longer. He had waited five years so he could wait a while longer, he said. He thinks he is a good man to have considered her feelings in this way. She does not see it like that.

Fran is already seated at a table by the time she arrives at the bar; Lucky is stretched out at her feet. She is drinking coffee.

'What do you fancy?' she asks.

'A gin and tonic?' Beth says.

'What, that bad?'

'Just joking, I'll have a coffee and maybe a croissant if they have any.'

She places her order with the waiter and sits down opposite her friend.

'So how are you today?'

'OK, I suppose. I didn't sleep much last night, wondering whether I should ring Tim again.'

'And?'

'I rang this morning. I thought I'd catch him before he left for work, but his phone was still off.'

'Could be he was still sleeping. We're an hour ahead here, remember.'

'Yes, that could be it, I suppose. Anyway, I'll be home in a few days.'

'Will you go and see him?'

'I suppose I'll have to; he's still in the flat, as far as I know. We'll have to sort things out no matter what happens. We've only just bought it,' she says, her voice faltering at the memory.

'Don't worry. He may have changed his mind about the baby, by now. Sometimes men need time to get used to the idea of being a father. It's a big responsibility, you know.'

'Exactly. A responsibility he's not facing up to.'

She drinks up the last dregs of her coffee and bends down to give Lucky the left-over crust of bread.

'What's going to happen to Lucky when you get to Santiago?' Beth asks, trying to change the subject away from Tim.

'Oh my God, that's another thing I haven't worked out. What am I going to do with her? I can hardly take her back to England but I can't abandon her now, not after all these miles. She's been such wonderful company.'

She bends down again and strokes the dog's ears.

'Good girl,' she murmurs.

'*Algo más?*' the waiter asks.

'No, nothing, thanks, just the bill,' Beth replies.

She takes out her pills and swallows them in one gulp, washing them down with the coffee.

'Headache?' Fran asks.

'No, it's just something the doctor gave me.'

She sees Fran waiting for an explanation.

'I've got cancer,' she says. 'He would only let me come on the *Camino* if I promised to take these pills.'

'Oh my God, I am so sorry.'

Fran seems genuinely distressed. This is what Beth hates, that look of horror on people's faces, as though they are looking into the face of death itself. This is why she cannot bring herself to tell Luke that the cancer has returned.

'Do you want to talk about it?' Fran asks her.

239

'Maybe later.'

'It's time we were on the move, anyway,' her friend says, standing up and hitching her rucksack onto her back.

Beth and Fran follow the waymarks to the edge of the town and immediately are in a dense forest of eucalyptus trees. These foreign usurpers have virtually eradicated the natural oak and beech in the area but, with their mottled, peeling bark and their airy, leafy branches, make a pleasant environment to walk through, helping to hide the nearby motorway and the proximity of the international airport. The carpet of fallen leaves makes a crisp crunching noise as they trudge on. After a few kilometres they drop down into a deep cutting that skirts the end of the runway and watch as a giant Airbus comes looming into view. The noise is overwhelming; a thunderous monster, it blots out the sky as it passes overhead, winging its way to other European cities: Madrid, Venice, London. With every step Beth seems to be returning to civilisation, getting closer to the hurly-burly of modern life. Soon the solitude of the *Camino* will be a distant memory. For five short weeks she has lived a life separate from all that is familiar to her. Now it is almost time to return.

Beth wonders how many pilgrims are on the Airbus and where they are headed. She has not booked her flight yet; she has an open ticket. In a few days she will be up there, heading for home and she feels a kind of peace at the idea. Yes, she is almost ready to leave this country. But not yet; first she has to reach the city of St James.

It is different walking with Fran; apart from the occasional meeting with other pilgrims, Beth has walked most of the *Camino* alone. Fran likes to talk; she comments on places that they pass, on the state of her feet, on the likelihood of more rain, on the people they have met. She points out birds that she recognises, flowers that she must examine, buildings that capture her attention; her eyes flick here and there taking everything in, missing nothing and commenting on it all. Surprisingly Beth is not irritated by this stream of chatter; if anything she finds it soothing. It distracts her from herself.

'What have been the best and the worst things about this trip? For you?' Fran asks.

Beth thinks for a minute; there are so many.

'I suppose the worst thing was the day I got lost. I felt so disorientated and lonely; I just wanted to sit down and cry. I imagine it was partly due to being so dog tired. It was early on in my journey and I hadn't really learned how to pace myself. When I realised I had walked miles in the wrong direction I just wanted to howl with frustration. That and the sore feet.'

She grimaces at the memory.

'And the best?'

'Oh without doubt, the people I've met. Something about the *Camino* makes people more open and friendly. Even those that you only meet briefly have time to talk. And everyone has a tale to tell,' she adds.

She thinks of Roxanne and how kind she was to wait for her the day she felt so ill.

'What about you? What was your best thing?' she asks.

'Like you, making new friends,' Fran says without any hesitation. 'And finding Lucky.'

'And the worst?'

'That's easy too, bedbugs.'

She pulls up her sleeve and shows Beth the scars on her arm.

'It happened near Logrono. God, what a night that was. I don't think any of us could sleep; we were itching and scratching all night long. I missed a day's walking because of it. There was no way I could go on until I was sure I had got completely rid of them. The next morning I got up early, to make sure there was plenty of hot water and I showered and washed my hair. I washed all my clothes and tumble-dried them at the highest heat possible, then I ironed all the seams. That's where they tuck themselves away, in the seams of your clothing. Nasty little buggers, they're so difficult to shift. Then I dumped my sleeping bag and went out and bought a new one. I also bought a big bottle of spray and after that I sprayed the mattress every night, before I made up my bed. It seemed to work; I wasn't bitten again.'

Beth looks down at Lucky, realising, for the first time, that she is wearing two collars: one with her *Camino* badge and another plain, rubber one.

'So Lucky is protected as well?' she asks.

'Not against bed bugs, but yes I bought her one of those collars to keep away fleas and ticks. I don't like those either. In fact I don't like anything that crawls.'

She laughs and adds:

'Except babies.'

Beth looks up at her, surprised at this comment.

'So you're going to keep it?'

'Yes, I've decided. I can't face the thought of parting with it. If I'm going to have it then I couldn't possibly abandon it, afterwards. Not my own child.'

'What about Tim?'

'Well Tim will have to accept the fact that we're having a baby. If he wants to be part of our lives then it's up to him. If I have to choose between them then it has to be my helpless child. Even he should understand that.'

'What's changed your mind?'

'I don't think it's really been changed. I just don't think I was clear about my relationship with Tim. I still feel the same way about him but I know that if I had an abortion just so that we could stay together, it would always be between us. Deep down I would never forgive him, nor myself. It's as you said the other day. I've got to stop running away from the truth.'

They have come to a crossroads and by the side of the road stands a large stone cross. Beth plumps herself down beside it and stretches out her legs.

'God, I'm tired and we've only done five kilometres.'

Fran fills up her water bottle from a fountain, then takes a plastic bowl out of her rucksack and pours some water into it for Lucky. The dog laps it up greedily. As she watches them, Beth realises just how old Lucky is. They have walked at a slow pace today. At first she thought it was because Fran was not feeling too well but now she sees it is because of Lucky. The dog walks slowly, her arthritis hampering her progress; besides which, she likes to stop and sniff the air, to investigate who has passed along this way before her, to chew a favoured piece of grass, to root in the hedgerows for little animals, be they mice, shrews or even rabbits. She is in no hurry. So they walk at an erratic pace, stopping and starting according to Lucky's whim. This is what is making her feel so tired. On her own she would be in Lavacolla by now.

She is pleased that Fran has made up her mind about the baby. She knows it is a good decision. Fran is not as hard as she tries to make out she is; you only have to see how she looks after that mangey dog to realise what a caring person she really is. If she can make one old dog's life so much better, what would she do for a child.

As though understanding her frustration at their slowness, Fran says:

'It's not much further to Lavacolla. We could stop and have a coffee there.'

She points to the fountain.

'In the meantime, have some fresh water; it's lovely and cold.'

Beth fills up her water bottle and then splashes some of the water over her face.

'Are you feeling OK?' Fran asks.

She nods.

'How old is Lucky, do you think?' she asks.

Fran shrugs.

'Can't say. Probably not as old as she looks; she's had a hard life. It's funny but it was because of those damn bedbugs that I found her. If it hadn't been for them I wouldn't have been kicking my heels in Logrono and we'd never have met. So you see, something good can come out of the the worst situations.'

'Well she certainly is one lucky dog,' Beth says.

She is fond of dogs.

'We used to have a dog,' she tells Fran. 'Benny, a retriever. He died when he was ten.'

She remembers that awful day, how Luke had cried; they all had. After ten years Benny had been a fixed member of the family.

'That's the worst bit, they don't live as long as us. Did you get another one?'

'No, Luke was away at university by then. There didn't seem much point.'

They walked on in silence for a while then Fran says:

'You don't talk much about your family. Luke is your only child, is he?'

'Yes, he's twenty-four now.'

'What about your husband? You never mention him at all. What's his name, John, Jim?'

'Joe.'

'That's right, Joe. What does he do?'

She pauses then blurts out:

'What does Joe do? Joe lies to me, that's what he does.'

Fran does not know what to say to this. Beth is sorry she has let it out; now she will have to explain. She owes it to Fran to be a bit more forthcoming.

'Joe doesn't know I have cancer.'

'You haven't told him?'

Fran looks incredulous. Even Lucky stops and looks up at her.

'No. He stood by me when I had cancer the first time; he was great. But he doesn't know that it's returned. He thinks I'm OK.'

'When are you going to tell him?'

'I don't know. Maybe I'll wait until he finds out.'

'But why? If he stood by you the first time, he'll be there for you now, surely,' Fran says.

'Yes, I know he will, but that's not what I want.'

'Why ever not?'

'He's told me he's leaving me; he's met someone else. Of course he doesn't know I'm ill, or he wouldn't have said anything.'

Fran says nothing.

'So what can I do now?' Beth continues. 'If I tell him the cancer's back he will stay, I know he will. But I'll know he'd only be feeling sorry for me, doing the right thing. Joe believes in doing the right thing. He won't stay because he loves me. So you see, I can't tell him. If he's going to leave me, I want him to go.'

'What about your son? Have you told him?'

'No, not yet.'

'And does he know about Joe leaving you?'

'I don't think so. I haven't said anything. I wanted to come to terms with it myself before I told him.'

'But wouldn't it have been easier to share it with your son? He would stand by you, wouldn't he?'

'I don't know. What if he sided with his father? I couldn't bear that. Losing Joe and Luke. No that would be too much for me.'

'There's no reason why he should take his father's side. After all it's him who's in the wrong, not you. Don't be ridiculous Beth. Of course your son will stand by you. Just give him a chance. He's not a child anymore. What did you say he was, twenty-four? Well I think he's old enough to understand that marriages break up and it's not necessarily anybody's fault.'

Beth flashes an angry glance at her friend.

'Well it's not my fault,' she snaps.

'Sorry. I'm sure it's not but that's not what I meant. Luke is old enough to understand that these things happen. You can't protect him from them anymore.'

'I suppose not.'

Somehow the thought of telling her problems to Luke does not seem so difficult now. She needs to face up to it. After all he has a right to know what is happening to his family.

The sun is shining by the time they reach Lavacolla. Here they can sit and rest by the chapel of San Roque before starting the steady climb up the hill to Monte del Gozo. The chapel is in a grove of trees. It was here that the pilgrims, in years gone by, stopped to wash and purify themselves before continuing into Santiago de Compostela. Although, as Fran is quick to point out, the literal translation of the name Lavacolla, '*lava' 'colla*', suggests that they only washed their necks.

'Perhaps that was all that was needed to guarantee them absolution,' she adds. 'Anyway, a paddle will be enough for me.'

She takes off her boots and plunges her feet into the icy water.

'Wow, that's wonderful,' she sighs, leaning back and letting the water run through her toes.

Beth cannot resist copying her and soon the two of them are splashing up and down the stream like a pair of two-year-olds. This is too much for Lucky who, being more adventurous, jumps in to join them then lies down and wallows in the flowing water.

'Oh no, you know what's going to happen next, don't you,' Fran says, scrambling out of the stream and trying to get as far away from Lucky as she can.

But Lucky thinks this is just part of the game and rushes up to her and begins to shake herself vigorously.

'Well I didn't intend to wash my clothes, but I see Lucky has other ideas,' Fran says. 'She's soaked me.'

'Oh, you'll soon dry. Don't be such a wimp.'

Beth takes out her notebook and makes a few notes about Lavacolla. She adds a brief sketch of the river and the chapel to the opposite page.

'What are you doing?' Fran asks.

'I decided to take Rob's advice. I'm writing a diary about my journey. It's only a few jottings. If I decide to do anything with it, I'll fill it out at home. I don't think I'm going to forget these last few weeks in a hurry.'

'Nor the people, I bet,' says Fran with a laugh. 'Here, pass it over.'

Beth hands her the battered notebook.

'This is great. Hey, you've got Roxanne off to a 't', and Lucky. Look Lucky, she's made you a very beautiful dog.'

She holds the sketch in front of the dog, who smells it briefly then turns away.

'There you are. Literary acclaim.'

'Well I thought I might contact my old boss and see if he wanted me to do a piece on the *Camino*. Lots of people are interested in that sort of thing.'

'Sounds a great idea. You could email him and ask him.'

Beth holds out her hands in mock astonishment.

'And how exactly? We're miles from anywhere and as you know, I don't have a computer with me.'

'Oh ye of little faith. What do you think this is?'

Fran holds up her iPhone.

'You can send him an email on this. Just make sure you give him your own email address as well.'

She hands the iPhone to Beth.

'OK, why not? He can only say no, after all.'

She types out a brief message and sends it. That simple action makes her feel better.

'I'm glad I did that. I was getting to the point where I was dreading to go home because there was nothing to look forward to, just an empty house.'

'I know what you mean. We have been away so long; it seems strange to think that in a few days we'll be sleeping in our old beds again and trying to pick up where we left off.'

'At least you've got a good job,' Beth says. 'My career never really got off the ground. I gave it all up for my husband and son. I put them first. Now my son has grown up and moved on and my husband has left me.'

She sighs and adds:

'I should never have married him.'

'You don't mean that. Try to think about the good times you had. And then there's Luke. You wouldn't have had Luke if it wasn't for Joe,' Fran says, trying to ease her

248

friend's pain. 'I know it's hard but you can get your life back. It's not too late.'

'You don't know that. First of all I've got to get well.'

Beth puts the notebook away and takes out her guidebook. It is looking very tattered; the plastic bag, that was supposed to protect it, has long since been put to other, more urgent purposes. Five weeks of constant use and exposure to rain and sun have given the cover a faded, well-worn look that she regards with pride. This is a testament to all her efforts.

'According to this we have five kilometres to go until Monte del Gozo. So we might as well press on,' she says.

'OK. Just let me give Lucky some more water and we'll be on our way.'

It was while she was in hospital the first time that the idea to walk the *Camino de Santiago* came to her.

She opened her eyes and saw a woman looking down at her; she was wearing a hospital nightdress and her long, straggly grey hair was held back from her face with two kirby grips, like a child's.

'Good, you're awake,' the woman said. 'I was worried about you; you were moaning.'

'Hello.'

'No need to talk. I'll ring for the nurse.'

The woman started to move away.

'No, I'm fine. Honestly, I'm fine. I know I make a noise when I'm asleep, or so my husband tells me,' Beth said.

She looked around but there was no-one else in the room but the old woman.

'Good. I'll just let the nurse know you're awake, anyway,' she said and pressed the button by Beth's bed.

'Ah, Mrs Stuart, you've come round. Excellent,' said the nurse. 'Your husband is here somewhere; I think he just went down for a coffee.'

She adjusted the drip in Beth's arm.

'Back in bed now Mrs Greenwall; you should be resting.'

'Plenty of time for that when I'm dead,' the woman said with a chuckle.

She climbed back into her bed and pulled out a magazine; there was an unusual red cross on the cover.

'Planning another pilgrimage, are you Mrs Greenwall?' the nurse asked.

'That all depends on the doctor. I thought I might just manage to do one more before I'm too old and decrepit.'

'Pilgrimage?' Beth asked. 'Are you a nun?'

'No, my dear, I'm a retired school teacher.'

She chuckled again.

'Kate here went on a pilgrimage to Spain last year. Seventy-six years of age and she walked all that way,' the nurse told her.

'Nearly five hundred miles,' Kate Greenwall reminded her.

'Quite an achievement, eh? And she did it for charity. What was it again?' the nurse asked as she straightened the covers on Beth's bed.

'The Lost Boys' Society. It's a Christian charity for homeless boys. I raised seven thousand pounds.'

'Where did you go?' Beth asked.

Her voice sounded strange, croaky; it must have been from the anaesthetic, she told herself.

'Right across the top of Spain to Santiago de Compostela,' Kate said. 'Best experience of my life.'

'And you walked all the way?'

It seemed incredible; she looked almost too frail to cross the room.

'All the way. It took me nearly two months and I was glad when it was over but now I feel like giving it another go. Here, you can read about it.'

She passed the magazine to Beth.

Something about the woman, or maybe it was just the idea of going on a pilgrimage, appealed to Beth straight away. It seemed such a brave thing to do. The idea lodged itself in the back of her mind. One day she would do that, she told herself.

They stand on the gorse-covered hilltop and look out over the plain to Santiago de Compostela. The three spires of its cathedral stand proud against a skyline softened by rising eucalyptus trees and modern buildings; at last the city is in sight. White clouds float across a clear blue sky; the rain is banished. Beth feels a thrill of excitement at the prospect of actually arriving at her destination. Only another three kilometres and they will be there. She is tempted to keep going. In another hour she could be standing at the door of the cathedral. But that is not what she has planned. She wants to do it properly and arrive in time for the midday Mass. After thirty-three days, what does one more day matter?

'So, do we press on to Santiago?' Fran asks.

'No, let's stick to our plan.'

'OK. Come on Lucky, time to go.'

The dog is reluctant to move; she is lying flat, her back legs stretched behind her, like a frog.

'I know sweetheart, you're hot and tired, but it's not much further.'

Gently she tugs at her lead and slowly Lucky gets up and follows them. They leave behind them the bronze images of two pilgrims, gazing across towards the cathedral, and continue down the hill to the *albergue*. Beth glances back. With the sun behind it, the foremost of the pilgrims looks just like her pilgrim guide. So he got here before me, she thinks.

The *albergue* is big and modern, purpose built to house the ever-growing numbers of pilgrims that find their way to Santiago each year, the young woman tells them as she stamps their *credenciales*, for the penultimate time.

'We have a leisure complex and sports facilities,' she says. 'I don't think the bishop is too happy with the place; he says it's not in the spirit of the *Camino*, too commercial and more like a holiday camp than a place of pilgrimage. But we say what matters is what is in your heart, not where you sleep. We get thousands of visitors every year and even more in Holy Year. They reckon there were 270,000 pilgrims in 2010. Santiago is not a very big city. Where would they all stay if they had not built this facility?'

It is her livelihood, of course she is in favour of this new development and Beth can see the logic in what she says but it is difficult to equate this enormous, barracks of a hostel with the romantic image conjured up by the name Monte del Gozo. The developers have tried to install reminders of the spiritual significance of the site but have failed to create any real sense of history. They lopped the top off the hill with bulldozers and built a large stone and bronze monument. Fran has taken a photograph of it; on one side it commemorates the visit of Pope John Paul in 1989 and on the other St Francis of Assisi, who came here as a pilgrim in the thirteenth century. Apart from the tiny chapel of San Marcos, that has thankfully remained untouched, there is nothing here to inspire any religious fervour. She recalls Jim's carping comments about the *Camino* and hopes that her expectations about tomorrow are not about to be dashed.

'We stopped by the statues,' she tells the woman. 'Is there a story about them?'

'No, they're just supposed to represent two pilgrims, a man and a woman. They could be anybody. You two, even.'

'I think you'd better be the man,' Fran whispers. 'Given my condition.'

She pats her belly.

'Some do say that there are pilgrims that haunt the *Camino*,' an old man says.

He is sitting at a table in the corner, a newspaper folded in front of him.

'Really?' asks Fran, always ready for a story.

'They do. They say that some are the souls of pilgrims that died on the way and never made it to Santiago, others are the spirits of pilgrims that sinned and died without receiving forgiveness. Their spirits roam the *Camino* looking for people to help, hoping that by doing so, they will receive absolution.'

Could her pilgrim be one of these spirits? It is strange that in all this time Beth has never seen him close up; he is always ahead of her, leading her on, easing her solitude, helping her. She feels that without him she might have given way to despair and abandoned this journey. If he is the spirit of a poor pilgrim, seeking forgiveness she hopes that he will now receive it.

CHAPTER 22

He had met another woman. Beth could hardly believe it was true. At first she thought he was talking about someone else, not about them, not their family. She thought he was talking about someone at work, someone who had cheated on his wife, someone she was supposed to know.

She laid the knife carefully on the chopping board and looked up at him.

'What are you telling me, Joe?'

'Look, sit down,' he said and took the knife away from her. 'I have something to confess to you and it's not going to be easy.'

A master of the understatement, our Joe, no it wasn't going to be bloody easy. She sat and looked at him. Already she could feel her insides turning to water.

'Beth, you know how much I care for you. Well, I..,'

He hesitated. For a man who made his living by the written word he was suddenly very inarticulate. She could feel that something awful was coming and remained silent. She would not help him say those words.

'I'm in love,' he blurted out. 'I'm sorry. I don't know how it happened, but it has. I love someone else.'

He looked to see her reaction but she was impassive. Her head was whirling; she could not think straight. How had this happened? When did it happen? How was it possible that she did not know? A thousand questions raced around her head.

'I'm so sorry Beth, really I am. I, we, couldn't help it. It was love at first sight.'

At this juvenile expression something inside her exploded. She leapt to her feet and shouted:

'I don't want to know all the sordid details, Joe. You're not a teenager.'

But no, he was trying to confess to her; he had found his voice and now he would not stop until it was all said. He loved her, this unknown woman, he had always loved her, he said, since he first met her. And he loved Beth too, but in a different way.

'What way?' she asked.

She thought she would be sick.

He didn't reply.

'What way?' she repeated. 'How do you love me differently to the way you love this woman?'

He started to cry. She hated that. Joe was not the sort of man to cry. Joe was a man's man, someone who was right at home in the changing rooms of the local cricket team, or leaning on the bar with a pint after the match. Joe did not cry. Joe took life on the chin. Joe found solutions to problems, mended things, fixed whatever was broken. All her life she had relied on Joe whenever anything went wrong. Where was that Joe now? Now he was telling her how sorry he was. Sorry? It didn't mean anything to her; she could not believe this was happening. Any minute now she would wake up, she told herself.

'Beth, speak to me. For God's sake, don't make this any harder than it already is. I'm sorry. How many times do I have to tell you that? I didn't want it to happen, it just did.'

She did not cry. What was the good of crying? There would be plenty of time for crying later, when he had gone.

255

'I met her in South Africa when I was on a trip. Her name's ..'

Before he could say it she screamed:

'Don't tell me her name. I don't want to know.'

If she knew her name then she became real. She wanted her to stay in the realm of nightmares, an unseen, unidentified monster that was threatening to destroy her world.

'OK. OK. Calm down. I was just going to explain that she was working for the 'The Independent News' when I met her and was in Johannesburg looking into their education system,' he said.

Another journalist. It was always a danger, she knew that. Joe was away from home for weeks on end; he was bound to meet other people, other women, but she had trusted him. Her life would have been impossible if she could not have trusted him.

As Beth made no comment he added: 'Her piece was entitled 'Education after Apartheid'. It got really good crits. She's a brilliant writer.'

Had this woman turned his brain? Did he really think she was interested in knowing this? So, his new love worked for a rival newspaper. South Africa? Something stirred in her memory.

'When were you in South Africa?' she asked. 'You haven't done a trip there for years.'

'I know. That's when I met her.'

'But that's eight, nine years ago.'

She was having difficulty coming to grips with this.

'Ten. It's ten years ago. That's when we met.'

'You've been seeing this woman for ten years?'

He looked shame-faced for a moment.

'Yes. That was where we met, at a press reception, in Johannesburg.'

'And you've been seeing her all this time?'

He nodded.

'While you were living with me? Sleeping with me?'

'I'm sorry.'

'A journalist with 'The Independent News',' she muttered. 'A bloody journalist.'

She had almost applied for a job with them, before Luke was born, of course.

'She's freelance now,' he told her. 'It works better with the kids.'

'Kids?'

The word shot out of her mouth like a rocket.

'You have children?'

'A boy and a girl,' he admitted, looking away as he told her. 'They're both at school; the boy is nine and the girl is five. They're great kids.'

'You have two children?' she repeated.

This was worse than she could ever have imagined. One child was, she assumed, a mistake, but the second? Did people make that sort of mistake more than once? The little one was five. That means she was conceived around the time that Beth was diagnosed with cancer.

'Yes. So you see,' he told her, 'I couldn't abandon her, could I? Her and the children.'

He looked to Beth for understanding.

'And what of Luke?' she asked. 'Luke is your child. Were you prepared to abandon him?'

'Luke was fourteen by then,' he said. 'Not really a child any more.'

'Why didn't you tell me? Why didn't you leave then, when you knew she was pregnant? Why have you waited until now, until I am fifty, until the year of our twenty-fifth wedding anniversary?'

She could see that he had not remembered either of those dates.

'I was going to. We had everything prepared; I was going to move into her flat in Ealing until the divorce went through.'

'Divorce.'

She felt that she was under siege; some evil force was bombarding her with weapons that were each designed in a different way to make her suffer but not actually kill her. Each time he opened his mouth he cut a piece out of her heart. Soon there would be nothing left of it. But she let him continue; she had to know why this was happening.

'I was going to ask you for a divorce.'

'So why didn't you?'

'Well, Luke was still at school. He'd only got two years until his GCSE's. I thought he might take it badly.'

'How considerate of you.'

She could not keep the sarcasm from her voice.

'When he went into the Sixth Form I thought I'd tell you then but you told us you had cancer. I couldn't leave then. I'm not a monster, you know.'

She remembered how upset he had been when she told him about the cancer. She thought it was because he loved her. Now she had been given an alternative hypothesis: maybe the real reason was that she had ruined his plans.

'So, actually, it would have been a lot simpler, and cheaper, if I hadn't survived,' she said. 'No messy, expensive divorce, just shed a few tears for the departed wife and, after a discrete wait, move in with the new one.'

'Don't be ridiculous. Nobody wanted you to die. I've told you, I still love you. You're the mother of my eldest son.'

So that was what it came down to. After twenty-five years of marriage she was just 'the mother of his son'. Not even that, she was 'the mother of his *eldest* son', no more and no less.

It's easy for Fran to say 'look back on the good times'. But how can she? Now she finds herself looking back over her marriage and questioning everything that they have done. Joe's absences from the family home usually went unremarked; it was the nature of his job, she knew that. But now she realises that even when he was not working he always had someone to see, meetings to attend and, when it was not work, there was cricket to play. In their early years she had been a dutiful supporter of his hobby, sitting on the grass with Luke and the other mums, watching her husband play and hoping that he would get bowled out early so that he could be with them. She joined the other cricketers' wives in making sandwiches for their hungry men after the match was over; she even baked cakes. But then, when Luke was older, she began playing golf and left Joe to attend the cricket matches on his own. She wanted Joe to join her in this new sport but he refused.

'I don't get enough time to play cricket as it is,' he explained. 'There's no time for golf as well.'

Now she understands. How could he fit in an afternoon of golf when he was juggling with the needs of two families?

She remembers the months after her operation when she was at home. That was when she first really became aware that Joe was never around much and, whenever he was, he seemed to be looking for excuses to get out of the house. He was very solicitous of her, always volunteering to go to the shops, or pick up her medicine or meet Luke from school but he never had time to just sit and be with her. She remembers how he was constantly popping out because he had run out of cigarettes or wanted to fill the car with petrol.

Silly little tasks that kept him out of the house for an hour at least. If she asked what had taken him so long he would say he had met someone he knew or he had fancied a quick pint at the local. It was round about that time that they bumped into Fred and Mary. They had gone to talk to Luke's teacher about which university would suit him best and their old friends were just leaving.

'Hi strangers,' Mary said. 'Never see you on Sundays anymore.'

Fred had played cricket with Joe for years and, when their children were growing up, both couples had seen a lot of each other. As the children grew older and went their separate ways, the families had drifted apart.

'Golf has taken over now, I'm afraid,' Joe said. 'Sunday is golf day. I'm married to Anita Sorenson these days.'

They had laughed politely and the conversation swerved away to a new topic: the sudden death of a mutual acquaintance. It was only afterwards that Beth thought it strange; Joe did not play golf but he had managed to leave Fred and Mary with the impression that both he and Beth played. As far as she was aware, while she trudged down the fairway with her golf clubs, he was scoring runs for Bideford's second XI, alongside his good pal, Fred. Now she wonders where he was on Sunday afternoons and whether Fred knew anything about it.

How many other clues have there been, that she has failed to notice? Ten years is a long time to keep something like that a secret, especially in a small market town like Bideford. She remembers a couple of cancelled holidays because of a sudden increase in his work load, were they because of her? The need to stay late, was he seeing her when he said he was at work? Everything has become tainted with the smell of deceit. She can taste it in her mouth.

At first she did not want to know about his second family; she wanted to eradicate it from her mind. But once the knowledge was there, her mind would give her no peace. Where did she live? How old was she? More importantly, was she younger than Beth? Was she pretty? What did her children think about having a father who was never there? In the end she gave him no rest until she knew it all.

His children, the innocent fruit of their relationship, knew nothing about Beth and Luke. They too, thought their father's absences from the family home quite normal.

'But what about Christmas?' she asked him. 'Don't they think it's strange that you're never there for Christmas?'

Now she remembers the times he would fly off somewhere on Boxing Day; to be in good time for a meeting the following day, was the usual excuse. She wishes she had followed Test cricket more carefully now, then she might have found that there were many occasions when he could have come home a week or two earlier than he told her. She regrets now that she did not go along to the numerous cricket dinners that Joe was invited to and listen to the boring speeches, just to be with him. But she had been happy staying at home in Bideford, looking after Luke, and Joe had been content for her to do so.

Luke. Did he know about his father's affair? Joe swore that he did not. The thought that her friends and neighbours might have known that Joe was cheating on her was humiliating enough but she cannot bear to think that Luke knew and never told her. It would break her heart to have him deceive her as well.

'Why would he?' Joe said. 'I never told him anything about them and they never came to Bideford.'

He had told her that they lived in Exeter. The woman was virtually on their doorstep.

'But someone else might have said something,' she protested. 'He might have read something on Facebook.'

'I don't think so. The kids are too young for Facebook and who else is going to post things about my family? Look, ask him yourself, if you're worried.'

So far she has said nothing to her son, but she will have to one day, just as she will have to tell him that his mother has cancer again.

CHAPTER 23
SANTIAGO DE COMPOSTELA

Beth is just coming out of the shower when Fran comes in. She is fully dressed and looking agitated.

'Lucky's not outside. There's no sign of her. Her blanket is still there and her water bowl, but she's gone. I'm going out to look for her. I'll meet you in the café next door. I won't be long.'

She grabs her rucksack and is gone.

Beth gets dressed and packs up her belongings then goes down to the café and orders a coffee. After half an hour she begins to get worried.

'Excuse me,' she asks the woman at the reception desk. 'Did you see which way my friend went?'

'You mean the girl with the dog?'

'Yes, that's her.'

'She went back up to the top of Monte de Gozo, but she didn't have her dog with her.'

'No, it's gone missing. She's looking for it.'

She climbs up the wooded path until she reaches the statues of the pilgrims. Fran is sitting at the foot of one of them with Lucky in her lap.

'Hey, Fran. Are you alright?' she calls. 'I was getting worried about you.'

As she approaches she realises that Lucky is not moving.

'Is Lucky OK?'

'She's dead. I just found her lying here as peaceful as can be; her head was resting on her paws and at first I thought she was sleeping. But she's cold. I think she's been dead for a few hours.'

She strokes the dog's head and whispers something to her. Beth sees a tear drop onto her hand; Fran brushes it away and says:

'She was such a lovely dog.'

'I'm so sorry. I know how fond you were of her.'

'It's almost as if she wanted to come up here to die. She could see the cathedral from here,' she explains.

'She was quite old,' Beth adds, hoping to comfort her.

'Yes, I know. But don't you think it's strange that she followed me all this way, just to die here on Monte del Gozo, the Hill of Joy? Is it possible that she knew what she was doing?'

'It was probably just a coincidence. You said yourself she hasn't had an easy life; I expect the journey was too much for her in the end.'

'Yes, I expect you're right.'

Fran continues to stroke Lucky's head, murmuring to her, all the while.

'So what do we do now? We can't leave her here.'

'Well you can't carry her in your condition.'

'She's not that heavy.'

'Well I'll carry her back to the *albergue* and we'll see if they can help. There must be a local vet who can dispose of her body.'

'OK, I have to pick up my rucksack anyway; I left it in reception.'

264

Beth picks up Lucky's lifeless body. She is not a big dog but she is heavy; there is some truth in the phrase 'a dead weight'. She lies in her arms like a twenty kilo sack of potatoes.

'Good job it's downhill all the way,' she says.

The people at the *albergue* are sympathetic and arrange for Lucky's body to be collected.

'It's not the first time we've had a stray dog die on our doorstep,' the woman tells them. 'It's curious how many of them end up here on the *Camino*. You are not the only pilgrim to be adopted by a dog. Sometimes they arrive here with their paws bleeding from the stony paths, or swathed in bandages but they don't give up until they reach Santiago. There are people who say that the dogs carry the souls of pilgrims who were never able to make the pilgrimage. Others say that they are pilgrim dogs, that want to make the pilgrimage themselves.'

'That sounds a bit anthropomorphic to me, but I will admit Lucky was one determined dog, that's for sure,' Beth says.

Fran is quiet.

'I'm going to miss her,' she says at last.

'Well you would have had to say goodbye to her soon anyway. You said yourself that you couldn't take her back to England with you. Maybe this is what she wanted. Maybe she was one of those pilgrim dogs.'

Beth would not be surprised at anything any more. The journey has opened her mind to a lot of things. Who is to say that there are not pilgrim dogs walking the *Camino*, or the ghosts of pilgrims seeking forgiveness, trapped on its paths? Anything seems possible now. María has experienced her miracle, not the one she was hoping for, but a miracle nonetheless. Who knows what lies in store for them all?

Once Lucky's body has been disposed of and the vet compensated for his trouble, Beth and Fran set off for Santiago. It is still early, so they have plenty of time before the Mass starts.

'I don't fancy staying in an *albergue* tonight,' Beth says. 'Shall we see if we can find a couple of rooms in a hotel, instead.'

'That's a good idea. We can splash out as it will be our last night together.'

Beth feels a twinge of sadness at losing her new friend so soon.

'Well we can keep in touch. You have to let me know when the baby's born, at least.'

'Of course. I suppose you do have a mobile?' Fran asks and for a moment her mischievous smile returns.

'Yes, of course; it's at home. I just didn't want to bring it with me.'

Fran already has her iPhone out and is zipping through information on Santiago de Compostela.

'How about this one? It's right near the cathedral and has some vacancies.'

She holds the mobile phone in front of Beth.

'That looks fine.'

'Shall I book it?'

'Yes, why not. Then we can dump off our stuff and start looking around the cathedral.'

'Yes and get our last stamps in our *credenciales*.'

'And the certificate. We have to get our certificates.

Entering the city is not the uplifting experience she had anticipated. The streets are busy with traffic and they have to circumvent both the motorway and a dual carriageway before eventually arriving in the suburbs of the modern city that

Santiago is today; the pavements are crowded with pilgrims, all heading for the cathedral. The two women walk on, passing the site of an old leper colony, located far enough away to protect the inhabitants of the city from infection. Beth wonders if any of the lepers ever made it to the cathedral seeking the miracle that would cure them or if they had to be content with praying to St James from outside the old city walls. They pass a bus station, its buses disgorging passengers from all over Spain; it is as though the whole world has been drawn to Santiago de Compostela today. She wonders if they will be able to see anything at all when they eventually arrive at the cathedral.

'There're so many people,' she says, despondently.

'Don't worry. We'll check in at the hotel and then go straight to the cathedral. We can do all the other stuff later,' Fran says. 'We've loads of time.'

She looks tired and walks along with her arms cupped under her stomach as though carrying her unborn child in her arms.

'We ought to get our *compostelas* first. It won't take long. The Pilgrims' Office is on the way,' Beth says.

'OK, then to the hotel.'

'It's not much further,' Beth reassures her. 'Look this cross marks the start of the old town.'

They have reached St Peter's cross and before them they can see the spires of the cathedral. It is the first view they have had of the cathedral since they left Monte del Gozo. The sight of the towering spires, glowing in the early morning sunlight, revive her spirits and she walks with more determination. Her journey is almost over.

It is just after ten o'clock when they arrive in the *Praza do Obradoiro*. Beth stands at the bottom of the stone steps and looks up at the great Baroque facade of the cathedral. Now she feels the anticipation. It is not a religious moment, rather a feeling of fulfilment, a job well done, a challenge successfully completed. She smiles. Who would have thought that she could do it. Certainly not Joe.

'Well we've made it,' Fran says. 'What do we do now?'

She has walked the whole *Camino* without once referring to a guidebook and now looks to Beth to direct her.

'Traditionally we would place our hands on the Tree of Jesse, but that's not allowed nowadays,' Beth tells her, her battered guidebook in her hand.

She points to the carved stone pillar in the doorway. It is easy to see why they are asked not to touch it; in one spot, the intricate marble carvings, that are supposed to depict the ancestors of Jesus, have been worn smooth by the hands of the pilgrims. She has a strong urge to reach out and touch it, like thousands of pilgrims before her have done over the centuries. But instead she says:

'This doorway is called the *Portico de Gloria*, the Door of Glory. It is very old, twelfth century.'

She walks round to the other side of the column and says:

'We can touch this though.'

She bends down and touches her forehead against a carving of the man who had sculpted the pillar, Master Mateo.

'Now maybe I'll pick up some of his artistic genius.'

'Well I'll have a go at anything,' Fran says, copying her. 'Now what?'

'We have to give the Apostle a hug.'

'Really?'

'Follow me.'

Beth leads Fran up to the high altar and the statue of St James. They both give the tall statue an embarrassed hug.

'Where is he then?' Fran asks. 'Where are his remains?'

'They're in the crypt under the altar.'

They have to wait quite a while until it is their turn and the tiny room that houses the remains of St James is empty then they go down to make their homage to the saint. His bones are stored in a silver gilt chest.

Beth is not superstitious, nor overly influenced by anything religious but she is compelled, like all the thousands of pilgrims before her, to kneel before the reliquary. She closes her eyes and tries to empty her mind of all the distractions around her: the queues of people waiting for their turn to kneel before the saint, Fran, kneeling at her side and her own unresolved problems. She does not want to think about anything; she just wants to be there, to experience a feeling of peace. She would like to pray but she does not know how.

A movement attracts her attention; Fran is getting up.

'Sorry,' she whispers. 'I can't stay down here. I need some air.'

'I'll follow you in a minute,' Beth says.

She is waiting for something; she does not know what it is, but she is expecting something to happen. Why have so many people made the pilgrimage to this shrine if nothing happens when they get here? She is not so naive as to expect a blinding flash of light or to see the solution to her problems clearly laid out before her, but she does expect something. She closes her eyes again and murmurs a childhood prayer then leaves. She cannot stop herself feeling just a little disappointed.

Fran is waiting by the entrance.

'I'm sorry about that. I just felt as though I was going to faint; it was so hot down there.'

'Shall we go and sit down? The Mass will be starting soon.' Beth says.

Already the pews are beginning to fill up so they find themselves somewhere to sit and wait. Beth is not a Catholic; she is not even a regular church-goer although her parents had her baptised in the Church of England. The Mass is foreign to her. She stands when the others stand and sits when they sit; she listens to the priest but understands very little even though the priest swings from one language to another in an attempt to communicate with his multi-lingual congregation. It all sounds the same to her; even his attempts at English are distorted by his strong Spanish accent.

'What is he saying?' Fran asks.

'I think he is reading out a list of the pilgrims who have arrived today and where they're from.'

'Where does he get them from?'

'The Pilgrims' Office, I expect.'

'I haven't heard our names.'

At that he reads out: 'Frances Rutherford from the United Kingdom.'

Fran grabs Beth's arm and giggles.

'That's me,' she whispers.

The organist begins to play the Hymn to Santiago and a nun, dressed in a traditional black habit, stands   and begins to sing in Gallego, the language of the region; she has a pure, clear voice. Beth can feel the hairs on the back of her neck tingle; it is very emotional. Now is the moment that they have all been waiting for; now the men begin to swing the *Botafumeiro* out across the congregation. This huge silver thurible, almost the size of a man, contains burning incense and the smoke and smell from it soon fill the air above them. Six robed men pull on the ropes and the *Botafumeiro* makes longer and longer passes across them until it is at full stretch, swinging almost from its own momentum. The cathedral is packed; pilgrims, tourists and communicants stretch their necks upwards, following its flight. Gradually it begins to slow and the passes become shorter and shorter until, as the nun sings the final words of the hymn, it stops. The spectacle is over. Beth gazes at its resting form, the silver gleaming dully in the artificial light, the rope pullers standing beside it, the ropes slack in their hands; she is spellbound.

Then the priest breaks the silence, inviting the pilgrims to take communion and the congregation slowly shuffles up towards the altar.

'Wow,' Fran whispers. 'That was something, wasn't it.'

Beth nods. The atmosphere in the cathedral, despite the crowds with their mobile phones and cameras, is electric. It is as though something special has happened here. A tradition repeated day in, day out, yet it still retains its power to enthral.

'What was all that about, the smoke and that?' Fran continues.

'Originally I think it was a way of fumigating the pilgrims. Remember they must have stunk like hell by the time they arrived here. Maybe some enterprising monk thought up the idea because he couldn't stand the stench,' Beth replies.

They make their way through the crowds towards the main doors.

'Isn't that your mobile?' Beth asks, as the raucous tune, that she has come to recognise as Fran's, thumps out its beat.

Fran flicks it open.
'Hi?'
'Tim?'
She sounds incredulous.

'Yes, I'm fine. No really, I'm fine. Getting a bit plump but otherwise OK. And you? How are you?'

'Good. That's great.'

'So don't you want to know where I am?' she asks, a smile on her face.

'What? You know? How do you know?'

'You can see me? What do you mean you can see me? No, I don't believe it. Oh my God.'

Beth can only hear Fran's side of the conversation but she can guess at the rest. Fran is rushing to the door, pushing her way through the tourists trying to enter the cathedral.

'Whereabouts? Where are you?' she is calling.

Then the phone is forgotten. She is running towards him; it's Tim. Beth can see them now; he is holding her in his arms and they are both laughing and kissing. So miracles do happen, she thinks. She walks over to them.

'Look Fran, I'll meet you back at the hotel, later on,' she says.

'No wait. Tim I want you to meet my new friend Beth. We've been together nearly all the time; we met in Larrasoaña.'

'Hi,' he says and gives her a peck on the cheek. 'I'm Tim.'

'I thought you must be.'

'He came to look for me,' Fran says, her face beaming with pleasure. 'He missed me.'

'Well I'm sure you have lots to talk about, so we'll catch up later.'

'Good idea. We'll all have dinner together,' Fran says. 'You'll be OK, won't you?'

'I'll be fine. See you later. Bye Tim,' she adds.

She looks at the cathedral clock; it is almost one o'clock, too soon to eat. She decides to explore the city a bit before

272

having some lunch. She knows she should be thinking about what she is going to do next but doesn't want to spoil her mood. The Mass has left her feeling very positive. She feels ready to face the world. Maybe that's what it is all about: nothing mind-shattering, no blinding revelation, just a reaffirmation of what is already in her heart.

There are four squares surrounding the cathedral, each accessible from inside the building, so she wanders back through the *Portico de Gloria* and out through the *Porta Santa* into the *Praza da Quintana*. The pilgrims are still arriving in their hundreds, so she sets off down a narrow street to explore. Many of the pilgrims are heading for the Pilgrims' Office, hoping, no doubt, to collect their certificates of completion. As she passes the office and sees the queue of weary pilgrims, sitting, slumped and standing outside, their backpacks beside them, she is glad that she and Fran went there early.

'Hey, Beth.'

It is Roxanne.

'I can't believe it's you,' she cries with delight. 'I never thought I'd run into you here; there are so many people.'

She gives Beth a hug.

'I thought you'd have left by now,' Beth says. 'Doesn't your flight go today?'

'Yes, at three. I had to get my certificate. I'd forgotten all about it. Can you believe that?'

She waves the rolled up certificate in the air.

'Have to have the proof that I've been here.'

'So you're going to visit your aunt?'

'Yes, if I don't miss my flight. I don't know what's the matter with me today; I feel like I'm floating.'

Beth frowns.

'No, it's nothing like that; I haven't smoked anything for days. It's just being here, the atmosphere, the buzz. It's been wonderful.'

'Where's Mike?'

'Oh he's gone on to Finisterre with Rob. I didn't want him to come with me in the end. Like you said, why complicate things by lying to my aunt. She will have to accept me as I am.'

'And Brisbane?'

'Later. I thought I'd stay in London for a while; see how the other half of the world live.'

'What about Jan?'

'I'll write to her.'

She looks at her watch.

'Sorry Beth, I've got to dash. It's been so good bumping into you.'

She hugs her again.

'Take care of yourself,' she whispers. 'God bless you.'

Beth feels her eyes fill with tears.

'Bye Roxanne. Have a good life.'

She kisses her on the cheek and then Roxanne is gone, haring down the road after a taxi, her rucksack flapping about on her back and the *compostela* gripped tightly in her hand.

Beth walks on, away from the queueing pilgrims; she turns a corner and there are Helen and Walter, walking hand in hand.

'Hey. Fancy seeing you,' she says, going up to them.

'Beth. Hello. You made it then?' Helen says.

'Fran and I arrived this morning. We've just been to Mass. It was very impressive. What about you?'

'Yes, we've done it all now: the Mass, the *compostela*, the lot. We just collected our certificates,' Walter adds

'We arrived yesterday, too late for the mid-day Mass, but we went to an evening one,' Helen says. 'It was quieter, not so many tourists.'

'We're just going to get some lunch. Why don't you join us?' Walter says.

'I'd love to.'

They find a small restaurant down one of the back streets; it looks as though it is frequented by locals and there is not a pilgrim in sight. A cold counter in the window displays the usual array of octopuses, their purple-tinged tentacles entwined in supplication.

'The local dish, I imagine,' Walter says. 'It's on all the menus.'

They find a table near the air conditioning fan and order some drinks.

'So everything alright with you two?' Beth asks.

She is dying to know how things are between them. Fran has been speculating on their relationship for a while now.

'A bit of romance going on there,' she said each time they saw them together.

'We're fine. We're going home tomorrow. Arranged the flights this morning, straight to Gatwick and then by train,' Walter says.

'What, both of you, together?'

Helen looks across at Walter and blushes. He smiles and reaches across the table for her hand.

'We might as well tell Beth,' he says. 'People have to know sooner or later.'

Helen nods shyly. The years seem to have dropped away from her and she looks more like a girl than a fifty year-old spinster.

'Well, we're both on our own now,' she says. 'So we thought ....'

'Helen is coming back to my place for a few days, until she has to go back to work. We thought we'd see how we got on back in the UK. Might have a trip up to the Lakes or somewhere at half-term. Get to know each other better.'

'We're not rushing into anything,' Helen adds. 'We just thought we'd give it a try. I've still got my job to get back to and the house to sell.'

'I'm very happy for you,' Beth says and she means it.

Now that their poorly guarded secret is out, they relax and smile at each other. Walter even leans across and kisses Helen on the cheek.

'I certainly never expected this,' he admits. "I came on the pilgrimage for something to do, because, I suppose, I was lonely without Nora and I wanted to do something in her memory. I never expected to meet someone like Helen.'

Helen smiles and tells Beth:

'He's going to visit his daughter in Australia.'

'That's wonderful. She'll be so pleased to see you.'

'I haven't seen any of the children since the funeral and even then they couldn't stay very long. Gareth was needed for the launch of a new television programme, Megan wanted to get back to her family and, as I've said before, Anwyn's work is her life; she flew out the next day.'

'But they asked you to visit them,' Helen reminds him. 'You know that you're very welcome in their homes. It's just you haven't made the effort to go. Every Christmas Megan invites you.'

She seems to be chastising him.

'Yes, I know.'

He turns to Beth.

'Helen has made me see how selfish I've been, sitting at home feeling sorry for myself. So I'm going to stay with Megan and her family for Christmas. Nora would have liked that. She always wanted to go but I kept finding excuses not to. I feel bad about it now.'

'He's been feeling guilty,' Helen explains. 'About us. But I've told him not to. I'm sure his wife wouldn't have wanted him to spend the rest of his life on his own. He has to go out and make new friends.'

'Of course. Life has to go own,' Beth says, thinking of her own broken marriage.

Walter takes Helen's hand and squeezes it. This is too much for Helen, who blushes an even deeper shade of pink and says:

'I think we should order now.'

Beth does not know what to say. First Fran and now Walter and Helen, everyone is finding happiness. Maybe she will wake up soon and find that it has all been a dream, that Joe is still in love with her and the cancer has gone away. Maybe she will be happy again, too.

It is almost eight o'clock when Fran knocks on her door.

'Hey, sorry it's so late. We had a lot to catch up on. I haven't seen him for such an age,' she adds apologetically.

'No problem. Are we going out?'

'Yes. Tim'll join us later; he has to check out of his hotel and sort out the flights. We're going home tomorrow morning, so he'll sleep here with me tonight.'

'So it's all on again?'

'Yes. It turns out you were right all along. It was just too soon for him; he needed time to get used to the idea. He wants to marry me.'

'Wow. I wasn't expecting that. Have you accepted?'

'I'm thinking about it.'

For a minute Beth sees the old Fran, cautious and independent.

'I know I can manage on my own with the baby. These last few weeks have taught me that. If I can do this, I can do anything. If Tim really loves me and wants the baby then that's great, but there's no way I'm marrying him just to give the child a father.'

'So what will you do?'

'I'll go back to the flat and we can live together as before. If it all works out then maybe, maybe we'll get married.'

'You'll never guess who I bumped into after I left you.'

'No, who?'

'Helen and Walter.'

'Well?'

'You were right, they are having a relationship. I think they're very fond of each other'

'Oh my God. That's wonderful.'

As they leave the hotel, Beth tells her about her conversation with them and their plans for the future.

'It's like a fairy-tale,' Fran says. 'I just can't believe it's all happening.'

'Guess what.'

'What? Not more romance?'

'No, much better. I checked my emails at the hotel and there was one from the newspaper. The editor wants my articles. He wants me to run it as a daily diary. I explained that the pilgrimage was over now but he said that didn't matter. They'll run it as though it's live.'

'Wow. That's great. So you'll be reliving the *Camino* a second time.'

'Yes, but without the sore feet.'

'And no bedbugs.'

'Exactly. So where are we going?' Beth asks.

'Tim suggested this bar in Rua Jeronimo.   He explained how to get there.   He's been here for three days, waiting for me to arrive.'

'How on earth did he expect to find you?'

'He just worked it out.   He knew I'd stick to the recommended stages of the walk, so he calculated when I'd get here.'

'But he didn't account for Lucky, or the bed bugs or the night at Monte del Gozo, did he,' Beth says.

'No. He said he was going to wait one more day then he was going to phone me.'

'So why didn't he phone you in the first place?'

'He wanted to surprise me.'

'He certainly did that.'

They have barely left the hotel when they bump into Dave.

'Hey Beth.   Good to see you.' he says, crossing the road to greet them.

For once he is on foot and without his helmet.   Beth scarcely recognises him.

'Hi. I thought you'd be long gone by now. When did you get here?' she asks in surprise.

'A few days ago. I decided to go up to Finisterre and I've just got back again. Having come this far, I wanted to go on to the coast.'

'Why don't you join us for a drink and you can tell us all about it,' Fran says.

The bar that Tim has recommended is not easy to find and they make a few wrong turnings before discovering it, tucked beneath an archway at the end of a narrow alley.

'This looks a grotty place,' Beth says.   'Are you sure you got the name right?'

'He put it on my iPhone.'

Fran flicks her iPhone on and checks.

'Yes, this is it alright. Maybe it's nicer inside.'

They go in and sit at a table by the door. The place is quiet but someone is setting up a microphone in the corner of the room.

'Looks like we're in for a musical evening,' Dave says, indicating for the waiter to come across. 'OK, ladies, what'll you have?'

'Wine for me,' Beth says.

'Just water, please.'

'Water? What's the matter with you?' Dave asks. 'It's our last night together.'

Fran points at her belly.

'I've decided to be good. No more wine and no more cigarettes until the baby's born.'

'OK, two glasses of Albariño and a bottle of water,' Dave tells the waiter.

'So what was it like going on to Finisterre?'

'Pretty easy really. It's dead flat and you see hardly anybody on the way. Not many pilgrims bother to carry on after they've arrived in Santiago, so the roads are pretty empty. I can't say I blame them, but it is worth the effort. When you get to the lighthouse at Finisterre you really do feel that you're at the end of the world. The scenery is awesome. Somehow it puts the rest of the journey into perspective. You forget the crowds and the traffic that you had to plough through when you got near Santiago and you have time to think. It's easy to imagine the pilgrims of years gone by walking along the same route.'

'But not cycling.'

'No, not cycling. Although maybe some of them went by donkey.'

'It sounds great, but I don't think I want to walk anywhere now for some time. My feet have been complaining for weeks,' Beth tells him.

'So when did you two arrive?'

'This morning.'

Fran tells him about Lucky.

'I knew there was something different about you,' he says. 'Well, I'm sorry to hear that. She was a nice dog.'

'Have you seen anyone else?' Beth asks.

She is interested to know what has happened to the people she has met over the past five weeks and how many more miracles have been performed.

'Andrew's still here. That is, he's still in Spain, not Santiago. You remember he had a girlfriend?'

'Yes, she ditched him, I believe,' Fran says, as direct as ever.

'She's in Madrid doing a course in tourism, isn't she?' Beth adds.

'Yes, that's her. Well she rang him to say she had some days off and why didn't he get the train across to see her.'

'So he's in Madrid?'

'Yes, he said he'll fly home from there.'

'Wow, do you think it's back on then?' Fran asks, her voice eager for news of more romance.

'No, I don't think so. I think they're just friends. Andy made it quite clear that he doesn't want to be encumbered with a new relationship. He can't bear the idea of anyone fussing over him. He says it's bad enough when he goes to see his mum.'

'Well he's young enough yet. He might change his mind when he's older,' Beth says. 'He's certainly one determined young man. I don't know how he's managed to pull his life around after what has happened to him. It takes a lot of courage.'

Dave nods.

'Yes, he's a pretty plucky bloke. I wouldn't like to be in his place, I can tell you.'

'What about his friend, Eric? Is he still here?' Fran asks.

'No Eric's gone home. He left last night, by train.'

'I wonder if you'll see him again,' Beth says.

It seems sad that people meet like this and then move on, never to see each other again.

'Unlikely. He lives somewhere up north. Anyway, what about you? Have you got your ticket home yet?' he asks Beth.

'No. I'm going to ring the travel agent in the morning and book something. I'm not in any hurry.'

'Me neither. I'm off on the bike tomorrow. Going to ride along the coast to Santander and get the ferry to Portsmouth.'

'That's the *Camino del Norte*, isn't it?'

'That's right, only I'll be doing it in reverse. Then back to work the following week. What a thought. Sitting behind a desk again after all this freedom.'

'There's always next year.'

The door swings open and Tim comes in.

'Hi there,' he says, bending down and kissing Fran. 'So you found it alright.'

'No problems,' Fran says with a giggle. 'What made you choose this out-of-the-way place?'

'They do wonderful seafood and tonight is music night.'

The evening is a great success. Dave and Tim get on well. To everyone's amazement, it turns out that they both work for McGrinleys, Tim as a consultant and Dave in IT, but have never run into each other before. The music is noisy but fun and, all in all, Beth finds it a good way to spend her last evening. Tomorrow she will buy her ticket and go home. But first she must ring Luke.

'What time is it?' she asks them.

'Ten thirty,' Fran says.

'I think I'll head on back to the hotel; I've got some things I want to do before I go to bed.'

'I'll walk with you,' Dave says. 'I need to get an early start tomorrow anyway.'

'So it's goodbye then,' Fran says.

''Fraid so. Parting of the ways and all that.'

Beth feels sad at saying goodbye to Fran. She gives her a hug and says:

'Don't forget to let me know when the baby arrives.'

'I will. Have a safe journey and I hope everything turns out alright for you.'

Beth knows she means: 'I hope you recover; I hope you don't die.' but she cannot say it.

'And for you, both of you,' Beth replies.

There are tears in her eyes, but she blinks them away. It has been an emotional day.

'Well nice seeing you again, Fran,' Dave says.

He turns to Tim.

'I'll look out for you at work, Tim. Any IT problems, just give me a bell.'

'Will do. Safe journey.'

They leave Tim and Fran sitting at the table, their hands linked, their heads touching. Maybe it will work out alright for Fran after all, Beth thinks.

It is almost eleven o'clock by the time she gets to her hotel room, ten o'clock in England; there is still time to telephone Luke. She dials his number from her bedside phone; it rings twice and then she hears his voice:

'Hello?'

'Luke?'

'Mum, is that you? Where are you? We've been so worried about you. Where are you?'

'It's OK Luke, I'm in Santiago del Compostela.'

'Santiago? Where's that? South America?'

'No, Spain. I'm in Spain, but I'm coming home tomorrow.'

'How are you? Are you alright? It's been weeks since we've heard from you. You just disappeared. Dad's been worried about you too,' he adds.

'I doubt that.'

There is a pause. She can imagine her son wrinkling his brow as he wonders what to say next.

'He's told me, Mum.'

'What? What's he told you?'

'About his other family.'

She has not expected this.

'How could he do this to us? To you?' he asks. 'All this time and we never knew. I just can't believe it.'

She can tell from his voice that he is hurt by his father's betrayal.

'It just doesn't seem possible that I've got a brother and a sister that I never knew existed. I tell you, Mum, I'm finding it hard to get my head round it.'

'I'm sure you are, sweetheart. I can't believe that he could do that to us, either, but he did.'

'He says he's sorry for hurting you.'

'Not as sorry as I am,' she says bitterly.

'No, really, he was very upset when he told me.'

'Upset that it's all come out, I expect. Well good luck to him. Let him have his new family.'

'You don't really mean that, do you Mum?'

'I most certainly do,' she replies.

Luke does not know what to say, so she asks:

'Is he still in the house or has he moved out?'

'He's gone.'

So that is that. It is over. Twenty-five years of marriage have come to an end. Her marriage, like a dying candle, has spluttered and gone out.

'There's a letter here for you; I think it's from his solicitor,' he adds.

'He didn't waste much time, did he,' she says, bitterly.

Maybe this is for the best. Now she can concentrate on getting well. Joe has lied to her for ten years; he has cheated on her while pretending to be in love with her; he has destroyed her memories of their life together. He has left her with nothing, no future and no past. It is time for her to move on without him. She realises that she no longer loves him. It is impossible to love someone who has treated you like that. She is free of him. The Joe she loved no longer exists. Maybe he never existed; maybe he was a figment of her imagination.

'I have something to tell you, Luke.'

'You've met someone else,' he blurts out.

'No, of course not. No, It's nothing like that.'

She can hear his sigh of relief. He does not know how hard it is for her to tell him.

'It's not good news, I'm afraid. The cancer's returned.'

'Oh Mum.'

There is pain in his voice.

'When did you find out?'

'Ironically, a couple of days before your father dropped this bombshell about his other family. I was working up to telling you both but then I just couldn't do it. When I realised how long his affair had been going on, I couldn't talk to him about my problems. I didn't know how he'd react. And I didn't want his sympathy. It just seemed too much, too cruel, one thing after another. That's why I had to get away. I had to get away from everything that could remind me of his betrayal. I'm sorry if I worried you, I am really, but I didn't know what else to do. I've spent all my married life putting you and your father first; this time I had to put myself first. You understand, don't you?'

'I understand, Mum. But you're coming home now?'

'Yes, I'll ring you with my flight details as soon as I've got them.'

'Jenny and I'll come and pick you up.'

'That'd be nice.'

The thought of seeing her son again makes her cry.

'Are you OK, Mum?'

She wipes her eyes and says:

'I'm fine. I've missed you.'

'I've missed you too, Mum. Hurry home.'

CHAPTER 24
GOING HOME

Beth has managed to get a direct flight to Bristol. She tells Luke she will get the train to Barnstaple, but he insists on driving to Bristol to meet her. She does not try too hard to dissuade him.

She hopes to see Fran before she leaves, but there is no sign of the love-birds this morning when she goes down to breakfast. After five weeks of rough living it is good to luxuriate in the trappings of civilisation; her hair feels clean for the first time in ages and her skin, burnt almost black by the sun, has been liberally coated with the hotel's best lotions. Her feet have been soaked and the hard skin scoured from them; they are still far from normal but are already beginning to heal.

She eats her breakfast quickly, pays her bill and takes a taxi straight to the airport.

At last she is on her way home. She feels as though she has been away forever. Homesickness grips her like a fever; she cannot wait to be back in sleepy, little   Bideford.   She welcomes the rain and grey skies that the weather forecast has predicted.   It won't be long now until she is home and then she will go to see her doctor as soon as she can. She has to start the treatment before it's too late.   Her hand moves automatically to her right breast; she thinks the tumour feels smaller. It is hard to be sure. She has lost a lot of weight in the last couple of months, so maybe it is just because of that or maybe the cancer is actually shrinking. She wants to believe it is true. She does not want to die. If nothing else, this pilgrimage has made one thing abundantly clear to her: life is for living. She is not going to give up easily. She wants to live for Luke's sake and for the sake of his unborn children, her grandchildren. She wants a future.

Her thoughts drift back to that day on the Meseta when she thought she was lost; it would have been so easy to have given up then but she had got through it. She is still not sure how she made it, but she did. Then there was the morning in Palas de Rei, when she thought the cancer was taking over, when she needed someone to lean on and there was Roxanne, sitting by the roadside waiting for her. Little miracles. She had come to Spain, looking for something; she knew not what. There had been no big miracle for her; it had impossible to turn the clock back and make it all as it was before, before the cancer, before Joe's treachery. Instead, what she has found is inner strength, the strength to face the future and accept what it will bring. That is her miracle.

Once she is well she will think about what to do with the rest of her life, a life without Joe. The thought no longer pains her. She sent the first episode of her Pilgrim's Diary to the newspaper last night; they will start running it from Monday. She is looking forward to writing for them. After all, if there is one thing she is good at, it is writing. She thinks of Walter and Helen; it isn't too late for them to make a fresh start. If they can do it, then so can she. Yes, it is time for her to have a new career and a new life.

The air hostess brings her a gin and tonic. It is ice cold and has a large slice of lemon, exactly to her taste. She sips her drink and thinks of the people she has met on the *Camino*.

María and her lost son, will she ever find him? It seems unlikely, so many years have passed since his disappearance yet María continues to hope. Andrew who, despite his disability, needs to prove that he is still a man. Helen and Walter, two lonely people who have found happiness in each other's company. Dave, kind and helpful, who spreads goodwill and cheerfulness wherever he goes. Roxanne, bubbly, pretty Roxanne trying to come to terms with her own sexuality. And of course Fran, tough, independent Fran who thought she had to choose between her child and her lover. And many more: Darren and Sheri, Denis and Jill, Jim, people she met briefly but their lives had touched. Everyone has a reason for walking the *Camino* and she has learnt something from them all.

Printed in December 2022
by Rotomail Italia S.p.A., Vignate (MI) - Italy